Robert Green Ingersoll, James Baird McClure

Mistakes of Ingersoll and his Answers

Robert Green Ingersoll, James Baird McClure

Mistakes of Ingersoll and his Answers

ISBN/EAN: 9783337401207

Printed in Europe, USA, Canada, Australia, Japan

Cover: Foto ©Andreas Hilbeck / pixelio.de

More available books at **www.hansebooks.com**

MISTAKES

OF

INGERSOLL

AS SHOWN BY

PROF. SWING,   J. MONRO GIBSON, D. D.,
W. H. RYDER, D. D.,   RABBI WISE,
BROOKE HERFORD, D. D.,
AND OTHERS.

INCLUDING INGERSOLL'S LECTURE

ON THE

"MISTAKES OF MOSES."

EDITED BY

J. B. McCLURE.

CHICAGO:
RHODES & McCLURE, PUBLISHERS.
1879.

A religious faith at present so generally pervades the civilized world that it seems almost amazing that any one should dare speak as Mr. Ingersoll does in his several lectures about the Bible. It is this singularity, no doubt, rather than intrinsic worth, which gives any significance that may attach to his words. That the Bible is in the least endangered is out of the question. It is too late now for that. The words herein compiled from good and able men, who have made the great Book, in its early language, import and history, a careful study for long years, will show how futile are Mr. Ingersoll's efforts in parading what he calls the "Mistakes of Moses," etc. Indeed, it would seem that, possibly Mr. I. is guilty of a mistaken identity, for he is severely accused of false assertions and misrepresentations concerning the *real* Moses. This reminds us of a "mistake" which was made on a certain occasion by the celebrated Archbishop of Dublin, the gifted author of the work so widely known, entitled "The Study of Words." He was not in robust health at the time, and for many years had been apprehensive of paralysis. At a dinner in Dublin, given by the Lord Lieutenant of Ireland, his grace sat on the right of his hostess, the Duchess of Abercorn. In the midst of the dinner the company was startled by seeing the

(3)

Archbishop rise from his seat, and still more startled to hear him exclaim in a dismal and sepulchral tone, " It has come! it has come!"

" What has come, your Grace?" eagerly cried half a dozen voices from different parts of the table.

" What I have been expecting for twenty years," solemnly answered the archbishop—" a stroke of paralysis. I have been pinching myself for the last twenty minutes, and find myself entirely without sensation."

" Pardon me, my dear archbishop," said the duchess, looking up at him with a somewhat quizzical smile—" pardon me for contradicting you, but it is *I that you have been pinching!"*

Messrs. Gibson, Swing, Ryder and Herford, of Chicago, and Rabbi Wise, of Cincinnati, whose replies are herein given, are too well known as scholars and divines, to require any introduction to a reading public. Their words are wise and timely, and are put on record in this form to show the weakness of modern infidelity and the stability of Divine Truth.

J. B. McClure.

Chicago, April 22nd, 1879.

CONTENTS.

David Swing

MISTAKES OF INGERSOLL

AS SHOWN BY

PROF. SWING,   J. MONRO GIBSON, D. D.,
W. H. RYDER, D. D.,   RABBI WISE,
BROOKE HERFORD, D. D.,   AND OTHERS.

PROF. SWING'S REPLY.

THIS discourse is not spoken regarding the man, Robert G. Ingersoll, but regarding the addresses which he is delivering and is otherwise publishing. The man Ingersoll is said to be, in his private life, kind, neighborly, humane, and in many ways an example which might be imitated with great profit by thousands who represent themselves as holding the Pagan or the Christian religion. But, were this author and lecturer a mean, wicked man, I should still be bound to consider his thoughts apart from the thinker just as we deal with Bacon's ideas apart from his moral qualities, and the politics of Alexander Hamilton apart from the infirmities of his moral sentiments. The intel-

(7)

lect of such an individual as the one before us is a thinking machine. It makes a survey of the religious landscape. Objects strike it that escape you and me. His eyes are not those of a preacher, not those of a bishop, nor those of an evangelist like Mr. Moody; not those of a moralist like Dymond or William Penn, nor those of Theodore Parker or Emerson, but they are a vision purely his own, and our task is limited to the inquiry what this peculiar sense discovers in our wide and varied world.

The Lawyer vs. The Philosopher—Ingersoll's Professional Proclivities in Making a Part equal to the Whole!

We perceive at once that these addresses do not offer us any system of philosophy for woman, or child, or State, and therefore they cannot aspire to be any valuable Mentor to tell each young Telemachus how to live. They are the speeches of a lawyer retained by one client of a large case. Men trained in a profession come by degrees into the profession's channel, and flow only in the one direction, and always between the same banks. The master of a learned profession at last becomes its slave. He who follows faithfully any calling wears at last a soul of that calling's shape. You remember the death scene of the poor old schoolmaster. He had assembled the boys and girls in the winter mornings and had dismissed them winter evenings after sundown, and had done this for fifty long years. One winter Monday he did not appear. Death had struck his old and feeble pulse; but, dying, his mind followed its beautiful but narrow river-bed, and his last words were: "It is growing dark—the school is dismissed—let the girls pass out first." Very rarely does the man in the pulpit, or at the bar, or in statesmanship, escape this molding hand of his pursuit. We are all clay in the hands of that potter which is called a pursuit. A pursuit is seldom an ocean of water; it is more commonly a canal. But if there be a class of men more modified than others in language and forms of speech, the lawyers compose such a class, for it is never their business to present both sides. It is their especial duty so to arrange a part of the facts as that they shall seem to be the whole facts, and next to their power of presenting a cause must come their power to conceal all aspects unfavorable to their purpose. A philosopher must see and set forth at once both sides of all questions, but a lawyer must learn to see the one side of a case, for there is another man expressly employed to see the reverse of the shield. But few of us are philosophers. When we wish to exhibit something, we instantly cut off all light except that which will fall upon our goods. If we are to display only a yard of silk, we will veil the sun and move about to find the right position, and then light a little more gas, that the fields, and hills, and heavens may all withdraw, and permit us to see the fold of a bride's dress. Thus all the professions, honored by being called learned, do more or less cut off the light from all things except the fabric that is being unfolded by their skillful fingers.

Men of intense emotional power like Mr. Ingersoll, and men who, like him, have hearts as full of colors as a painter's shop, are wont, beyond common, to pour their passion upon one object rather than diffuse it all over the world. These can awaken, and entertain, and shake, and unsettle, but then, after all is over, we all must seek for final guides men who are calmer and who spread gentler tints with their brush. I am, therefore, of the opinion that none of us should follow any one man, but rather all men; should seek that general impression, that wide-reaching common-sense, which knows little of ecstacy and little of despair. These

" Addresses " under notice are wonderful concentrations of
wit, and fun, and tears, and logic, but concentrations upon
minor points.   They are severe upon a little group of men,
upon literalists and old Popes, and old monks, but they do
not weigh and measure fully the religion of such a being as
Jesus Christ, nor touch the ideas and actions of the human
race away from these fading forms of human nature.

Seven Mistakes of Moses Left out!— Injustice to Hebrew History.

These addresses do injustice to the Hebrew history.   A
lawyer has a right to be one-sided and narrow when he is
presenting the cause of his client, but when he is addressing
a public upon a religious, or political, or social question,
narrowness in his discourse must be considered an infirmity,
or else an act of injustice.   These speeches betray either
unconscious narrowness or willful injustice.   But Mr. Ingersoll is the embodiment of sincerity, according to those who
enjoy his acquaintance, and therefore we must conclude
that the cast of his mind is such that it is led hither and
thither by that narrowness which belongs no more to a high
Calvinist than to a high infidel.   If the lecture upon
" Moses " had been more thoughtful, it would have confessed that there were several forms of the man " Moses,"—
the historic " Moses," the Hebrew " Moses," and the Calvinistic " Moses; " and then, after this concession, he might have
assailed the " Calvinistic Moses."   .   .   .   .
But if the addresses had been broad, and spoken for that
larger audience called humanity, they would have asked us
to mark the mistakes of the Moses of Hebrew times and of
common history.   But they did not dream of this.   Standing in the presence of one of the grandest figures of Egyp-

tian and Hebrew antiquity, Mr. Ingersoll failed to see this
personage, and permitted nothing to come upon his field of
vision except those sixteenth century theologians who distorted alike the mission of Moses and of Christ, and even
of the Almighty. To set forth the mistakes of the historic
"Moses" would not be any easy task. One doing this
would be compelled to ask us to mark the blunders of a
leader who planned freedom for slaves; who bore complain-
ings from an ignorant people until he won the fame of unusual meekness, one who did in reality what infidels only
have dreamed of doing—living and dying for the people;
the mistakes of one whose ten laws are still the fundamental
ideas of a State, of one who organized a nation which lived
and flourished for 1,500 years; the mistakes of one who
divested the idea of God of bestiality and began to clothe it
with the notions of wisdom and justice, and even tenderness;
the follies of one who established industry and education,
and a higher form of religion, and gave the nation holding
these virtues such an impulse that in the hour of dissolving
it produced a Jesus Christ and the twelve Apostles; and
thus did more in its death than Atheism could achieve in all
the eons of geology. Seven mistakes of Moses left out!

There is, it is true, a time and a place for irony, but after
it has done its work amid the accidental of a time or a place,
there remains yet much to be studied by the sober intellect
and loved by the heart which really cares for the useful and
the true. It is essentially a small matter that some poetic
mind, some Froissart or some Herodotus, came along perhaps after the reigns of David and Solomon, and gathered up
all the truths of old Hebrew tradition, and all the legends,
too, and wove them together, for out of such entanglements
the essential ideas generally rise up just as noble pine trees
at last rise up above the brambles and thickets at their base,

and evermore stand in the full presence of rain, and air, and
sun. Above the brambles and thorn of legend, at which
the narrow eye may laugh, there rises up from the Mosaic
soil a growth of moral truth that catches at last full sunshine and full breeze; a growth that will long make a good
shadow for the graves of Christian and infidel beneath.
The errors of legend are so unimportant that even a Divine
Book may carry them.

It will thus appear that the method of the addresses is
very defective. It is not a wide survey of a two-thousand-
year period in human civilization, a period when the Hebrews were making imperishable the good of the Egyptians
who were dying from vices and despotism, but is only the
ramble of a satirist having a sharp eye for defects and a most
ready tongue. All the by-gone periods may be passed over
in two manners. We may go forth for our laughter or for
our pensiveness and wisdom. Juvenal saw old Rome full
of dissolute men and women. Virgil saw it full of literature. Tacitus found it not destitute of patriots and heroes;
and when Juvenal found the husbands all debauchees, and
the wives all hypocrites, there the most calm and elegant
historians found the most excellent Agricola, and found a
wife of spotless fame in the daughter Domitia. Thus in
the very generations in which the lampoons of Juvenal
found only vice, behold we see beauty and virtue in full
bloom around the homes of Tacitus, and Agricola, and
Pliny. Thus all the fields of human thought lie open to
the invasion of those who wish to mock, and of those who
wish to admire. And beyond doubt when Mr. Ingersoll
shall have uttered his last thought over the Mistakes of
Moses, some other form of intellect could glean in the same
field, and leave covered with the truths of Moses, a nobler
and larger tablet.

**Swing Puts Himself in Ingersoll's Place and Attacks the
Seventeenth Century.—How it Works!**

Permit me now, in imitation of the style of these addresses,
to ask you to look at the seventeenth century: Why, it all
drips in blood! Horror upon horrors! The King of Persia
put to death some of the Royal family and put out the eyes
of all the rest—even the eyes of infants. Russia begins her
cruel oppression of Poland. Prussia, the hope of Europe,
is desolated by war, which never lifted its black cloud for
thirty years. In this wretched century came the massacre
of Prague and the forcible banishment of 30,000 Protestant
families. Allowing five persons to a family, it will thus appear that 150,000 were driven from their homes and country.
Further south, in France, a few years before, 700,000 Protestants had been murdered in twenty-four hours. Afterward came the licentious court of Louis XIV.; while over
in England noble men and women were being beheaded or
otherwise slain in dreadful numbers. The beautiful Queen
Mary is beheaded just as the century begins, and Essex is
beheaded in its full opening. And in its close France re-
enters the scene, revokes the edict of Nantes, and sends into
exile 800,000 of her best citizens.

Thus dragged along the seventeenth century, as it would
seem, bleeding, and weeping, and gasping in perpetual
dying. What a picture! Amazing indeed, but narrow and
false! I have been thinking only of the "mistakes" of a
time. Just look at that century again with a wider survey
and a happier heart, and lo! we see in it a matchless line
of immortal worthies. There flourished Gustavus, laying
the foundations of our liberty; there lived Grotius, writing
down the holiest principles of duty; there we see Galileo
inventing the telescope, and beholding the starry sky; there

sits Kepler finding the highest laws of astronomy; near these are the French preachers, Bossuet, Fenelon, and Massilon, whose fame has not been equaled; there, too, Pascal and Corneille. But this is not all. It is not one-third the splendor of that one epoch, for, cross the Channel, and behold you meet Shakspeare, and Lord Bacon, and Milton, and Locke, and while these divine minds are composing their books, Cromwell is overthrowing despots, and a Republic springs up as by enchantment. Thus the seventeenth century, which awhile ago seemed only a period that a kind heart might wish stricken from history, now comes back to us as the sublime dawn of poetry, and science, and eloquence, and liberty.

The truth is we must move through the present and the past with both eyes wide open, and with a mind willing to know all and to draw a conclusion from the whole combined cloud of witnesses. The author of the addresses does not do this. He does not make a wide survey nor draw conclusions from widely scattered facts; and hence, after he has spoken about the horrors of the Mosaic age, or of the church there remains that age or that church emptying rich treasures into the general civilization, purifying the barbarous ages, awaking the intellect, stimulating the arts, inspiring good works, elevating the life of the living, by setting before man a God and a future existence. Our Christianity has a Hebrew origin. The sermon on the Mount was begun by Moses.

The eloquence of Mr. Ingersoll is much like the art of Hogarth or John Leech,—an acute, and witty, and interesting art, but very limited in its range. Hogarth was without a rival in his ability to picture the "mistakes" of marriage, and of a "Rake's Progress," the peculiarity of "Beer Lane" and "Gin Lane"; and his art was legitimate in its

field, but its field was narrow, and took no notice of the
eternal beauty of things as painted by Rubens or Raphael.
After Hogarth had said all he could see and believe about
marriage, there stood the holy relation in its historic greatness, filling millions of homes with its peace and friendship, notwithstanding the mirth-provoking pencil. Thus
the ideas of "Moses," and "Church," and "Heaven," and
"God" lie before Mr. Ingersoll to be pictured by his skillful derision, but after the artist has drawn his little Puritanic
Hebrew and his absurd Heaven, and has painted his little
gods, and has limned his own Papal Heaven and Hell,
another scene opens and there untarnished are the deep
things of right and wrong, the immortal hopes of man, and
a Heavenly Father which cannot be placed upon a jester's
canvas.

John Leech found the weak points in all English high
and low life. The fashions, and sports, and entertainments,
and the current politics, underwent for a generation the torture of his pictures, his sketches, his cartoons, but the
moment the laugh had ended, the homes of England, the
happy social life of rich and poor, the learning and wisdom
of her statesmen were back in their place just as the sun is
in his place after a noisy thunderstorm has passed by.

Ingersoll's Narrowness Shuts out God, Heaven and Immortality—Infidel Dogmatism.

This narrowness of survey which marks Mr. Ingersoll's
estimate of the Hebrew period and of the human Church,
follows him in his thoughts about another life and the existence of God. He denies that any regard whatever should
be paid to a second life. Heaven deserves no consideration at our hands. He says in his lecture on the Gods:
" Reason, observation and experience have taught us

2

that happiness is the only good; that the time to be happy
is now, and the way to be happy is to make others so. This
is enough for us.   In this belief we are content to live and
die."   Such assertions as these no broadly-reaching mind
could make, for the broad mind, not knowing but that there
may be a second life, having no positive information on that
point, is bound to admit all that uncertainty, and that hope
is a most lawful element in that strange mingling which
makes up the soul.   As Mr. Ingersoll does not know whence
man came, so he knows not whither he goes, and therefore
he must himself stand and permit others to stand in the
presence of death as in the presence of a great mystery that,
at least, should silence all dogmatism of priest or infidel.
The logic of the addresses may be fitted for the common
jury, but they are too rude for man who is weeping his
way along between birth and death.

   In some better hour the lawyer forgets his petit jury and
addresses the human soul.   On the title page of a recent
volume he says in substance that: "The dream of immortal life has always existed in the heart of man, and will
remain there in all its matchless charms, born not of any
book or creed, but out of human affection;" and being not
born of reason and sense, he can but reject its hope; he is
personally above being molded in thought, or action, by
such a fable of the heart.   In calling such a dream a fable,
he is guilty of that very dogmatism which he so hates in
Calvin and Edwards, for if Calvin was too certain that he
knew God's will, Mr. Ingersoll is too certain that he knows
God not to exist.   It often happens that the dogmatism
of the bigot must await its exact parallel in the dogmatism
of the atheist.   The ideas of a future life and a God are
thus in these addresses rudely set aside as though this
author had shown the real origin and destiny of the Universe, and had found out the secret of the grave.

He would pay no attention to the idea of God. He would not be guilty of any worship in this life. He says: "If by any possibility the existence of a power superior to and independent of nature shall be demonstrated, there will be time enough to kneel. Until then let us stand erect."

In such language we find only a perfect overthrow of the method of the human soul; for the soul has never dared wait for any such certainty in any of the paths before it. It has always been compelled to build up before itself the largest possible motives and hopes, and then live for them and abide the consequences. It is wonderful that a man who will pluck a violet and draw delight from its tender color and still more delicate perfume, will sternly command the human race not to hold in its hands any flower of immortality, lest by chance its leaves may at last wither. If this idea of a future life should at last fail, which seems impossible, the human heart will be all the purer and happier from having held all through these years a lily so sweet and so white.

Logic cannot make such short work of the religious sentiments. Mr. Ingersoll says: "If you can ever find a God, just let me know, and I shall kneel. Until then I shall stand erect." What injustice to that delicate form of reason, which has moved the world for perhaps 10,000 years! We do not propose to find God or a future life. What the world has found long since is the deep hope in a God, and the measureless hope that the dying loved ones of this world will meet in a land that is better. Nobody has come to the human race to let it know that a God has been found, but many have come to it saying: "My dear children, let us trust that all this matchless universe came from a Creator, and that from him we also came." So many and so holy were these voices, and so responsive was the heart, that upon this trust the living and the dying have knelt and have told their longings to the Invisible. The human race has not been haughty. It has been willing to kneel. Its heart has never been stone, nor its knees brass. It has stood erect in battle where liberty was to be won; it has been as erect as an infidel when a bosom was to be bared for arrows or bullets, or when the neck was to be unclothed for the fatal ax, but in moments of hope and longing it has bent willingly in hope and prayer. The advice of the Addresses not to kneel until you have reached and handled the Creator, is advice that civilization has always spurned, for it has woven all its gorgeous fabrics out of delicate probabilities,—gossamer threads spun by the heart. Fame, and learning, and art, and happiness are all simple possibilities before each youth. He does not dare say, Make me sure of results, and I will gird myself for the present. He casts himself upon the better of two possibilities, and is borne along toward an unknown end. Thus has the human race dealt with the intimations of religion. It has cast itself upon the better hope, and, being at perfect liberty to espouse Atheism, has always repudiated it as being a paralysis of the soul, and a perfect reversal of the common logic of society.

In the World's Great Freedom of Choice, Ingersoll is Counted out!

The world has always been perfectly free to use the form of reasoning which Mr. Ingersoll suggests. No Westminster Assembly, no Calvin compelled the human family from Old Egypt to Greece to think the universe had a Creator. The world has always been free to suppose that such seasons as day and night and spring and summer, such creatures as the nightingale and man, such a star as the sun, all came from mud and water and fire, mingling of their own accord; but the world has had no wide use for such conclusions. Of its own free choice, it has avoided Atheism, and has never made up anywhere a civilization without discarding the idea of waiting for a demonstration, and without espousing the idea that all noble society reposes upon lofty hopes. Out of beautiful possibilities the soul's garments are woven.

It thus appears that the Addresses are defective as guides for any man's life or death. They constitute a bill of exceptions against certain hard rulings in some local and ignorant courts, but as pleadings in the great tribunal where the whole human family stands assembled, to get the wisest decisions about duty and happiness, and the possibility of there being a God and a second life, the possible value of a hope for the dying—they each and all fall far short. They see only the religion of some fanatic, and think it the religion of Jesus or of mankind. They see a God damning honest men, and conclude that is what is meant by Jehovah. They see a Heaven with some little sect in the midst of it, and speak as though they were what is meant by the immortality of man. They note the follies of the Puritans and Papists, and infer that if there were no religion in the world, there would be no bad judgment or bad passions. They fail, too, to mark the delicacy of man's practical logic, which is not iron-like, waiting for the absolute end of all doubt, but which is bending and hopeful, and stands ready forever to found immense motives, and society, and church, and homes upon the greater and better of two probabilities that lie within this world of cloud. They assert the adequacy of earthly happiness as an end of being, and fail to mark that earthly happiness has always depended upon high morals, and father, and mother, and child, and social life, and all mental development have found their full meaning, until a warm and

broad religion has shed its cheering light.   The human race
cannot find its supreme good in having a few acres of ground,
and in seeing the grass grow, and in hearing the birds sing.
These make some days delightful indeed, but man, with his
retinue of art, and statesmanship, and morals, and tempta-
tions, and virtues, and joys, and sorrows, and partings, and
death, demands the assumption of a God, and the expecta-
tions of a resurrection from the dust.   Under such a temple
as society, the foundation must be deep.

To those who read or hear these addresses of Mr. Ingersoll, let me say: Hear them, read them if you wish, for they
will show you what a sad caricature of Christianity was that
which came down to us from the Dark Ages; but, having
thus been taught by an enemy, then dismiss the laughter,
and look at religion in the widest forms of its doctrine and
experience.   We are now warned daily not to follow partisans in politics, because they will eclipse a country by a
little chair in office—they will make a village outweigh a
continent.   These addresses of a talented lawyer warn us
equally against trusting the partisans in religion—the dim-
eyed zeal which makes a Deity as small as their own hearts,
a Bible as cold and as hard as adamant; but now, having
been taught to shun partisans in politics and in Christianity, let us learn to resist one more form of partisan—the
partisan of an atheism and a hopeless grave.   Let us at
times laugh with him, let us admire his acuteness, let us
confess the honesty of his life, but for our guides or ideas
in the world spiritual let us seek some mountain of thought
where the survey is broader, and tenderer, and more just,
from which height no good lies concealed; but looking from
which we can see the great landscape of the soul, some of
it bathed in light, some of it lying in shadow, but all of it
instructive and full of impressiveness.

DR. RYDER'S REPLY.

In the commencement of this review of Mr. Ingersoll's lecture upon "The Mistakes of Moses," I wish two things distinctly understood: First, that my controversy is not with the man, but with his address; and, second, that he has the same right to advocate his views as I have to advocate mine. On the question of religious liberty we are as one.

Furthermore, I do not wonder that certain minds, having passed through peculiar experiences, become thoroughly disgusted with particular forms of theological thought. My only surprise is that more are not. Such material ideas of the Deity as are sometimes put forth in the name of Christianity; such offensive literalizing as is sometimes applied to the future life,. and such thoroughly untenable positions as are sometimes taken as to what the Scriptures actually are, has long been a fruitful cause of infidelity, and will continue to be so as long as they receive the indorsement of any branch of the Christian Church.

But intensity of conviction may degenerate into preju- dice, and this prejudice practically unfits one to discuss the subject to which it relates. From what the distinguished lecturer says of himself, of his determination in every ad- dress he makes, no matter what the topic, to denounce cer- tain views, and from the specimen of his work now brought under review, I conclude that Col. Ingersoll occupies just this position.

While, then, the right to speak one's honest thought is thus frankly conceded, and the provocation to employ strong language in reference to certain theological opinions is also conceded, it will be admitted by all candid minds that certain subjects from their very nature, and from interest which they involve, are to be treated with seriousness and fairness. If not so treated, the influence of the discussion is almost certain to be harmful. The lecture under notice, though nominally on the errors of a particular character in the Old Testament, is virtually an assault upon all revealed religion, and especially that contained in the Bible.

Ingersoll's Unfairness—Attributes to Moses Statements not in the Bible.

Now, my first position is this: Whoever publicly attacks the sacred books of the Christian world, and attempts to destroy faith in them, should treat the subject fairly. I regret to say that the lecture does not seem to me so to treat its great theme, but is, on the contrary, a conspicuous illustration of prejudice and unfairness. No small portion of the lecture is unworthy a reply. There is nothing to reply to. Of fair argument there is a lamentable lack,—no inconsiderable portion of the time seems to have been spent in knocking over a man of straw of his own manufacture. If his lecture be regarded simply as an entertainment, it is a success, for the Colonel knows how to amuse an audience as well as the best; but if it were intended to be a fair and able discussion of an important subject, it is not simply a failure, but a failure so obvious as to leave no room for any other opinion. In proof of my statement that the lecture does not treat the topic which it professes to discuss fairly, I offer these specimens as evidence:

The first specimen is: Attributing to Moses language
and statements not to be found in any of his writings.
Speaking of Moses, he says: "The gentleman who wrote it
(Genesis) begins by telling us that God made it (the world)
out of nothing." And then he proceeds to ridicule the idea.
But Moses says neither that nor anything like it. The
lecturer thus misrepresents the very first sentence in the
Pentateuch. What Moses says is, that "In the beginning
God created the heavens and the earth." What he created
them out of, or when "in the beginning" was, he does not
say. The simple thought is that the heavens and the earth
were not self-evolved, but were created by the Omnipotent
Jehovah.

"You recollect," he says, "that the gods came down and
made love to the daughters of men," etc. Where does Moses
say that? Plenty of that kind of talk is Grecian and Roman
mythology, but what has that to do with "The Mistakes of
Moses?" "They built a tower (Babel) to reach the heavens
and climb into the abodes of the gods." Another of the
Colonel's mistakes. The Tower of Babel was not built for
any such purpose. From the frequent references of this
kind to the gods in connection with the religion of Moses,
it looks as if the lecturer was not aware that the Jews were
not particularly in favor of idolatry. Again he says:
"There is not one word in the Old Testament about woman
except words of shame and humiliation. It did not take
the pains to record the death of the mother of us all. I have
no respect for any book that does not treat woman as the
equal of man."

It is true that Moses does not record the death "of the
mother of us all;" but it is also true that the first account
of the burial of any person in the book of Genesis is that
of a woman, Sarah, the wife of Abraham. Moses simply

says of Adam: "The father of us all," "And he died;" and in a similar summary manner are all the other men disposed of; but when it comes to this woman Sarah, a special lot has to be purchased for her, and secured to the family, so that her remains might not be disturbed; and even now in remembrance of the cave of the field in which she was buried, a certain part of our modern cemeteries is called Machpelah. By the side of this fact how does the declaration look that "there is not one word in the Old Testament about women, except words of shame and humiliation?" Suppose I turn the tables upon the lecturer, and say, I have no respect for any book that does not treat man as the equal of woman. My words, if applied to the Bible, would be hardly less libelous than his.

His Temporary Insanity Occasioned by Heavy Rains— Intellectually Submerged in the Deluge—Damaging Blunders—Ingersoll up the Wrong Mountain.

My second specification is that he not only makes Moses say what he does not say, but he frequently misrepresents what he does say. I name these particulars: First, in speaking of the flood, he gives the impression that, according to the Scriptural account, all the water that covered the earth and inundated it came out of the clouds in the form of rain. He says: "And then it began to rain, and it kept on raining until the water went twenty-nine feet over the highest mountains. How deep were these waters? About five and a half miles. How long did it rain? Forty days. How much did it have to rain a day? About 800 feet." Now what are the facts? In the verse which precedes the one which says, "And the rain was upon the earth forty days and forty nights," we have this record,—Gen., vii., ii.—"In the 600th year of Noah's life, in the second month, the 17th day of

the month, the same day were all the fountains of the great
deep broken up, and the windows of heaven were opened."
Why did not the lecturer mention this statement of the
" breaking up of the fountains of the great deep," which is
generally supposed to refer to the upheaval or subsidance of
some large body or bodies of land, perhaps to portions of
this western continent, and is considered to have been the
principal cause of the deluge? Why omit the supposed
principal cause of the deluge, unless it was his purpose to
make out a case without regard to the facts?

Furthermore, what authority has he for saying that the
ark rested on the top of a mountain seventeen thousand feet
high, and that the water upon the earth was "five and a
half miles deep?" Has he committed the ignorant blunder
of confounding Agri-Dagh with the hilly district to which
the name was formerly applied? The lofty peak that now
bears the name of Ararat has no such designation in Bib-
lical history, and it is the name given to it in comparatively modern times. The Bible record is: "Fifteen cubits
upwards did the waters prevail." The Hebrew cubit is
about twenty-two inches. If we may trust the conclusions
of science, deluges have been no unusual events in the history of this globe. Most of the land, if not all of it, no
matter how high at present, has been at some time submerged. Whatever one may think about the accuracy of
the narrative in reference to the building of the ark and the
uses to which it was put, there is certainly no physical
improbability in the statement that that part of the earth
which was then above water was thoroughly inundated.

Again, the gentleman makes merry over what he calls the
" rib story," and imagines two persons before the bar of
God, one believing the " rib story " and the other denying
it. The believer of it is accepted by the Judge as belonging

in Heaven, and the denier of it as belonging in Hell. And
this he puts before the public as Bible doctrine—as if any
man of common sense, whether Jew or Gentile, ever defended
so ridiculous a theory.   As a further specimen of this unfairness, I present you this: " Do you believe the real God—
if there is one—ever killed a man for making hair oil?
And yet you find in the Pentateuch that God gave Moses a
receipt for making hair oil to grease Aaron's beard; and
said if anybody made the same hair oil he would be killed."

There could hardly be written a more complete misrepresentation and perfect caricature of the whole subject than
this.   The reference in Scripture is to an anointing oil, to be
applied, not simply to the persons of the priests, but to the
sacred vessels as well; and, thus anointed, they were set
apart for what they regarded as holy uses.   But if this custom which Mr. Ingersoll seeks to hold up to ridicule, was
simply Jewish, there would be some show or plausibility for
talking about it as he does; but he has not even that to justify his attack.   For this custom of using anointing oils in
connection with religious services, and sacred persons, and
utensils, was common among the idolatrous nations, and
even conspicuous among the rites of the Romans.   And
even now one often meets with the spirit of the same custom.   I do not know whether the Colonel is a member of
the Masonic fraternity, but he must have seen representatives of that ancient Order pour out anointing oil upon the
corner-stone of some building which they were engaged in
laying.   Why not ridicule that, and why not also ridicule
the beautiful custom of that Order of dropping upon the
uncovered coffin of a deceased member the little sprigs of
evergreen that the brethren bear in their hands as they
march around his open grave?   It is easy to see that with
reference to every such custom, however sacred, one who

takes the naked fact apart from its associations, may find abundant material for ridicule. But whether a fair-minded man will allow himself to treat any serious subject in that manner, is a question upon which there is no occasion that I should pronounce judgment. Mr. Ingersoll makes a similar blunder in what he says about the custom of sacrificing doves for the use of priests, since the practice did not exist among the Hebrews until hundreds of years after the event which he seeks to ridicule.

Top-Heavy—Too Broad a Structure Reared on a Too Narrow Base.

My third specification is, that he treats a particular interpretation of the Bible as the undisputed word of God. He assumes that this or that is Bible doctrine because somebody may at some time have taught it, and then denounces the whole Bible as unworthy the respect of mankind. This feature of the address runs through the whole of it. But, in this respect, candor compels me to say his method is that of Thomas Paine in his "Age of Reason," and of a certain class, but not the better class, of so-called infidel writers. Mr. Paine reproved the world for believing what he showed to be unreasonable doctrines, and called upon the people to throw away their Bibles for teaching such sentiments; but it was Mr. Paine, and not the Bible that was in fault, for the doctrines which he shed so much ink to condemn are not taught in the Bible. Mr. Ingersoll's method is precisely the same. If he wishes to hold up to the contempt of mankind certain doctrines that some sect may have believed, or even does believe, let him announce his subject, keep to his text, and go ahead; but to go from place to place, exhorting the people everywhere to throw away their Bibles, under the pretense that these representations of his are the undisputed word of God, is simply an outrage upon the Christian public, and unworthy any man who claims to be fair-minded.

Mr. Ingersoll's references to the clergy disappoint me. He speaks of them as if they were a set of fools, and does not add that they are all graduates of prisons, and a pack of scoundrels generally. To which gentlemanly references we need only say, that in this slanderous speech he is guilty of the same offense against fairness and good breeding that is committed by any nominal Christian who, either through blindless or perversity, can see nothing good in the services of the distinguished infidels of history, and who, to prejudice the public against them, resort to the mean subterfuge of misrepresenting their positions, and telling falsehoods about them. If any man, in an address before this community, should treat the writings of Voltaire as shabbily as Mr. Ingersoll has treated the writings of Moses,—and as to that, the entire Bible,—the Colonel would have to go outside the Psalms of David to find imprecations to express his contempt. His references to Andover have, of course, nothing to do with "The Mistakes of Moses," but they relate to an important subject, and are a pertinent illustration of the eminent unfairness of the general address. This is what he says: "They have in Massachusetts, at a place called Andover, a kind of minister factory; and every Professor in that factory takes an oath in every five years that, so help him God, he will not during the next five years intellectually advance; and probably there is no oath he could easier keep. They believe the same creed they first taught when the foundation stone was laid, and now, when they send out a minister they brand him, as hardware from Birmingham and Sheffield. And every man who knows where he was educated knows his creed, knows every argument of his creed, every book that he has read, and just what he amounts to intellectually, and knows that he will shrink and shrivel and become more and more stupid day after day until he meets with death."

My personal sympathy with the Andover Theological School is not, as you may suppose, very deep and ardent. I respect the generosity and self-sacrifice of the five noble minds—one of whom was a woman—that founded the institution in 1807, and the aid which it has given to liberal and exact scholarship. On the whole, I do not like the rule to which Mr. Ingersoll refers. Probably many of those in charge of the institution do not. I understand it to be a custom contingent upon certain endowments made long ago, and which is observed as a matter of form. But the rule is not fairly open to the objection that Mr. Ingersoll makes against it. First, it simply relates to the theological professors, and does not concern the students. Second, it compels no man to take it who does not wish to. The University says, in effect, we believe in certain doctrines; we desire the instruction of this institution to be in accordance with these ideas. Can you conscientiously teach them? If so, we wish you; if not, we do not wish you. But if you come to us, you are not compelled to remain, but can go where you will, and when you will, and teach what you please; but so long as you remain in the service of this institution we expect you to carry out the purposes of its founders. What is there in this that is particularly narrow and dementing? But the Colonel repudiates his own positions. He says: "The common school is the bread of life, but there should be nothing taught in the school except what somebody knows; anything else should not be maintained by a system of general taxation."

Ingersoll's Inconsistency!

But, let us inquire, who is to decide "what somebody knows?" Practically, the answer is, the people, or their

representatives, in school boards, committees, etc. They
select the text-books, and they expect instructors whom they
engage to follow them, for the text-books are assumed to
embody what is true on the subjects to which they relate.
What would the lecturer say of a teacher in one of our public
schools who should to-day teach the rejected doctrine that
the sun revolves about the earth? What, but this: turn
him out and put some one in his place who teaches the
truth—which, being interpreted, means, teaches according
to the authorized text-books. Why, on the very occasion of
the lecture itself, after the Colonel had denounced Andover
for pledging loyalty to certain doctrines, and which act he
characterizes as so harmful to freedom of thought, he himself demands of the people whom he is addressing that they
will never support a certain form of doctrine, nor give money
to aid in building any church in which they are taught.
His language is: "I would have every one who hears me
swear that he will never contribute another dollar to build
another church in which is taught such infamous lies."
Mark you, not simply a pledge for five years, but they are
never to change their views. My friends, is there no such
thing as consistency in belief? Is one a bigot because he
says, This is what I believe, and this, therefore, I defend?
Are these men to be ridiculed and assailed, and only those
who shirk such responsibility to be held up as patterns and
guides? Brethren, I am not speaking of some sophomoric
oration, but about the deliberate thought of a man who has
made himself famous in this line of labor, and of whom our
townsman who gracefully introduced him said, "a man who
does his own thinking, and who thinks before he says."
Now, of every such man it is safe to say, he knows that
organization is essential to the welfare of society, and is
perfectly consistent with liberty of thought. The free-
thinkers of this country are organized as well as others;

and it is their right to be if they have anything to teach or defend. A Christian combination, against which some people hurl their anathemas, is simply the grouping together of those who have a similar mind and purpose, the better to do this work which they have in common. Of course there has been in connection with some of these denominations a fearful amount of bigotry. When we come to that topic we are quite at home. Bigotry is no friend of ours: we owe him no service. The denomination which this church represents has received from the dominant sects about us a pretty large share of persecution and abuse. But, for all that, we do not propose to follow the lecturer's example and call our brethren hard names, simply because they apply such epithets to us.

He Has no Poetry in His Soul; Ergo, etc.

My fourth specification is, that he misrepresents the writings of Moses. and, as to that, the entire Bible, by treating its metaphoric language as literal statements.

Think of a man, in this age of light, speaking of the pictured representation of the Old Testament in this way: "They believed that an angel could take a lever, raise a window, and let out the desired quantity of moisture. I find out in the Psalms that he bowed the heavens and came down." I wonder if the gentleman can see anything but mere literalism in this passage? "As the mountains round about Jerusalem, so the Lord is round about His people from henceforth, even forever." Like other nations, the Hebrews have their patriotic, descriptive, didactic, and lyrical poems in the same varieties as other nations; but with them, unlike other nations, whatever may be the form of their poetry, it always possesses the characteristic of religion. Even their patriotic songs are a part of their religion. The Jews have taught the world its devotional poetry. If there is to be

3

found anywhere conceptions of the Deity and of the universe
more remarkable for their sublimity and grandeur than are
met with in the sacred books of the Jews, I know not where
to look for them.   Certainly when they are compared with
the religious poems of other countries, most nearly contemporaneous, as those of Homer and Hesiod, they are so vastly
superior as to lead to the belief that, if the poets of idolatrous Greece drew their inspiration from human genius and
learning, those of Judea had a higher illumination.

Additional Misrepresentations.

My fifth specification is, that the representation given in
the lecture of the Hebrews as a people, is almost wholly in-
correct, both as to the work undertaken by them and the
effect of that work upon mankind.

We have no disposition to shut our eyes to the ignorance,
cruelty and superstition of the Hebrew race in the early
periods of their history.   There was but little in them that
gave the promise of a great nation when Moses led them
out of Egypt.   They were low in the scale of civilization.
Many of the things done by them we cannot justify, and
we are not required to do so.   But what arrests our attention is, that almost from the first they show a gradual improvement in their condition, and finally reach that proud
pre-eminence when Jerusalem became the Athens of its
day.   There are two points of view from which to judge of
the early history of any people: one is, to compare it with
that of contemporary nations, and the other is, to compare
it with our own time.   It is manifest that the former is the
proper basis of judgment.   Consider, then, as already inti-
mated, who the people were that Moses thus led out of
Egypt.   Reflect that they were but children in intelligence,
and that the higher forms of thought had but little influence
over them; and that if they were held to the law of duty,

and organized into a nation, it must be by such material forms and simple customs as they could comprehend. Reflect, furthermore, that these people had been brought up in the midst of idolatry, and that in leaving Egypt they did not get away from its influences, but that, wherever they went, they were assailed by it; that idolatry was almost the universal form of worship, and that it was a mighty task to educate these people in the doctrine of the one only living and true God, and hold them to it. Reflect, furthermore, that to secure this end much might then be done which, under the circumstances, would be at least excusable, that should not be done now. Fairness requires that we consider whether the custom originated with the Jews themselves, and what was its spirit and purpose.

Prominent mention is made in the lecture of polygamy in connection with the Jews, and one would infer from what he says that the custom of plurality of wives originated with them, and that it was a custom peculiar to them. This is his language: "Is there a woman here who believes in the institution of polygamy? Is there a man here who believes in that infamy? You say 'no, we do not.' Then you are better than your God was 4,000 years ago. Four thousand years ago he believed in it, taught it, and upheld it." The facts appear to be these: Polygamy has existed from time immemorial. Even in the Homeric age of the Greeks it prevailed to some extent, and, though not known in republican Rome, it practically prevailed under the Empire, owing to the prevalence of divorce; but in what we call the Eastern nations the custom has been almost universal, being sanctioned by all religions, including that of Mohammedanism. In this regard the Hebrews, to a certain extent, followed the prevalent custom viz: the law of Moses did not forbid it, but did contain many provisions against its worst abuses, and such as were intended to

restrict it within narrow limits; and, as the spirit of the
Hebrew religion advanced the civilization of the nation,
the practice more and more fell into disuse, until it finally
died out; and in the glimpses of Jewish life which the New
Testament gives us, there are no traces of it discernible.
Since the Hebrew race the world over, for some 2,000 years,
has as much as any other people discountenanced such
practices, though still firmly believing in Moses as the
prophet of God, it is clear that they do not consider polygamy any part of the Jewish system, but a custom permitted for a season because so universally practiced by the
surrounding nations.

Doctor Ryder Propounds a Question.

But just here comes in a question of high importance.
If there is nothing in Judaism to exalt woman—and every
reference to her in their sacred books is one of " humiliation
and shame "—how happens it that the Jews discarded the
custom of polygamy some two thousand years ago, while
the practice still prevails among the nations of the East,
and notably in Mohammedanism, which, in so many respects,
takes the external form of Judaism? The truth is, that great
injustice has been-done to the real religion of the Hebrews,
by both Christians and unbelievers. We have judged it too
exclusively by the Mosaic law, and the mere letter of it at
that. Real Judaism is not the Old Testament, but that
which has come out of it—the result of its growth, and the
expansion of its inherent forces. Long before the advent
of our Lord the Mosaic law had virtually given way to the
Jewish religion, and it is that religion, the spirit of which
in the beginning so largely came from the great law-giver
himself that has had three thousand years of existence to
certify its right to live, and which to-day assigns it a most
honorable place among the religions of humanity. And in

dismissing this branch of our subject, it seems pertinent to inquire, where did Moses obtain his religious ideas? The Egyptians had reached high advancement in the arts and sciences in the time of Moses, but their degradation in reference to religion is unmistakable. It is said of Moses that he "was learned in all the wisdom of the Egyptians, and was mighty in words and deeds;" and he was no doubt greatly aided by what he had learned from them, but it seems too evident to admit of discussion that he did not get his religious ideas from that source. Whence came they? But, whatever may be our answer to this question, there can be, it seems to me, but one opinion as to the respect due to the illustrious religious leader who has made upon the race so profound an impression for good.

The five specifications now before you cover the evidence we offer of the correctness of our general proposition, viz.: that the address upon "The Mistakes of Moses," is a conspicuous illustration of prejudice and unfairness.

Ingersoll Admits His Sad Need of Inspiration.

Col. Ingersoll uses this language: "Nothing needs inspiration but a falsehood or a mistake. A fact never went into partnership with a miracle." "A fact will fit every other fact in the universe, and that is how you can tell whether or not it is a fact." Suppose we test this rule. How about good and evil, truth and error, the mysterious and the evident, divine sovereignty and human freedom, heat and cold, art and asceticism, economy and benevolence, government and freedom, each of which is an undisputed fact, but each two facts that we thus group together no more fit each other than the centripetal and centrifugal forces, which, acting in opposite directions, hold the universe together? My friends, there is a recognizable distinction between the knowable and unknowable. But the line that separates the two is

not sharply defined. The border land between them seems
sometimes near and at other times very far away. The
realm beyond the knowable is the realm of mystery, and
out of it come some of the most potential forces that sway
our lives. What we call the knowable is those things that
can be demonstrated—can be proved to be true by a practical method. But consider how small a portion of our real
life is covered by any such form of real evidence. For
neither our affections, nor our tastes, nor our judgments,
nor our beliefs, nor our ambitions, nor the higher expressions of our moral natures, can be thus demonstrated.
They do not in any way depend upon the classification of
facts in nature, but are cognizable by our consciousness,
and are so widely operative in our daily life, that it almost
seems as if what we call the knowable never touches us at all.

Science has nothing to say about, or to do with, either
morals, religion, benevolence, duty, or inspiration. The
sources of life, the cause of thought, of affection, passion,
hope, and love, are all incomprehensible to science, and will
remain so till the end of time. "There is no science of the
soul, any more than there is a prayer in mathematics." How
utterly, then, does one misapprehend and misstate the real
facts of human experience, who teaches that "nothing needs
inspiration but a falsehood, or a mistake," and that one is to
accept nothing as true which cannot be demonstrated. How
much wiser and how much better are the words of St. Augustine, when he says: "God exists more truly than he can
be thought of; He can be thought of more truly than he
can be spoken of." For myself, I reverently believe that
the Bible contains a revelation from God. I say contains
a revelation from God, not that it is in itself such a revelation, for the Bible, as such, was not revealed. The inspiration that breathes through its pages is of some of the things
written, but not of all; the inspiration is rather of the

thought, purpose, the leadings of God, than of the letter in which they are expressed. There is, to my mind, no appeal from the words of Christ once satisfied that he uttered the sayings which are attributed to Him in the Gospels, and they are, to me at least, infallibly true, and literally "the words of eternal life."

Ingersoll's "Religion of Humanity" All Right Except the Religion.

The influence of such an address is to completely destroy the religious faith which the people now have, and give them nothing in return. It is true Mr. Ingersoll commends to his hearers "the religion of humanity." But what does he mean by it? The answer is, he means simply Atheism, which is virtually the rejection of all religion, since it is the denial of the being of God himself. Now with God dethroned, the name religion has no further use. What, then, is the religion of humanity to those who deny the existence of God, and leave everything either to chance or inexorable law? One might infer from the assumption of these Atheistic teachers that free-thinkers are the only people who have any religion of humanity, or who practice it. The general impression made by the Colonel's lecture is that Christians are a bad lot—mean, hypocritical, demented kind of folks; and that bright and progressive people. such as "have brains" (though it does not require a large supply of that article to qualify one to ridicule another person's religion) and "do their own thinking," reject all such absurdities as revealed religion, and are governed by some sort of a higher law.

Now that this view of human nature, so complimentary and congenial, withal, is "quite taking" is very likely true. One likes to be patted on the back in this way, and be called "progressive," and not hide-bound like those old fogies, and stupid theological graduates, and owlish ministers, and such sort of folks. But somehow it does not seem to stay upon the public stomach after it is taken. For this is just the kind of talk in which noisy infidels have indulged for the past 300 years. "Christianity is virtually extinct," they say, "and now we are to have a new order of things." But, for some reason, Christianity does not die, and the world moves forward in much the old way."

The truth is, some things seem very well as declamation that utterly elude you when you attempt to embody them in vital forms. As theories they look well, but in practice they are worthless. They are as beautiful as foam and just as substantial. Where are the monuments of free religion? In the struggle for religious liberty in France I recognize the powerful influence of Voltaire; and an advocacy of a true democracy in this country, very few, if any, did more by their pen than Thomas Paine; but, aside from these general benefits to society, where are the testimonies of the work they wrought? What did they do for the more perfect organization of society, and for the elevation and purity of the public morals? I repeat, where are the monuments of this free religion? Has it nothing to show in its own behalf but slanderous assertions? And has its most distinguished advocate in this country degenerated into a jesting scoffer? Who built the institutions of learning throughout the Christian world, and who supports them? Who organized the institutions of charity, and who sustains them? I repeat, this "religion of humanity," whatever that may be, does well enough to talk about, but, somehow, when there is solid work to be done nobody wants it, and somehow, nobody seems to do or pay much towards supporting it. The leading universities in Germany that did so much forty years ago in disseminating Rationalism are now comparatively empty, while those of the religious schools are patronized. To-day every prominent university in Germany except that in Heidelberg is controlled in the interests of revealed religion, and Heidelberg has but very few theological students left. And, if one may judge of the effects of teaching by the deportment of those taught, it will be, I think, nearly the unanimous opinion of travelers that they are very badly instructed, for a prominent part of the business of the students of that institution seems to be to get up quarrels with each other and with the public, and fight duels. The truth is, that the sober second thought of the thinking world has shut its " colossal shears" upon the theories of Bauer, Strauss, and Renan, and no wisdom of man will ever reunite the dissevered fragments.

Dr. Ryder tells a Little Story for the Sake of Illustration.

How strange it is that nearly all the world should be such simpletons, and that human nature persists in exploding all these fine theories that have no real religion in them. But then, you know, some people are wise in their own conceits. Let me relate an incident: " An eminent lawyer had in court a very clear case. After presenting an array of testimony, law, and precedents that he thought was unanswerable, he submitted his case. To his utter astonishment, the Judge, who was bigotedly and dogmatically on the opposite side in prejudice, decided every point of the case against him. After he had recovered from his amazement, he arose and proceeded to read Blackstone and leading jurists, the statute law, and judicial decisions, flatly contradicting the decision of the Court. The Judge pompously interrupted him with: ' That will do you no good; the mind of the court is made up; cannot change it.' The lawyer replied: ' I have no expectation of changing the opinion of the court. I do not question the infallibility and the infallible accuracy of its decision. I only want to show what consummate fools Blackstone, Kent, and all jurists, our legislators, and all the judges, except the judge of this court, must have been.'"

Friends of humanity, lovers of the truth as it is in Jesus, can we afford to trifle with such a momentous issue as this? Is there nothing sacred, nothing but the mere husk of things in which it is safe for us to place our faith? Is there no permanent joy this side the grave, and only the blackness of darkness beyond? Is the religion in which so many millions trust simply a delusion, and the God whom we adore merely a myth? If so, why are we in this world, and what is this world? What is anything for but to lure us into disappointment?

Nay, we believe in God, the Father everlasting, and in Jesus Christ, His Son. In the love which They awaken, we desire to live; and in the trust which They inspire, we hope to die.

DR. HERFORD'S REPLY.

ALL through my life I have felt a very deep sympathy for those who have become alienated from Christianity by the irrational and unworthy things often taught in its name. It seems such a miserable, gratuitous loss, as if there was not enough to make even the purest faith often dim and doubtful without it being made more so by the follies of those who should strengthen men in it! But so it is. And of course one cannot expect men in that strong reaction to be very discriminating in what they attack. But there are limits! A man is not absolved from the duty of thinking and speaking fairly by having come to reject the popular opinions of society. Now it seems to me that this recent lecture of Col. Ingersoll's overpasses all just limits. I frankly own its brilliant eloquence, its irresistible humor, and the passionate impulses of tender human sympathy which flash out in it. I can quite understand many being carried along by these. But afterward has to come the sober thinking and the honest questioning. What does it amount to? Are its positions true? Are its arguments fair? It seems to me that they are glaringly the opposite. The whole test that he applies to his subject is a mistake; the way in which he applies it is not even moderately just; its representations are one-sided; its illustrations are caricature. And the worst of all is that there is no sign even of any desire or attempt to be fair!

The Ingersoll Paradox.

The first of Col. Ingersoll's mistakes, is in the whole point of view in which he places the Bible in order to make it the easier target for his wit. He starts by repudiating any idea of its having been written by God's inspiration; and yet all through talks as if God were responsible for it—as if God had said this and threatened that—and becomes quite heroic in his declaration that God may damn him, but he won't believe such things! When once inspiration is put aside, such declarations are mere clap-trap! When you look through all this, you find that in reality he simply regards the Bible as the work, the ideas of men. Very well; then take it so, and judge it fairly in that light! If the book of Genesis is, as Col. Ingersoll believes, the writings and the ideas of ancient men, then do not attack it because the ideas are not those of men to-day. But that is what he is constantly doing. He is very fond of saying, "The question is not, is it inspired, but is it true?" That sounds very plausible, but you know, as applied to any ancient book, it is simply nonsense. It is a test which you don't apply to any other ancient book in the world. You do not try Homer's "Iliad" by the test of whether it is true. When a clay tablet is dug up at Nineveh, or a papyrus is found in some mummy-wrappings, you don't ask, Is it true? and if not, throw it away. The question about all such things is not, "Are they true?" but "Are they genuine relics and representations of the thought of the ancient world?" By-and-by indeed will come the question, how far any records or statements in such ancient writings can be taken to throw light on actual history—how far their statements are allegorical or poetical, or mere ancient tradition? Well and good. And by all means let those questions be applied to Genesis; apply them just as you would to any other ancient

writings; but in the name of common fairness don't pick it
to pieces by a minute verbal criticism, and a strained liber-
ality which would only be justifiable on the ground of its
being verbally inspired. That is a mistake which may be
merely a mental confusion, but a graver one lies beyond.

Ingersoll's Exaggerations and False Assertions.

Mr. Ingersoll not only applies a kind of test to the book
of Genesis which he would not think of applying to any
other book, but he does not even apply his own test fairly.
He stands upon the very letter, but he constantly misrepresents and twists the letter. He exaggerates, makes things
worse than they are; if he can make a bad meaning anyhow
he does so. He says: "The gentleman that wrote Genesis
begins by telling us that God made the universe out of
nothing." It does not say so. It simply says: "In the
beginning God created the heaven and the earth." A little
further on he makes great fun of the grass being created on
the second day, while the sun was not created till the third
day, so that the grass was growing without having "ever
been touched by a gleam of light." Yet right before him
were these words, at the beginning of all: "And God said,
let there be light, and there was light." Of course, the
whole idea is that of the world's childhood, but why strain
a point to make it ridiculous? It is a far worse perversion
where he says: "You will find by reading the second chapter that God tried to palm off on Adam a beast as his helpmeet." Now there is absolutely no justification for such a
representation. The whole thing is a gratuitous invention
of his own. These are small verbal matters, but they show
the utter unscrupulousness with which those ancient traditions are exaggerated and distorted to make better point for
his ridicule.

And then, even in larger things, he cannot be decently

fair, though the explaining truth may lie on the very surface. He quotes the first part of the command against making any graven image, and then goes off into one of its
tirades about that being a law which was "the death of all
art " among the Jews. Not a word about the closing part
of the command—really the essence of it: " Thou shalt not
bow down to them, nor worship them! " Why, even if it
were as he implies, that Moses utterly prohibited all the art
of sculpture, the making of idols being merely one part, still,
which was of most importance to the world—that the Jews
should have cultivated art a little more, or that they should,
even at the cost of art altogether, be kept from idolatry?
But then Mr. Ingersoll is not even true in his fact. The
command was only understood as a command against idol-
making, not against other forms of sculpture, and the best
proof of this is that they did have other forms of sculpture
even in Moses' time, and later had art of no ignoble kind.
Even there in the wilderness we read how the sacred ark was
by Moses' command shadowed over by the images of two
cherubim, with outstretched wings made of pure gold, and
the candlestick was made with branches which were shaped
like almonds, alternately a bud and a flower. And later,
when Solomon built the temple, we not only read of two
similar cherubim, but of colossal size, extending their wings
over the shrine, but also that " he carved all the walls of the
house round about with carved figures of cherubim and palm-
trees and open flowers; " while in his own palace we read of
sculptured pillars, with pomegranate capitals, and images
of oxen and lions, round the great brazen "laver."

Or, take his representation of Christians thinking of
Heaven as a place where their happiness will be enhanced
by seeing the tortures of the damned. · Here he rises to the
height of his most fiery indignation. And · it is a horrible
idea. But then, who holds it—who preaches it? It is an

idea of Heaven that was prevalent among one sect of Christians a century ago. But even they have not preached it for a century. And yet he says, without a word of limitation, "This is the Christian view of Heaven," and makes a powerful appeal to his hearers not to give a "dollar to any man to preach that falsehood." Why, there is not a church in all the land where he could find a man preaching that to give his dollar to; no, not even if the person were only a stump politician, turned preacher in the slack season between campaigns.

And the same of his representation of the attitude of Christianity toward those who do not believe in the early traditions of Genesis. He represents Christianity as teaching that any man who does not believe the "rib story" will go to Hell, however good he was in other respects. Is that an honest representation? Why, even if all orthodoxy preached that, orthodoxy is not all of Christianity. Has Col. Ingersoll ever heard of Channing and Parker and Starr King? Are the bodies of the Unitarian church, the Universalists, the Christians, the Quakers, not worth a passing word? Did he not know when he put that champion joke about the "rib story" that he was representing as the teaching of the churches what many entire churches, and the best men in all churches, never have held, nor preached, nor countenanced in any way? Yet he comes rampaging into the field, with a whoop and a yell, brandishing his shillelah, defying Christianity, calling ministers "owls" and "idiots," and swooping round as if he were the first who had found out a little common sense about the Bible! But after all, the real matter at issue is not as to this or that exaggerated or unfair criticism of the Old Testament, but has it any real, substantial worth? It has. It gives us the origin of the world's noblest religious faith; it shows us the purest faith of to-day in its first roots in the far-off ancient world;

and so I think it strengthens our conviction that that faith is not a temporary or isolated thing that may be mistaken, but part of that long development of man which surely corresponds to the truth and fact of the universe.

Dr. Herford's Story of Moses, with an Apt Illustration— The Germinal Power of the Pentateuch.

When I hear people treating the Pentateuch as something they would like to see done away, I cannot help wishing that it could be dug up afresh in these days of curious research into the past. Why, suppose that the Jews had no such books; and had not known anything of their origin except a vague tradition of some sort of migration under one Moses, and curiously fitting to this the Egyptian tradition—which is, you know, that some thirteen hundred years before Christ a great multitude of people had gone out of Egypt led by an Egyptian priest, who taught them many things contrary to the Egyptian religion, and afterward changed his name to Moses. Well, supposing then these books of the Pentateuch should be discovered somewhere —why, the world would go wild over them. What would it matter whether it could be settled that Moses did or did not write them—or that possibly they were really not written till centuries after, and only preserved what was believed about him at that later date—still the fact would remain that they take us by traditions, at any rate, so much further back into the past, and show us there one of the very noblest stories of the world;—for that is what the story of Moses is. Take off all the discount you will for exaggeration—I dare say the numbers are immensely exaggerated—suppose the idea of his having been led by God speaking to him to have been only his own intense consciousness of what was best, ascribed to God; suppose the idea of his having been helped by miracles to have been only his own reverent impression, ascribing every trouble that came on Egypt, and every favoring circumstance to his own people, to some purposed and direct help from God; all that does not touch the essence of the story of Moses! There it stands—how those Hebrews through many generations had sunk into the Pariah and Helot class of that great rich Egyptian civilization; and how at last this Moses rose up, to rally them to a mighty effort to get right away into some other land. He had been somehow brought up among the Egyptians, trained in the sacred city, educated among the priests—an adopted son of Pharaoh's daughter—but he had given it all up, identified himself with his down-trodden people, and at last won for them the liberty *to go!* And they went out—out into the great desert waste. What does it matter that the tradition of their numbers got perhaps enormously exaggerated? If there were only a hundredth part—thirty thousand instead of three millions in all—there were quite enough to task their leader's fortitude to its utmost; and through those books we have at least very living glimpses of him, in his efforts to keep them from grumbling and getting disheartened; in his efforts to keep them true to his simple teaching of the one Almighty God; in his lonely hours when he was listening for the eternal word, and shaping his best thoughts which he believed came to him from God, into laws for his people. And there is the great fact, you know— however he did it—he *did* guide and lead them through that long migration, and at last brought them to the land from which their fathers had gone out long before, and bade them go in and possess it! And that multitude whom he led out of Egypt a race of slaves, servile with long oppression, at every difficulty talking of going back, he had in that forty years knit into a brave, hardy, fierce race—who did go in and possess the land and became the progenitors of one of the world's noblest races. That is the story of Moses

4

—just the barest skeleton of it—taking one, the largest, most unmistakable features; and I say again there is no finer story in history. And what will you say of a man who will make fun of it?

Why, what would you think of a man who would go around the country, making fierce fun of Abraham Lincoln, holding up his gaunt, lank figure to ridicule, burlesquing his speeches, denouncing as lies some of those quaint little anecdotes, and holding him up as a fool and an idiot? And yet that glorious work that makes Lincoln's name dear—not to Americans only but to the lovers of freedom and of man in every nation—that work of his was only the modern counterpart of what Moses did in the morning of the world!

But the Pentateuch is most valuable, not for the light it throws upon the origin of a people, but for the light it throws upon the origin of ideas. In the teachings of Moses, in the religion of that little migrating tribe, by-and-by fighting for its foothold in Palestine, we have the beginings of those thoughts from which have sprung the three greatest, most living religions of the world—Judaism, Christianity and Mahommedanism. Granted, the beginnings are only rude, is that any reason for making fun of them? What would you think of a man who should take one of those rude urns that they dig out of the mound builder's graves and put it side by side with some beautiful porcelain of to-day, and scoff and sneer at those early dwellers on the earth because the best decoration they could make was a few rude scratches in the clay with their flint-knives?

Already, even so far off, the idea of one Almighty God, that which the priests of Egypt held as a sacred mystery— if they *did* hold it—that leader of the Hebrews taught his people as the truth for all, and the truth to be kept evermore before them. Already, too, in the old world, where every race shaped out its thought of God in some idol form, that leader was giving them as the second of his great commands that they should make no idol images at all to worship. Already, too, they had that idea of a God of Righteousness! True, their idea of righteousness was not yet very high, but the best they knew they ascribed to God. Where in all the ancient world will you find such a description of Deity as that which Moses brought with him out of the solitudes of Sinai?—"The Lord; the Lord God, merciful and gracious, long suffering and abundant in goodness and truth; keeping mercy for thousands, bearing with iniquity, transgression and sin, but that will by no means clear the guilty."

The Mosaic Religion of Humanity.

Nor is this divine side of that old Hebrew religion all. Mr. Ingersoll is very strong on the religion of humanity. Indeed, that is the only real religion, he says. Well, where did the religion of humanity begin? Why, it began there—among those same old Hebrews. The religion of a truer thought of God and of a better thought of man went together even in their beginnings, as they did afterward when they both reached their culmination together in Christ, with His great teaching of love to God and love to man.

Mr. Ingersoll, however, has nothing but the bitterest contempt for the morality of the Pentateuch, because it is behind the morality of to-day! "See, you are better than your God," he cries; "for four thousand years ago He believed in polygamy, and you don't!" The truth of which simply is that four thousand years ago polygamy existed among the Jews, as everywhere else on earth then, and even their prophets do not come to the idea of its being wrong. But what is there to be indignant about in that? Simply men—whom Mr. Ingersoll regards, in other lectures, as having come up from the brutes—had then got only so far in their ideas of marriage. But if their religion is a good one, what do you expect to find it doing? Altogether altering, even so 'early, the marriage relation, or purifying and elevating it? Surely this is all we can look for, and this we find. I know that Mr. Ingersoll says: "There is not one word about woman in the Old Testament, except the words of shame and humiliation." Well, though he says he has read the Bible over again this year, I can only conclude he has read it very hurriedly and slightly, for not only are there such passages as that of Naomi and Ruth, the Shunamite woman, Hannah, the mother of Samuel, and that most beautiful picture at the close of the book of Proverbs of a good wife, but I think that throughout woman is spoken of in the Bible, not as the slave, but as the companion and the helpmate. The "wise-hearted women" share the work of making that goodliest of the tents which was in the desert wanderings to be the tabernacle; Miriam, the sister of Moses, holds the place of a prophetess, and other prophetesses we read of; and the whole law of marriage in the Pentateuch, with its stern punishment of death for adultery, either on the part of man as well as woman, shows the process of elevation towards that higher law of one wife and one husband which had become universal by the time of Christ.

Or take the slavery question again. Slavery was universal in the ancient world. Men had not come anywhere to a sense of any inherent wrongfulness in it for a thousand years or two after the time of Moses. But mark where this finer humanity of the Mosaic religion comes in; it already brings glimpses of the idea of an inalienable right to liberty—though not a perfect sight of it. The law of the Pentateuch abounds with laws about the relation of master and slave, which, as compared with what we know of slavery, *e. g.*, among the Greeks and Romans a thousand years later, were simply a marvel of noble humanized thought.

And then as to the general tone and character of that Mosaic law. Mr. Ingersoll pooh-poohs the Ten Commandments as merely what men knew before; knew all along. But such a law as this: "Thou shalt not have in thy bag divers weights, a great and a small; but thou shalt have a perfect and just weight—a perfect and just measure shalt thou have—for all that do such things, and all that do unrighteously, are an abomination unto the Lord thy God;" and this: "If a man shall steal an ox or a sheep he shall restore five oxen for an ox and four sheep for a sheep;" and this: "Ye shall have one manner of law, as well for the stranger as for one of your own country, for I am the Lord your God;" and this: "Thou shalt not oppress an hired servant that is poor and needy—whether he be of thy brethren, or of the strangers that are in the land; at his day thou shalt give him his hire; neither shall the sun go down upon it, for he is poor and setteth his heart upon it." There is a good deal of the religion of humanity about these, isn't there?

And other laws come in here and there with such a kind consideration for poverty and need. When a man harvested he must not reap the corners of his field, nor gather up the gleanings, and if he forgot a sheaf and left it in the field he must not go again and fetch it. "Thou shalt leave them for the poor and the stranger." And this: "When a man hath taken a new wife he shall not go out to war, neither shall he be charged with any business; but he shall be free at home one year and shall cheer up his wife whom he hath taken." And even in regard to war—in which certainly they were fierce enough—what a gleam of kindness comes in in that command that when they were besieging a city they must not cut down the fruit trees about it for their war purposes, but only trees that they knew were not for fruit. Why, I might go on for an hour quoting these more merciful laws and showing you the large, grand thoughts of duty that pervade that whole system which the Jews believed had been given to them by Moses.

But there is nothing really to fear. For the moment many may be led to throw the Bible away, and to give up religion as the weak nonsense he so scornfully proclaims it. Religion will abide in the heart of man. And the Bible will stand because in it we have the accumulated utterance of religion in its best beginnings and along its noblest line of development.

THE JEWISH RABBI'S REPLY.

We need not pray for Col. Robert Ingersoll's soul, for he says he has none; and in this instance we are bound to believe him, as he is judge, jury and witness in the case; and there may be men without souls, as there are some without conscience, others without reason, and quite a number without principle. The first man of whom the Bible says that he prayed, was Abraham. He prayed for Abimelech. But Col. Ingersoll, we suspect, is not smitten with that disease. He prayed for the wicked people of Sodom and Gomorrah, to which class belongs no American citizen, of course, as "Mitchell's Geography" substantially proves. Jacob prayed when his brother Esau approached him with an armed force; and the Colonel has come to us unarmed, and without any force except a few harmless agents of the Boston Lecture Bureau, who take the money, show the show, and depart in peace. Moses prayed for his sister Miriam when she was leprous, but Mr. Ingersoll is no woman, and his excellent exterior betokens no leprosy. Joshua prayed to make the sun and moon stand still, but Mr. Ingersoll is neither the greater nor the lesser light, and to the best of our knowledge nobody wants him to stand still at any place.

Speaking of imagination, it reminds me that Col. Ingersoll said he could not imagine the existence of a God. Imagine God! Any professor of philosophy would faint if he was told that illogical expression. How can God be imagined? Perhaps one of Mr. Ingersoll's manufactured gods could be imagined in a disorderly imagination, as only physical objects of nature or combinations thereof could be imagined—nothing else. What kind of a god would that be which could be submitted to the imagination of a man without a soul? It must be the miniature or pocket edition of an idol, made by man, such as Col. Ingersoll purchases and exhibits to amuse tall babies. It must be that sort of farcical gods which he describes in his burlesques. He is not the first quack who would not take his own medicines, although he is certainly among reasoners the first who would imagine Deity, for none tries to imagine that which reason only can grasp; none will permit himself to be led astray by imagination where pure reflection only can reach the aim.

The perversion of ideas springs from a mistake about Moses. A god or gods have been fabricated at the expense of Moses, until each little priest had his own snug little god that could be used as the Crusader's emblem or the license of the auto-da-fe, to massacre and glut in human gore, or the frail woman's last resort of love to make honest men out of rogues, pure souls out of the dregs of hell. The god or gods variously depicted, miscellaneously described, and promiscuously applied become objects of imagination, hence also of the farce. The mistake is that Moses was charged with all the follies of theological jugglers and sophistical bummers. The God whom Moses taught is emphatically the God whom no man can see and live,—the Great I Am, who is the I, the Ego, the Subject of the Universe, the law, the life, the love and the intellect of the cosmos, the Eternal Jehovah, essence itself, and the absolute substance, in whom all things are as all objects of a man's tender love are in his soul, of whom all things came and into whom all return. This is not a God fabricated by man, hence He could not

be imagined by man, as no man can imagine a being superior to himself. This is the God taught by Moses; the other
gods may be subjected to farce and ribaldry, while the true
Deity is too sublime even for the pyrotechnical displays of
Mr. Ingersoll's disentangled humor. It is a mistake about
Moses which feeds his boiler to tweedle the rusted think-
apparatus of twaddlers. The God of Moses is too great for
Mr. Ingersoll; he only deals in gods which can be imagined, and in speaking of mistakes of Moses he reverently
passes by the God of Moses. The man is not as bad as his
reputation.

I maintain that Col. Robert Ingersoll is not half as bad
as his reputation. The man was persecuted by his country-
men, was defeated in his political aspirations by church-
members, and thinks the Presbyterians have done it. He
is a man of prominent talents, belonging to the better class;
all on account of the Presbyterians, he was teased, persecuted, and wounded in his pride, and so he became a public
lecturer. But business is business; if one wants to make
money he must know how. He could imagine that people
go to the circus to see the clown, to the theater to laugh
over the comedian. People want fun to be amused, alcohol
to force the blood to the brain, to fill up the vacuum. He
could see that earnest men who reason on principles would
not take with the masses. Aware of his own talents as a
humorist and an orator, of the scarcity of humorists in this
country, and the plenitude of slang, low comedy, and uncul-
tivated taste, he could only choose the career which he did
choose—a career of ribaldry, to laugh over everything holy,
to sneer alike at human follies, frailties, virtue and piety;
and as a business man he has chosen well—he makes plenty
of money and hurts nobody. A moral effect he will never
have upon anybody, because there is no moral force in his
burlesque. He is no Thomas Paine, Thomas Jefferson, no

Voltaire, Strauss, Feuerbach, or even a Heinrich Heine, because he lacks the research, the erudition, the systematical learning, and the moral backbone of either of them. He will not set Rome on fire in order to sing from his balcony the destruction of Troy; he lacks the fire and the torch. It is all pyrotechnical ribaldry, which sweeps away many a consumptive superstition and laughs many a prejudice out of existence; but truth takes care of itself. Let the man alone; he is better than his reputation.

You think, perhaps, I ought to be very angry, because the gentleman spoke of the mistakes of Moses, and ridiculed the great lawgiver of the Jews. Let me tell you first, anything over which you laugh leaves no particular impression behind. That which goes not though the avenues of reason or the depth of the moral sentiment in a short time proves effectless. Scorn is a terrible weapon to achieve momentary success, but it is worse than worthless after a second sober thought or a healthy action of the feelings. Then let me say, the theology of Moses is certainly beyond the reach of Col. Ingersoll, for he is no reasoner; he can spit, but he could not think with philosophical minds. He never studied through or even read any of the philosophical systems of Germany, England, or France; nor has he the ability to do it. He is no naturalist of any description, has never troubled himself about any specialty thereof, and so he talks about matters and things in general as is the American custom, what the Germans call *Wurst-philosophie,* good enough as jokes or for beer-house reasonings. When he speaks of the infinite he becomes too ludicrous for anything, especially for men of thought to make anything out of it. He will not upset the theology of Moses.

The law of Moses is also secured against the Colonel's possible attacks. He will commence no trouble with his **Blackstone** or **Hugo Grotius,** or the other writers on law who maintain that all law rests upon the Mosaic legislation.

Thirty-five hundred years of history, and the common consent of the civilized world at this end of the nineteenth century, are a little too much for any man to upset. He says he could write a better Decalogue than Moses did, but that is said only—he is not going to do it; he will not even add a category of law to the ten.

Well, then, if he is not the man to attack successfully the theology or jurisprudence of Moses, I have no cause to object to his lectures. He ridicules Bible stories, but that concerns literalists only, not us. If all the stories of the Pentateuch be ridiculed, denied, or otherwise disposed of, it does not change an iota in the jurisprudence or theology of Moses. Let the literalists take up that part; it does not concern us so very much.

Here, again, is a point which makes me feel bad and badly disposed to the eloquent humorist. Why does he continually repeat that which others have said often before him; why does he not hit upon something original? He rehearses old rags in new shoddy, and that is unworthy of a man who has any pride about him. He does sometimes worse than that; he ignores his opponents, which no honest man must do. He speaks a long yarn about the history of creation, always assuming an air of originality, without having the honesty of mentioning even Dr. J. W. Dawson's work, "The Origin of the World," which upsets his whole twaddle. It is dishonest to make people believe that a thing said is indisputable, when it has been completely upset.

He appeals to the apotheosis of labor to impeach Moses, because it said in the Genesis that God cursed man. "In the sweat of thy brow shalt thou eat bread;" and labor is a blessing to man. Did all Socialists clap hands? If not,

some must have thought this is the language of a dema-
gogue, who is either a hypocrite or a self-deluded man.   Labor and hard labor are two different things, and the "sweat
of thy brow" points to hard labor, which rests like a curse
upon the poor man, and is the severest punishment imposed
on the criminal condemned to hard labor.

He talks about the creation of woman like an ignorant
man who has not the remotest idea of the difficulties among
biologists, considering the differentiation of man and the
origin of sexes.   So he talks about the littleness of the ark
and smites Charles Darwin in the face, instead of saying
this proves Darwin's theory on the origin of species.   He
scoffs at the God who destroyed His own children and
undertakes to teach the Colonel of Peoria how he should
educate his.   It all depends upon what kind of children one
wishes to bring up.   Usually every parent brings up his own
kind.   God wanted them to bring up God-like children, and
when they would not do it, he got them out of the way in
preference to destroying human freedom or perpetuating
wickedness.   If it is only to bring up such children as Robert Ingersoll, of Peoria, Ill., no such stringency is necessary.
Musquashes grow spontaneously in abundance.   Then he
speaks about 600 pigeons a day for three priests, and does
not know that there were no pigeons in the wilderness, and
the Mosaic sacrificial polity was not introduced till Joshua
had taken the Land of Canaan, and then there were more
priests than there are to-day humorists in America, for
Joshua gave them quite a number of cities, and I would
not be astonished if those American humorists could eat
more pigeons than they can do good in this world.

But what is the use to speak of the mistakes of Moses?
Speak of the mistakes about Moses.   Did Moses write the
Genesis?   Says Col. Ingersoll, "I do not know;" and he
does not know a great many other things.   Did Moses write

the historical portions of the Pentateuch? Says the Illinois Colonel again, "I do not know." If he has written all that, did the translators and commentators which the Colonel read represent correctly the ideas of Moses? "Do n't know," says the Colonel. If those writers do represent the matter correctly, have those points which the Colonel ridicules never been discussed and refuted? "Do n't know," says the Colonel; and decent men must not curse; still they are permitted to say, "Why do you talk of matters of which you know so preciously little? That is all excusable, however, in this case. The humorous and eloquent gentleman is out on a lecture tour, and wants to succeed. This can be done by reckless ribaldry only. It makes no difference whether Hell or gods, Devil or Moses, Pope or Presbyterian church —anything that will pay must be pressed into the service. The Colonel's field is small; he has no great choice of subjects, and he must take the first best to ridicule it and make it pay. He has that particular talent, and could not do the same work in another field. He cannot criticise Aristotle and Emanuel Kant and make it pay, because he cannot read them. He cannot ridicule Carlyle or Stuart Mill, because he cannot understand them. So he picks up some small stories which the children know, and dishes them up in his own humoristic way for the amusement of big babies. The man understands his business to the T. I tell you, he is not as bad as his reputation. I beg a thousand pardons of Col. Robert Ingersoll if I have wronged him. I did not mean to make fun of him any way.

Juel Gibson

[Photographed by Mosher.]

DR. GIBSON'S REPLY.*

UNHAPPILY, the attention of Bible students has been almost exclusively directed to certain difficulties. These difficulties all arise, as it seems to me, from three sources, and the Bible is not to blame for any of them. First source: treating the passage as if it were history, whereas it is apocalypse. Second source: taking it as intended to teach science, especially astronomical and geological science. Third source of difficulty: the mistakes of translators. For example, the unfortunate word firmament continually comes to the front as one of the " mistakes of Moses." Strange that a Latin word should be a mistake of Moses! Did Moses know Latin? Did he ever write the letters f, i, r, m, etc.? Not only is the word "firmament" not in the Hebrew Bible, but it does not represent the Hebrew word at all. The word firmament means something strong, solid. The Hebrew word for which it is an unfortunate translation, signifies something that is very thin, extended, spread out; just the best word that could be chosen to signify the atmosphere.

Then there is the word "whales," that Professor Huxley made so merry over a year ago. But the Hebrew does not say whales. The Hebrew word refers to great sea monsters, and is just the very best word the Hebrew language affords to describe such animals as the plesiosaurus and ichthyosaurus and other creatures that abounded in the time prob-

---

*Portions of this reply recently appeared in the daily press signed "CANDOR;" other portions were selected by the Editor from his new work, just published by Randolph & Co., New York, entitled "The Ages Before Moses."

ably referred to there. Let us only guard against these three sources of error, and we shall not find many difficulties. If we would only avoid the mistakes of Moses' critics, we would not show our ignorance by talking about the mistakes of Moses.

We have said that almost everybody knows about the difficulties, but how few are there comparatively that know about the wonderful harmonies? So much is said and written about the difficulties, that many have the idea that the narrative is full of difficulties—nothing but difficulties in it —nothing that agrees with science as we know it now; whereas, when we look at it, we find the correspondencies most wonderful all the way through. Let us look at a few of them. And first, the absence of dates. The fact is very noteworthy that there is such abundance of space left for the long periods, not till quite recently demanded by science. And this does not depend on any theory of day-periods; for those who still hold to the literal days, find all the room required before the first day is mentioned. Not six thousand years ago, but " in the beginning." How grand and how true in its vagueness.

Another negative characteristic worth noticing here is the absence of details where none are needed. For example, there is almost nothing said in detail about the heavens. What is said about the heavens in addition to the bare fact of creation, is only in reference to the earth, as, for example, when the sun and moon are treated of, not as separate worlds, but only in their relation to this earth as giving light to it and affording measurements of time. There is no attempt to drag in the spectroscope!

Ingersoll Betrays His Ignorance.

A certain infidel lately seemed to think he had made a point against the Bible by remarking that the author of it had compressed the astronomy of the universe into five words. Just think of the ignorance this betrays. It proceeds on the assumption that the author of this apocalypse intended to teach the world the astronomy of the universe; and then, of course, it would have been a very foolish thing for him to discuss the whole subject in five words. Whereas, in this very reticence we have a note of truth. If this work had been the work of some mere cosmogonist, some theorist as to the origin of the universe, he would have been sure to have given us a great deal of information about the stars. But a prophet of the Lord has nothing to do with astronomy as such. All that he has to do with the stars is to make it clear that the most distant orbs of light are included in the domain of the Great Supreme, and this he can do as well in five words as in five thousand; and so, wisely avoiding all detail, he simply says, " He made the stars also." There was danger that men might suppose some power resident in these distant stars distinct from the power that ruled the earth. He would have them to understand that the same God that rules over this little earth, rules to the uttermost bounds of the great universe. And this great truth he lays on immovable foundations by the sublimely simple words, " He made the stars also." But passing from that which is merely negative, see how many positive harmonies there are.

Harmony of Science and Genesis.

First, there is the fact of a beginning. The old infidel objection used to be that " all things have continued as they were from the beginning of the creation." Nobody pretends to take that position now that science points so clearly to beginnings of everything. You can trace back man to his beginning in the geological cycles. You can trace back mammals to their beginning; birds, fishes, insects to their beginnings; vegetation to its beginning; rocks to their

5

beginning. The general fact of a genesis is immovably established by science.

Secondly, " The heavens and the earth." Note the order Though almost nothing is said about the heavens, yet what is said is not at all in conflict with what we now know about them. We know now that the earth is not the center of the universe. Look forward to Genesis iv. 2, and you will find the transition to the reverse order—quite appropriate there, as we shall see in the next lecture; but here, where the genesis of all things, the origin of the universe, is the subject, it is not the earth and the heavens, but " in the beginning God created the heavens and the earth."

Thirdly, there is the original chaos. " The earth was without form and void." Turn to the early pages of any good modern scientific book, that attempts to set forth the genesis of the earth from a scientific standpoint, and you will find just this condition described. Observe, too, in passing, how carefully the statement is limited to the earth. The universe was not chaotic then.

Fourthly, the work of creation is not a simultaneous, but an extended one. If the author had been guessing or theorizing, he would have been much more likely to hit on the idea of simultaneous, than successive creation. But the idea of successive creation is now proved by science to be true.

Fifthly, there is a progressive development, and yet not a continuous progression without any drawbacks. There are evenings and mornings; just what science tells us of the ages of the past. Here it is worth while perhaps to notice the careful use of the word " created." An objection has been made to the want of continuity in the so-called orthodox doctrine of creation, the orthodox doctrine being supposed to be that of fresh creation at every point. But the Bible is not responsible for many " fresh creations."

The word " created " is only used three times in the record.
First, as applied to the original creation of the universe,
possibly in the most embryonic state. " In the beginning
God created the heavens and the earth." Next, in connection with the introduction of life (v. 2), and last, in reference to the creation of man (v. 27). In no other place is
anything said about direct creation. It is rather making,
appointing, ordering, saying " Let there be." " Let the
waters bring forth," etc. Now, is it not a significant fact
that these three points where, and where alone, the idea of
absolute creation is introduced, are just the three points at
which the great apostles of continuity find it impossible to
make their connections? You will not find any one that is
able to show any other origin for the spirit of man than the
Creator Himself. You cannot find any one that is able to
show any other origin of animal life than the Creator Himself. There have been very strenuous efforts made a great
many times to show that the living may originate from the
not-living; but all these efforts have failed. And the origin
of matter is just as mysterious as the origin of life. No
other origin can be even conceived of the primal matter of
the universe than the fiat of the great Creator. Thus we
find the word " creation " used just at the times when
modern science tells us it is most appropriate.

Sixthly, the progression is from the lower to the higher.
An inventor would have been much more likely to guess
that man was created first, and afterward the other creatures
subordinate to him. But the record begins at the bottom
of the scale and goes up, step by step, to the top: again,
just what geology tells us. All these are great general
correspondencies; but we might,

Seventhly, go into details and find harmonies even there,
all the way through. Take the fact of light appearing on
the first day. The Hebrew word for " light " is wide enough

to cover the associated phenomena of heat and electricity, and are not these the primal forces of the universe? Again, it used to be a standard difficulty with sceptics that light was said to exist before the sun was visible from the earth. Science here has come to the rescue, and who doubts it now? It is very interesting to see a distinguished geologist like Dana using this very fact that light is said to have existed before the sun shone upon the earth as a proof of the divine origin of this document, on the ground that no one would have guessed what must have seemed so unlikely then. So much for the progress *toward* the Bible which science has made since the day when a sceptical writer said of the Mosaic narrative, " It would still be correct enough in great principles were it not for one individual oversight and one unlucky blunder! "—the oversight being the solid firmament (whose oversight?), and the blunder, light apart from the sun (whose blunder?).

I have spoken already about the words " created " and " made," in relation to the discriminating use of them. This word *raqia*, too, how admirable it is to express the tenuity of our atmosphere, especially as contrasted with the clumsy words used by the enlightened Greeks (stereoma) the noble Romans (firmamentum), and even by learned Englishmen of the nineteenth century (firmament)! And not to dwell on mere words, as we well might, look at the general order of creation: vegetation before animal life, birds and fishes before mammals, and all the lower animals before man. Is not that just the order you find in geology? More particularly, while man is last he is not created on a separate day. He comes in on the sixth day along with the higher animals, yet not in the beginning, but toward the close of the period. Again, just what geology tells us.

The Harmony of Genesis and Science, not the Result of Guess Work, but of Inspiration.

These are only some of the many wonderful harmonies between this old revelation and modern science. I would like to see the doctrine of chances applied to this problem, to determine what probability there would be of a mere guesser or inventor hitting upon so many things that correspond with what modern science reveals. I don't believe there would be one chance in a million! Is it not far harder for a sensible man to believe that this wonderful apocalypse is the fruit of ignorance and guess-work, than that it is the product of inspiration? It is simply absurd to imagine that an ignorant man could have guessed so happily. Nay, more. Let any of the scientific men of to-day set themselves down to write out a history of creation in a space no larger than that occupied by the first chapter of Genesis and I do not believe they could improve on it at all. And if they did succeed in producing anything that would pass for the present, in all probability in ten years it would be out of date. Our apocalypse of creation is not only better than could be expected of an uninspired man in the days of the world's ignorance, but it is better than Tyndall, or Huxley, or Haeckel could do yet. If they think not, let them take a single sheet of paper and try!

.... It is of great importance to remember that the symbolism attaches to the form, and not to the substance of the history. To call this whole story of the Fall a mere allegory, is to take away from it all historical reality. Let us distinguish carefully between the *reality* of the history, which is a very important thing, and the *literality* of it, which is of minor importance. It is very unfortunate that so much time is often spent upon the mere letter, regardless of the warning of the great apostle: "The letter killeth, but the spirit giveth life. This accounts for nine-tenths of the difficulties people have about it. Suppose a person, seeing a cocoanut for the first time, and being told it was good for food, should spend all his time gnawing away at the shell, and never get at the kernel. No wonder of his verdict should be, it is not fit to eat. So you will find that most of the people who have insuperable difficulties with the Bible are those who are busying themselves all the time about the shell and never get hold of the kernel. If they could only seize the kernel they would so readily see the beauty and enjoy the taste, and find the use of it; and then, perhaps, they would begin to see some beauty and some usefulness in the shell too. "The letter killeth, but the Spirit giveth life."

A very good illustration of this is found in the fifteenth verse of the third chapter, where we read about "the seed of the woman bruising the head of the serpent." The literalists get nothing more out of it than a declaration that in time to come serpents will annoy the descendants of Eve by biting at their heels, and on the other hand, the descendants of Eve will destroy serpents by crushing their heads! The mere shell of the thing manifestly. The reality, as pictured there, is of a great conflict to go on throughout all these ages of development; a great conflict between the forces of good on the one hand, and the forces of evil on the other. Of this conflict the issue is not doubtful. There is to be serious trouble all the while from the forces of evil, but in the end these forces will be crushed. There is One coming —a descendant of this same woman, called here "the seed of the woman"—who will at last "bruise the head of the serpent," and gain the victory, and bring in that glorious era when sin and suffering and pain and death shall have all rolled away into the past. There is a great deal more than this in that wonderful verse—more than we would have time to tell though we spent a whole hour on it. We only refer to it now as an illustration.

And now, what matters it whether you take the "serpent" that tempted Eve to be a real and literal serpent, or the mere (phenomenal) form of a serpent assumed by the Spirit of Evil for the purpose? or even whether the serpent form is connected with the old style of pictorial representation? All that is minor and subordinate. There is no use of wasting time on it. All we want to be sure of is the truth, that there was a tempter, an evil spirit, that in a seductive form tempted our first parents and they fell. Let us by all means beware of allowing our time to be frittered away by mere trivial questions of the letter, instead of making it our great aim to see and to seize the great spiritual truths set forth in this old and simple record.

There are many who represent this book of the Generations as a second edition of the Genesis, or separate account of the creation; and of course they find difficulty in comparing the two. All their difficulty, as we shall see, comes from their not understanding the passage as a whole, their not perceiving what it was intended to teach. It will help us to meet this difficulty if we follow the same order of ideas as in the exposition of Genesis i., viz.: God, Nature, Man. In all we shall find marked differences. But these differences, instead of presenting any difficulty, will have their reason made abundantly manifest.

God.

First, then, there is a different name for God introduced here. All through the Genesis it has been "God said," "God made," "God created." Now it is invariably, "Jehovah God" (LORD God in our version). And this is the only continuous passage in the Bible where the combination is used. How is this explained? Very easily. In the apocalypse of the Genesis, God makes Himself known simply as Creator. Sin has not yet entered, and so the idea of salvation has no place. In this passage sin is coming in, and along with it the promise of salvation. Now the name Jehovah is always connected with the idea of salvation. It is the covenant name. It is the name which indicates God's special relation to His people, as their Saviour and Redeemer. This name is introduced now, because God is about to make Himself known in a new character. He appeared in Genesis simply as Creator. He appears now in the book of the Generations as Redeemer; and so we get the name Jehovah in place of the name God. But lest any one should suppose from the change of name that there is any change in the person; lest any one suppose that He who is to redeem us from sin and death, is a different being from Him who created the heavens and the earth, the two names are now combined—Jehovah God. The combination is retained throughout the entire narrative of the Fall to make the identification sure. Thereafter either name is used by itself without danger of error.

Nature.

Look next at the way in which Nature is spoken of here. When you look at it aright, you find there is no repetition. Nature in the Genesis is universal nature. God created all things. But here, nature comes in, as it has to do immediately with Adam. Now see the effect of this. It at once removes difficulties, which many speak of as of great magnitude.

In the first place, it is not the whole earth that is now spoken of, but a very limited district. Our attention is narrowed down to Eden, and the environs of Eden, a limited district in a particular part of the earth. Hence the difficulty about there not being rain in the district ("earth") disappears. Let me here remind you once or all that the Hebrew word for *earth* and for *land* or *district* is the same. See Gen. xii., 1., where the word is twice used, translated "country" and "land."

Again, it is not the vegetable kingdom as a whole that is referred to in the fifth verse, but only the agricultural and horticultural products. The words "plant," "field" and "grew" (v. 5) are new words, not found in the creation record.* In Gen. i. the vegetable kingdom as a whole was spoken of. Now, it is simply the cereals and garden herbs, and things of that sort; and here instead of coming into collision with the previous narrative, we have something that corresponds with what botanists tell us, that field and garden products are sharply distinguished in the history of nature from the old flora of the geological epochs.

In the same way it is not the whole animal kingdom that is referred to in verse nineteen, but only the domestic animals, those with which man was to be especially associated, and to which he was very much more intimately related than to the wild beasts of the field. It may be easy to make this narrative look ridiculous, by bringing the wild beasts in array before Adam, as if any companionship with them were conceivable. But when we bear in mind that reference is made here to the domestic animals, there is nothing at all inappropriate in noticing that while there is a certain degree of companionship possible between man and some of those animals, as the horse and dog, yet none of these was the companion he needed.

In the first chapter of Genesis, nature is the great theme. We are carried over universal nature, and the great truth is there set forth, that God has created all things. In the second chapter of Genesis, man is the great theme, and conse-

---

* The correct translation of the fifth verse is: "Now no plant of the field was yet in the land, and no herb of the field was growing."

quently nature is treated of only as it circles around him, and is related to him. This sufficiently accounts for the difference between the two.

Man.

Passing now from nature to Man, we find again a marked difference. In Gen. i. we are told, "God created man in His own image; in the image of God created He him." And here: "The Lord God formed man of the dust of the ground." (ii. 7.) Some people tell as there is a contradiction here. *Is* there any contradiction, let me ask? Are not *both* of them true? Is there not something that tells you that there is more than dust in your composition? Is there not something in you that tells you, you are related to God the Creator? When you hear the statement that "God made man in His own image, is there not a response awakened in you—something in you that rises up and says, It is true? On the other hand, we know that man's body is formed of the dust of the earth. We find it to be true in a more literal sense than was formerly supposed, now that chemistry discloses the fact that the same elements enter into the composition of man's body, as are found by analysis in the "dust of the ground."

And not only are both these statements true, but each is appropriate in its place. In the first account, when man's place in universal nature was to be set forth—man as he issued from his Maker's hand—was it not appropriate that his higher nature should occupy the foreground? His lower relations are not entirely out of sight even there, for he is introduced along with a whole group of animals created on the sixth day. But while his connection with them is suggested, that to which emphasis is given in the Genesis is his relation to his Maker. But now that we are going to hear about his fall, about his shame and degradation, is it not appropriate that the lower rather than the higher part of his nature should be brought into the foreground, inasmuch as it is there that the danger lies? It was to that part of his nature that the temptation was addressed; and so we read here, "God formed man of the dust of the ground." Yet here, too, there is a hint of his higher nature, for it is added, "He breathed into his nostrils the breath of life," or as we have it in another passage, "The inspiration of the Almighty gave him understanding."

In this connection it is worth while to notice the use of the words "created" and "formed." "God *created* man in His own image." So far as man's spiritual and immortal nature was concerned it was a new creation. On the other hand, "God *formed* man out of the dust of the ground." We are not told He created man's body out of nothing. We are told, and the sciences of to-day confirm it, that it was formed out of existing materials.

Woman.

Then, in relation to Woman, there is the same appropriateness in the two narratives. In the former her relations to God are prominent: "God created man in His own image. In the image of God created He him; male and female created He them"—man in His image; woman in His image. In the latter, it is not the relation of woman to her Maker that is brought forward, but the relation of woman to her husband. Hence the specific reference to her organic connection with her husband.

Here, again, it is very easy for one that deals in literalities to raise difficulties, forgetting that there is no intention here to detail scientifically the process of woman's formation, but simply to indicate that she is organically connected with her husband. It is here proper to remark that the rendering "rib" is probably too specific. The word is more

frequently used in the general sense of "side." As an evidence that there is no intention to give here any physiological information as to the origin of woman, we may refer
to the words of Adam: "This is now bone of my bone and
flesh of my flesh. She shall be called Woman, because she
was taken out of man." And now, is there anything irrational in the idea that woman should be formed out of man?
Is there anything more mysterious or inconceivable in the
formation of woman out of man, than in the original formation of man out of dust? Let us conceive of our origin
in any way we choose, it is full of mystery. Though there
may be mystery connected with what is said in the Bible,
there will be just as much mystery connected with any other
account you try to give of it. Matthew Henry, in his
quaint and half-humorous way, really gets nearer to the
true spirit of the narrative than any physiological interpreter can, when he makes the remark that some of you
may be familiar with, "that woman was taken out of man,
not out of his head to top him, nor out of his feet to be
trampled underfoot; but out of his side to be equal to him,
under his arm to be protected, and near his heart to be
beloved." Another remark of his is worth quoting. Re-
ferring to the fact of Adam's being first formed and then
Eve, and the claim of priority and consequent superiority,
as made on his behalf by the apostle Paul, he says: "If
man is the head, she is the crown—a crown to her husband,
the crown of the visible creation. The man was dust refined, but the woman was dust double-refined—one remove
further from the earth."

But, Matthew Henry apart, one thing is certain, that this
old Bible narrative, while it has not done that which it was
never intended to do, while it has given no scientific explanation of either man's origin or woman's origin, has nevertheless accomplished its great object. It has given woman

her true place in the world.   It is only in Bible lands that
woman has her true place; and it is only there that marriage
has its proper sacredness.   Here as everywhere else, we see
the practical power of the Bible.   It was not written to
satisfy curiosity, but to save and to bless; and most salutary
and most blessed has been the influence of these earliest
words about woman, setting forth her true relation to man
and to God, to her earthly husband and her heavenly Father.

Mistakes Respecting Labor and Death, Corrected.

. . . The Bible has been charged with representing labor
as a curse.   The charge is not true.   On the contrary, we are
told that Adam was appointed in Eden to dress the garden
and keep it.   The law of labor came in among the blessings
of Eden, along with the law of obedience and the marriage
law.   It is a slander on the Bible to say that it represents
labor as a curse.   It is not the labor that is the curse.   It is
the thorns and the thistles.   It is the hardness of the labor.
" In the sweat of thy brow thou shalt eat bread."   Labor
would have been easy and pleasant otherwise.

Then in regard to death.   There are those who represent
the Bible as if it taught that death was unknown in the
world until after the Fall.   And then they point us to the
reign of death throughout the epochs of geology as contradicting the Bible.   Now, the Bible teaches nothing of the
kind.   On the contrary, there seems rather to be a suggestion
that death was in existence among the lower animals all the
way through.   Not to speak of the probability that one of
the divisions of animals, mentioned in the first chapter of
Genesis, corresponds with the carnivora, is there not something in the way the subject of death is introduced, which
rather suggests the idea that it was already known?   It was
a new thing to Adam.   It was not a new thing to animal
life.   Man had been created with relations to mortality

below him, but with relations also to immortality above
him. Had he not fallen, his immortal nature would have
ruled his destiny; but now that he has separated himself
from God by his sin, his lower relations, his mortal relations,
must rule his destiny. Instead of having as his destiny the
prospect of being associated with God in a happy immortality, he is degraded from that position, and is henceforth
associated with the animals in their mortality. We are told
that " death passed upon all *men*, because all have sinned."
But you do not find a passage in the Bible asserting that
death passed upon the animals because of man's sin.

The Deluge and its Difficulties — Not Universal — Ararat Originally a District (Alas! Ingersoll Calls it a High Mountain)—Other Deluges.

. . . We must here touch a little on the difficulties connected with the story of the flood. These difficulties are
almost all founded upon the idea that the deluge was universal; that it covered the highest tops of the Himalayas in
India, the Rocky Mountains here, and all the mountains over
all the earth. It is but reasonable, then, to ask if there is
good reason for insisting that it was universal?

I know of only three strong reasons that are given for this
position. The first is the use of the term " earth " continually throughout the narrative, which only proves that those
who translated the Bible into English, believed the flood to
have been universal. As we have had occasion already to
prove, the word " earth " in Hebrew means just as readily a
limited district. Why do not those who insist so strongly
on the wide signification of " earth " here, not insist upon
the same interpretation in such a passage as Genesis, xii. 1,
and make it an article of faith that Abraham left the world
altogether and went to another, when he left Ur of the
Chaldees and went to Canaan? The second argument for

universality is found in universal expressions, the strongest
of which is Gen. vii. 19: "And the waters prevailed exceedingly upon the earth, and all the high hills that were
under the whole heaven were covered." Now remember
that this is the account of an eye-witness, vividly describing
just what he saw, water on every side, water all around,
nothing but water—even the mountains to the farthest verge
of the horizon covered over with water. When, in the book
of Job, we read of the lightning flashing over the whole
heaven, the meaning surely can not be that a lightning flash
starts at a certain degree of latitude and longitude, and
makes a journey right round the world to the point where
it started. "The whole heavens" is evidently bounded by
the horizon. The third reason which has led people to suppose the whole earth was covered with water, is found in
the tradition that the ark rested on Mount Ararat. The
tradition, we say, for that is all the authority there is for the
idea. In Gen. vii. 4, we are told that the ark rested on the
mountains or highlands of "Ararat." The word "Ararat"
only occurs other two times in the Bible, and in neither
place does it refer to what was only long afterward called
Mt. Ararat. In Old Testament times Ararat was not a
mountain at all, but a district, on some of the highlands of
which the ark rested. A moment's thought will show that
it could not be on the top of Ararat. It would require one
of the hardiest mountaineers to perform such a feat as the
climbing of Ararat. It would be the most inconvenient
place you could think of for the ark to rest on. When you
look fairly at these three arguments that are urged in support of a universal deluge, you will find that none of them
really demand it.

On the other hand, there are things that seem to point
the other way. In the eleventh verse of the seventh chapter we are told that " in the second month, the seventeenth

day of the month, were all the fountains of the great deep broken up, and the windows of heaven were opened." There is no indication there of the sudden creation of such a body of water as would cover the earth to the depth of 30,000 feet above the old sea-level. The causes that are assigned are just such as could be most readily and naturally used. It may be worth while to notice here in passing, an attempt which has been made recently to cast ridicule upon the story of the flood, by representing the Bible as if it attributed the deluge to nothing else than a long, heavy rain, whereas the first importance is given to an entirely different cause: "the fountains of the great deep were broken up." That is just what would appear to one who was describing such a scene as we imagine this to be. Suppose there had been some great submergence of the land there, as has taken place in other parts of the world. There would be a rushing up of water from below, from "the fountains of the great deep."

Again, in the first verse of the eighth chapter, natural agency is made use of: "God made a wind to pass over the earth, and the waters assuaged." There is no reason why we should suppose a greater miracle performed than was necessary. Still further; turn to the tenth verse of the ninth chapter, where God says: "I establish my covenant with you, and with every living creature that is with you; from all that go out of the ark, to every beast of the earth." What were those beasts of the earth thus distinguished from those going out of the ark? Probably they were those that came from the area of land not covered by the flood.

Then again, attention is called to the purpose of the flood, which was simply to destroy the race of men, and it is not to be supposed they had traveled a great distance by this time from their original place of abode. The extent of the flood need not have been any greater than was necessary to submerge that area.

Further, when we take this view, not only do geological and other difficulties disappear, but there is decided confirmation from modern scientific research. There is no evidence in geology that there was in any period of the earth's history, a flood great enough to overtop the Rocky Mountains, but there are evidences of floods as great as this one must have been, for the purpose of destroying the race. I do not know how it is in the immediate region where the flood is supposed to have been. I do not know whether geologists have explored it sufficiently; but this is certain, that there are evidences of similar floods in other parts of the world. Some of our own geologists have discovered evidences of them in this very neighborhood. You have not to go very far from Chicago to find such traces of sudden, powerful, and transient diluvial action. Then, finally, this view of the deluge removes, of course, all difficulty about the number of animals in the ark, because all that was necessary was, that the species more nearly connected with man, those found in the region that was submerged, should be represented in the ark.

But after all, the question of extent is of quite minor importance so long as it is conceded that it was universal in the sense of destroying all but the family of Noah. *The reality* of the judgment is the great thing, and of this we have abundant confirmation from tradition. We find legends of a flood everywhere. We find them among the Semitic and Aryan and Turanian races. We find them east and west, and north and south: in savage nations and civilized nations; on continents and in islands: in the old world and in the new. And if Egypt is a solitary exception, which is very doubtful, but if it is, the exception is accounted for by the simple fact that in that country they have floods every year.

Here again, as in the traditions of the Fall, there is difference enough to show which is the original and true.

Other traditions of the flood are polytheistic, whereas here we have the one living and true God. Those are full of mythological elements, whereas here is a plain narrative, with the impressive scene vividly, but quite simply, depicted. In heathen traditions, too, you find many grotesque items and exaggerations, as for instance, when the ark is described as three-fourths of a mile long, and drops of rain the size of a bull's head; and, generally speaking, a conspicuous absence of that moral purpose which is so impressive and all-pervading in the narrative before us.

Faith in Jesus Christ the Essential Factor.

. . . There are those in our day who find a stumbling-block at the very threshold of the Christian life, in the fancy, that what is required of them in order to salvation, is the crediting of all the details of a long history extending from the first man to the last man, from Adam to the consummation of all things; and long accustomed to that sceptical attitude of mind which questions all things, they think it would take them a life-time (as indeed it would) to verify every statement that is made from Genesis to Revelation, and clear them from all possible objections; and so they do not venture at all. But remember, it is never said: " Believe everything that is in the Bible and you will be saved." Ah, there have been many who believed everything in the Bible, who never thought of questioning a sentence in it, who will find themselves none the better for their easy acquiescence in the statements of a book which they had been taught to accept as inspired. There is no such word written as, " Believe the Bible and you will be saved." No. It is " Believe on the Lord Jesus Christ and thou shalt be saved." Do not trouble yourselves in the first instance about questions connected with the book of Genesis, or difficulties suggested by the book of Revelation. Let the wars of the

Jews alone in the meantime, and dismiss Jonah from your mind. Look to Jesus; get acquainted with Him; listen to His word; believe in Him; trust Him; obey Him. That is all that is asked of you in the first instance. After you have believed on Christ and taken Him as your Saviour, your Master, your Model, you will not be slow to find out that "all Scripture is given by inspiration of God, and is profitable for doctrine and for reproof, and for correction, and for instruction in righteousness." You may never have all your difficulties solved, or all your objections met; but though difficulties may still remain, and interrogation points be scattered here and there over the wide Bible-field, you will be sure of your foundation; you will feel that your feet are planted on the "Rock of Ages," even on Him of whom God, by the mouth of the prophet Isaiah, said: "Behold, I lay in Zion for a foundation, a stone, a tried stone, a precious corner-stone, a sure foundation: he that believeth shall not make haste."

―――

Candor v. Injustice—Dr. Gibson's Pointed Summary.

The prevailing feeling among intelligent readers of the Bible in reference to the profane and coarse assaults made on it by Mr. Robert Ingersoll, is that few people are so ignorant as to be imposed upon by his vulgar witticisms. But, inasmuch as there are not a few who accept without inquiry his account of what is in the Bible, it may be well to give a few illustrations of his unscrupulousness in putting "mistakes" into the Bible which he either knows or ought to know, are not there.

He asserts positively that Moses must have understood by firmament something solid, though every one who has studied the subject knows, and the fact has been published again and again, that the Hebrew word means something exceedingly attenuated, being the very best word in the language to designate the atmosphere; while the mistake found in the English word "firmament," is due to the science of Alexandria, where in the third century before Christ, the "expanse" of Moses was translated "stereoma" (firmament) to suit the advanced astronomy of the time.

When, in speaking of the vegetation of the third day, he says, "Not a blade of grass had even been touched by a single gleam of light," is he dealing fairly with a narrative that makes light its first creation?

When he accuses Moses of compressing the astronomy of the universe into five words, is he dealing fairly with a narrative that does not profess to give any astronomy at all, but, after a general reference to the heavens and the earth as created in the beginning, restricts itself to the earth and its "environment?" Any intelligent person can see that this is the reason why sun, moon and stars are referred to only in their relations to the earth.

When he represents the first and second chapters of Genesis as a varying repetition of the same story, is it fair to withhold all reference to the different purport and object of the two narratives, which fully and satisfactorily explains the variation?

Is it fair to speak of the deluge to represent it as ascribed to nothing but rain, when the Bible expressly says, "All the fountains of the great deep were broken up," evidently pointing to such a subsidence of the land as is familiar to any one acquainted with geology.

Is it fair to make the Bible responsible for the Armenian tradition that the ark rested on the top of Mount Ararat, 17,000 feet high, when the Bible nowhere, from Genesis to Revelation, makes any such statement? The district of Ararat on the mountains or highlands of which the ark rested is not the "Agri-Dagh" to which the name Ararat

has in modern times been given; and Mr. Ingersoll's
ignorant mistake about it is of the same kind as that of the
bumpkin who should inquire for the Coliseum in Rome, N.
Y., or seek the tomb of Leonidas in Sparta, Wisconsin.

It will be at once seen that with this childlike ignorance
is connected the Ingersoll nonsense that the water was five
and a half miles deep. So says the ignorant critic, while
the simple and reasonable statement of the Bible is:
"Fifteen cubits upwards did the water prevail." As for the
submersion of even the hills to the utmost verge of the
horizon, the subsidence of the land was quite sufficient to
accomplish it without resorting to the supposition of any
unreasonable quantity of water.

Is it fair, when Mr. Ingersoll wishes to render ridiculous
the rate of increase among the Israelites in Egypt, to represent the length of their stay there as 215 years, when
Moses says (Exodus, xii., 40): "Now the sojourning of the
children of Israel who dwelt in Egypt was 430 years."
The only other place in the Pentateuch where the length of
their stay is referred to is in the prediction concerning it in
Genesis xv., where it is put in round numbers at 400
years. To do Mr. Ingersoll justice, it is admitted that
certain theologians, on the strength of one or two passages
in the New Testament and some genealogical difficulties,
have favored shortening the period, but the subject was not
the mistakes of Moses, but of theologians; and again we
ask, Was it fair, without a word of apology or explanation,
to deduct more than two centuries from the time Moses
gives, and then make all his coarse, not to say indecent,
ridicule turn on the shortness of the time?

One hardly knows how to characterize the infamy of such
a passage as that about the bird-eating priests during the
time of rapid increase, in view of the fact that there were
no priests at all, and no such rule as he refers to during the

entire 430 years! The consecration of Aaron, the first priest. did not take place till after the Law was given at Sinai, and the ordinance relating to the offering of the pigeons was still later. These are mere specimens of the mistakes and misrepresentations which form the warp and woof of this lecture.

WHAT DISTINGUISHED MEN SAY OF THE BIBLE.

SCIENTISTS.

THE grand old book of God still stands, and this old earth, the more its leaves are turned over and pondered, the more it will sustain and illustrate the sacred word.—*Professor Dana.*

INFIDELITY has, from time, erected her imposing ramparts, and opened fire upon Christianity from a thousand batteries. But the moment the rays of truth were concentrated upon their ramparts they melted away. The last clouds of ignorance are passing, and the thunders of infidelity are dying upon the ear. The union and harmony of Christianity and science is a sure token that the flood of unbelief and ignorance shall never more go over the world.—*Professor Hitchcock.*

ALL human discoveries seem to be made only for the purpose of confirming, more and more strongly, the truths contained in the sacred Scriptures.—*Sir John Herschel.*

THE Bible furnishes the only fitting vehicle to express the thoughts that overwhelm us when contemplating the stellar universe.—*O. M. Mitchell.*

IN my investigation of natural science, I have always found that whenever I can meet with anything in the Bible, on any subject, it always affords me a fine platform on which to stand.—*Lieutenant Maury*

If the God of love is most appropriately worshiped in the Christian temple, the God of nature may be equally honored in the temple of science. Even from its lofty minarets, the philosopher may summon the faithful to prayer; and the priest and the sage exchange altars without the compromise of faith or knowledge.—*Sir David Brewster.*

A NATION's intellectual progress has always followed—not preceded—some moral impulse. The history of the fine arts shows that some form of religion gave them their earliest impulse. There has never been a great genius but has been inspired in some sense by religion. The thoughts of the intellect are lofty in proportion as the sentiments of the heart are profound. If we begin the attempt to improve men with the intellect we end where we begun. Education will not remove corruption. It may guide vice as in ancient Rome and Athens, but will not uproot it. A godless education has no power to purify. Instruction in morality also has failed to regenerate. No man does his duty simply because he knows it unless he loves it; nor are political and social changes effective. Social evil has its root in the individual heart, and cannot be removed except by influences operating within it. This fountain of man's corruption must be purified to corrupt social vice.—*Prof. Seelye.*

STATESMEN.

THERE is a book worth all other books which were ever printed.—*Patrick Henry.*

THE Bible is the best book in the world.—*John Adams.*

So great is my veneration for the Bible, that the earlier my children begin to read it, the more confident will be my hopes that they will prove useful citizens to their country, and respectable members of society.—*John Quincy Adams.*

IT is impossible to govern the world without God. He must be worse than an infidel that lacks faith, and more than wicked that has not gratitude enough to acknowledge his obligation.—*General George Washington.*

POINTING to the family Bible on the stand, during his last illness, Andrew Jackson said to his friend: "That book, sir, is the rock on which our republic rests."

I DEEM the present occasion sufficiently important and solemn to justify me in expressing to my fellow citizens a profound reverence for the Christian religion, and a thorough conviction that sound morals, religious liberty, and a just sense of religious responsibility, are essentially connected with all true and lasting happiness.—*General Harrison's Inaugural Address.*

As to Jesus of Nazareth, my opinion of whom you particularly desire, I think the system of morals, and His religion, as He left them to us, is the best the world ever saw, or is likely to see.—*Benjamin Franklin.*

Do you think that your pen, or the pen of any other man, can unchristianize the mass of our citizens? Or have you hopes of corrupting a few of them to assist you in so bad a cause?—*Samuel Adams' Letter to Thomas Paine.*

CHRISTIANITY is the only true and perfect religion, and that in proportion as mankind adopt its principles and obey its precepts, they will be wise and happy. And a better knowledge of this religion is to be acquired by reading the Bible than in any other way.—*Benjamin Rush.*

When that illustrious man, Chief Justice Joy, was dying, he was asked if he had any farewell address to leave his children; he replied, "They have the Bible."

I always have had, and always shall have, a profound regard for Christianity, the religion of my fathers, and for its rites, its usages, and observances.—*Henry Clay.*

A few days before his death, "the foremost man of all his times," drew up and signed this declaration of his religious faith: "Lord, I believe; help thou mine unbelief. Philosophical argument, especially that drawn from the vastness of the universe, in comparison with the insignificance of this globe, has sometimes shaken my reason for the faith that is in me, but my heart has always assured and reassured me that the gospel of Jesus Christ must be a divine reality. The Sermon on the Mount cannot be a merely human production. This belief enters into the very depth of my conscience."—*Daniel Webster.*

"Hold fast to the Bible as the sheet anchor of our libererties; write its precepts on your hearts, and practice them in your lives. To the influence of this book we are indebted for the progress made in true civilization, and to this we must look as our guide in the future.—*U. S. Grant.*

Philosophy has sometimes forgotten God: as great people never did. The skepticism of the last century could not uproot Christianity, because it lived in the hearts of the millions. Do you think that infidelity is spreading? Christianity never lived in the hearts of so many millions as at this moment. The forms under which it is professed may decay, for they, like all that is the work of man's hands, are subject to the changes and chances of mortal being; but the spirit of truth is incorruptible; it may be developed, illustrated and applied; it can never die; it never can decline.

No truth can perish. No truth can pass away. The flame is undying, though generations disappear. Wherever mortal truth has started into being humanity claims and guards the bequest. Each generation gathers together the imperishable children of the past, and increases them by the new sons of the light, alike radiant with immortality.—*Bancroft.*

GREAT THINKERS.

It is a belief in the Bible which has served me as the guide of my moral and literary life.—*Goethe.*

I ACCOUNT the Scriptures of God to be the most sublime philosophy.—*Sir Isaac Newton.*

To give a man a full knowledge of true morality, I should need to send him to no other book than the New Testament.—*John Locke.*

I KNOW the Bible is inspired, because it finds me at greater depths of my being than any other book.—*Coleridge.*

A NOBLE book! All men's book. It is our first statement of the never-ending problem of man's destiny and God's way with men on earth.—*Carlyle.*

I MUST confess the majesty of the Scriptures strikes me with astonishment.—*Rousseau.*

"THERE is not a boy nor a girl, all Christendom through, but their lot is made better by this great book.—*Theodore Parker.*

TAKE the gospel away, and what a mockery is human philosophy! I once met a thoughtful scholar who told me

that for years he had read every book which assailed the
religion of Jesus Christ. He said that he should have
become an infidel if it had not been for three things:

"First, I am a man. I am going somewhere. I am to-
night a day nearer the grave than last night. I have read
all that they can tell me. There is not one solitary ray of
light upon the darkness. They shall not take away the
only guide and leave me stone blind.

"Secondly, I had a mother. I saw her go down into the
dark valley where I am going, and she leaned upon an unseen arm as calmly as a child goes to sleep upon the breast
of a mother. I know that was not a dream.

"Thirdly," he said with tears in his eyes, "I have three
motherless daughters. They have no protector but myself.
I would rather kill them than leave them in this sinful
world if you could blot out from it all the teachings of the
Gospel."—*Bishop Whipple.*

WHEN Daniel Webster was in his best moral state, and
when he was in the prime of his manhood, he was one day
dining with a company of literary gentlemen in the city of
Boston. The company was composed of clergymen, lawyers, physicians, statesmen, merchants, and almost all
classes of literary persons. During the dinner conversation incidentally turned upon the subject of Christianity.
Mr. Webster, as the occasion was in honor of him, was
expected to take a leading part in the conversation, and he
frankly stated as his religious sentiments his belief in the
divinity of Christ, and his dependence upon the atonement
of the Savior. A minister of very considerable literary
reputation sat almost opposite him at the table, and he
looked at him and said: "Mr. Webster, can you comprehend how Jesus Christ could be both God and man?" Mr.
Webster, with one of those looks which no man can imitate,

fixed his eyes upon him, and promptly and emphatically said: "No, sir, I cannot comprehend it; and I would be ashamed to acknowledge him as my Savior if I could comprehend it. If I could comprehend him, he could be no greater than myself, and such is my conviction of accountability to God, such is my sense of sinfulness before him, and such is my knowledge of my own incapacity to recover myself, that I feel I need a superhuman Savior."—*Bishop Janes.*

WHAT can be more foolish than to think that all this rare fabric of Heaven and earth could come by chance, when all the skill of art is not able to make an oyster?—*Jeremy Taylor.*

IT would not be worth while to live if we were to die entirely. That which alleviates labor and sanctifies toil is to have before us the vision of a better world through the darkness of this life. That world is to me more real than the chimera which we devour, and which we call life. It is forever before my eyes. It is the supreme certainty of my reason, as it is the supreme consolation of my soul.—*Victor Hugo.*

ONCE, had I been called upon to create the earth, I should have done as the many would now. I should have laid it out in pleasure-grounds, and given man Milton's occupation of tending flowers. But I am now satisfied with this wild earth, its awful mountains and depths, steeps and torrents. I am not sorry to learn that God's end is a virtue far higher than I should have prescribed.—*Channing.*

TO do good to men is the great work of life; to make them true Christians is the greatest good we can do them. Every investigation brings us round to this point. Begin here and you are like one who strikes water from a rock on the summit of the mountains; it flows down all the intervening tracts to the very base. If we could make each man love his neighbor, we should make a happy world. The true method is to begin with ourselves and so extend the circle around us. It should be perpetually in our minds.—*J. W. Alexander.*

FROM philosophy, from poetry and from art, is heard the acknowledgment that there is no repose for the rational spirit but in moral truth. The testimony that the whole creation groaneth and travaileth in pain, together, is as loud and convincing from the domain of letters, as it is from the cursed and thistle-bearing ground. From the immortal longing and dissatisfaction of Plato, down to the wild and passionate restlessness of Byron and Shelley, the evidence is decisive that a spiritual and religious element must enter into the education of man in order to inward harmony and rest.—*Dr. Shedd.*

"THE mother of a family was married to an infidel, who made a jest of religion in the presence of his own children; yet she succeeded in bringing them all up in the fear of the Lord. I one day asked her how she preserved them from the influence of a father whose sentiments were so openly opposed to her own. This was her answer: 'Because to the authority of a father I did not oppose the authority of a mother, but that of God. From their earliest years my children have always seen the Bible upon my table. This holy book has constituted the whole of their religious instruction. I was silent that I might allow it to speak. Did they propose a question, did they commit any fault, did they perform any good action, I opened the Bible, and the Bible answered, reproved or encouraged them. The constant reading of the Scriptures has alone wrought the prodigy which surprises you.' "—*Adolphe Monod.*

I PREACHED on Sunday in the parlors at Long Branch. The war was over, and Admiral Farragut and his family were spending the summer at the Branch. Sitting on the portico of the hotel Monday morning, he said to me, " Would you like to know how I was enabled to serve my country? It was all owing to a resolution I formed when I was ten years of age. My father was sent down to New Orleans with the little navy we then had, to look after the treason of Burr. I accompanied him as cabin-boy. I had some qualities that I thought made a man of me. I could swear like an old salt; could drink a stiff glass of grog as if I had doubled Cape Horn, and could smoke like a locomotive. I was great at cards and fond of gaming in every shape. At the close of the dinner one day, my father turned every body out of the cabin, locked the door, and said to me:

" 'David, what do you mean to be?'

" 'I mean to follow the sea.'

" 'Follow the sea! Yes, be a poor, miserable drunken sailor before the mast, kicked and cuffed about the world, and die in some fever hospital, in a foreign clime.'

" 'No,' I said, 'I'll tread the quarter-deck and command as you do.'

" 'No, David; no boy ever trod the quarter-deck with such principles as you have, and such habits as you exhibit. You'll have to change your whole course of life if you ever become a man.'

" My father left me and went on deck. I was stunned by the rebuke and overwhelmed with mortification. 'A poor, miserable, drunken sailor before the mast, kicked and cuffed about the world, and to die in some fever hospital!

That's my fate, is it? I'll change my life, and change it at once. I will never utter another oath, I will never drink another drop of intoxicating liquors, I will never gamble.' And, as God is my witness, I have kept those three vows to this hour. Shortly after, I became a Christian. That act settled my temporal, as it settled my eternal destiny."
—*Anon.*

A BIBLE well worn in that part which contains the Sermon on the Mount is the book which our age most needs. There the Will of the Father, those laws which save souls or damn them lie in perfect plainness. No commentary can throw light upon them, no science or learning can take their light away. They are a part of the universe, only more imperishable than the stars. Christ died for man because man would not respect these laws of the kingdom. Having died for sinners, He now invites them to come into these laws of the Father. Do not mistake the invitation.—*David Swing.*

You never can get at the literal limitation of living facts. They disguise themselves by the very strength of their life; get told again and again in different ways by all manner of people; the literalness of them is turned topsy-turvy, inside out, over and over again; then the fools come and read them wrong side upwards, or else say there never was a fact at all. Nothing delights a true blockhead so much as to prove a negative,—to show that everybody has been wrong. Fancy the delicious sensation to an empty-headed creature of fancying for a moment that he has emptied everybody else's head as well as his own! nay, that for once, his own hollow bottle of a head has had the best of other bottles, and has been *first* empty,—first to know nothing.—*Ruskin.*

It is not so wretched to be blind as it is not to be capable of enduring blindness. Let me be the most feeble creature alive as long as that feebleness serves to invigorate the energies of my rational and immortal spirit; so long as in that obscurity in which I am enveloped the light of the divine presence more clearly shines; and indeed, in my blindness I enjoy in no inconsiderable degree the favor of the Deity, who regards me with more tenderness and compassion in proportion as I am able to behold nothing but Himself. For the divine law not only shields me from injury, but almost renders me too sacred to attack, as from the overshadowing of those heavenly wings which seem to have occasioned this obscurity.—*Milton.*

A PRINCE said to Rabbi Gamaliel: "Your God is a thief; he surprised Adam in his sleep, and stole a rib from him." The Rabbi's daughter overheard this speech, and whispered a word or two in her father's ear, asking his permission to answer this singular opinion herself. He gave his consent. The girl stepped forward, and feigning terror and dismay, threw her arms aloft in supplication, and cried out, "My liege, my liege, justice! revenge!" "What has happened?" asked the prince. "A wicked theft has taken place," she replied. "A robber has crept secretly into our house, carried away a silver goblet, and left a golden one in its stead." "What an upright thief!" exclaimed the prince. "Would that such robberies were of more frequent occurrence!" "Behold, then, sir, the kind of thief our Creator was; he stole a rib from Adam, and gave him a beautiful wife instead." "Well said!" avowed the prince.—*Talmud Sanhedrim.*

ONCE there was a Judge who had a colored man. The colored man was very godly, and the Judge used to have him to drive him around in his circuit. The Judge used often to talk with him, and the colored man would tell the Judge about his religious experience, and about his battles;

and conflicts. One day the Judge said to him: "Sambo, how is it that you Christians are always talking about the conflicts you have with Satan? I am better off than you are. I don't have any troubles or conflicts, and yet I am an infidel and you are a Christian—always in a muss;—how's that, Sambo?" This floored the colored man for awhile. He did n't know how to meet the old infidel's argument. So he shook his head sorrowfully and said: "I dunno, Massa, I dunno." The Judge always carried a gun along with him for hunting. Pretty soon they came to a lot of ducks. The Judge took his gun and blazed away at them, and wounded one and killed another. The Judge said quickly: "You jump in, Sambo, and get that wounded duck before he gets off," and did not pay any attention to the dead one. In went Sambo for the wounded duck, and came out reflecting. The colored man then thought he had an illustration. He said to the Judge: "I hab 'im now, Massa; I 'se able to show you how de Christian hab greater conflict dan de infidel. Do n't you know de moment you wounded dat ar duck, how anxious you was to get 'im out, and you did n't care for de dead, but jus' lef' him alone?" "Yes," said the Judge. "Well," said Sambo, "ye see as how dat are dead duck 's a sure thing. I 'se wounded, and I tries to get away from the debbil. It takes trouble to cotch me. But, Massa, *you are a dead duck*—dar's no squabble for you; de debbil have you sure!" So the devil has no conflict with the infidel.—*D. L. Moody.*

INGERSOLL'S LECTURE

ON

"THE MISTAKES OF MOSES."

Now and then some one asks me why I am endeavoring to interfere with the religious faith of others, and why I try to take from the world the consolation naturally arising from a belief in eternal fire. And I answer, I want to do what little I can to make my country truly free. I want to broaden the intellectual horizon of our people. I want it so that we can differ upon all those questions, and yet grasp each other's hands in genuine friendship. I want in the first place to free the clergy. I am a great friend of theirs, but they don't seem to have found it out generally. I want it so that every minister will be not a parrot, not an owl sitting upon a dead limb of the tree of knowledge and hooting the hoots that have been hooted for eighteen hundred years. But I want it so that each one can be an investigator, a thinker; and I want to make his congregation grand enough so that they will not only allow him to think, but will demand that he shall think, and give to them the honest truth of his thought. As it is now, ministers are employed like attorneys—for the plaintiff or the defendant. If a few people know of a young man in the neighborhood maybe who has not a good constitution—he may not be healthy enough to be wicked—a young man who has shown no decided talent—it occurs to them to make him a minister. They contribute and send him to some school. If it turns out that that young man has more of the man in him than they thought, and he changes his opinion, every one who contributed will feel himself individually swindled—and they will follow that young man to the grave with the poisoned shafts of malice and slander. I want it so that every one will be free—so that a pulpit will not be a pillory. They have in Massachusetts, at a place called Andover,

7

a kind of minister-factory; and every professor in that factory takes an oath once in every five years—that is as long as an oath will last—that not only has he not during the last five years, but so help him God, he will not during the next five years intellectually advance; and probably there is no oath he could easier keep. Since the foundation of that institution there has not been one case of perjury. They believe the same creed they first taught when the foundation stone was laid. and now when they send out a minister they brand him as hardware from Sheffield and Birmingham. And every man who knows where he was educated knows his creed. knows every argument of his creed, every book that he reads, and just what he amounts to intellectually, and knows he will shrink and shrivel, and become solemnly stupid day after day until he meets with death. It is all wrong; it is cruel. Those men should be allowed to grow. They should have the air of liberty and the sunshine of thought.

I want to free the schools of our country. I want it so that when a professor in a college finds some fact inconsistent with Moses, he will not hide the fact, that it will not be the worse for him for having discovered the fact. I wish to see an eternal divorce and separation between church and schools. The common school is the bread of life; but there should be nothing taught in the schools except what somebody knows; and anything else should not be maintained by a system of general taxation. I want its professors so that they will tell everything they find; that they will be free to investigate in every direction, and will not be trammeled by the superstitions of our day. What has religion to do with facts? Nothing. Is there any such thing as Methodist mathematics, Presbyterian botany, Catholic astronomy or Baptist biology? What has any form of superstition or religion to do with a fact or with any science? Nothing but to hinder, delay or embarrass. I want, then, to free the schools; and I want to free the politicians, so that a man will not have to pretend he is a Methodist, or his wife a Baptist, or his grandmother a Catholic; so that he can go through a campaign, and when he gets through will find none of the dust of hypocrisy on his knees.

I want the people splendid enough that when they desire men to make laws for them, they will take one who knows something, who has brains enough to prophesy the destiny of the American Republic, no matter what his opinions may be upon any religious subject. Suppose we are in a storm out at sea, and the billows are washing over our ship, and it is necessary that some one should reef the topsail, and a man presents himself. Would you stop him at the foot of the mast to find out his opinion on the five points of Calvinism? What has that to do with it? Congress has nothing to do with baptism or any particular creed, and from what little experience I have had of Washington, very little to do with any kind of religion whatever. Now I hope, this afternoon, this magnificent and splendid audience will forget that they are Baptists or Methodists, and remember that they are men and women. These are the highest titles humanity can bear—man and woman; and every title you add belittles them. Man is the highest; woman is the highest. Let us remember that we are simply human beings, with interests in common. And let us remember that our views depend largely upon the country in which we happen to live. Suppose we were born in Turkey most of us would have been Mohammedans; and when we read in the book that when Mohammed visited heaven he became acquainted with an angel named Gabriel, who was so broad between his eyes that it would take a smart camel three hundred days to make the journey, we probably would have believed it. If we did not, people would say: "That young man is dangerous; he is trying to tear down the fabric of our religion. What do you propose to give us instead of that angel? We cannot afford to trade off an angel of that size for nothing." Or if we had been born in India, we would have believed in a god with three heads. Now we believe in three gods with one head. And so we might make a tour of the world and see that every superstition that could be imagined by the brain of man has been in some place held to be sacred.

Now some one says, "The religion of my father and mother is good enough for me." Suppose we all said that, where would be the progress of the world? We would have the rudest and most barbaric religion—religion which no one could believe. I do not believe that it is showing real respect to our parents to believe something simply because they did. Every good father and every good mother wish their children to find out more than they knew; every good father wants his son to overcome some obstacle that he could not grapple with; and if you wish to reflect credit on your father and mother, do it by accomplishing more than they did, because you live in a better time. Every nation has had what you call a sacred record, and the older the more sacred, the more contradictory and the more inspired is the record. We, of course, are not an exception, and I propose to talk a little about what is called the Pentateuch, a book, or a collection of books, said to have been written by Moses. And right here in the commencement let me say that Moses never wrote one word of the Pentateuch—not one word was written until he had been dust and ashes for hundreds of years. But as the general opinion is that Moses wrote these books, I have entitled this lecture the "The Mistakes of Moses." For the sake of this lecture, we will admit that he wrote it. Nearly every maker of religion has commenced by making the world; and it is one of the safest things to do, because no one can contradict as having been present, and it gives free scope to the imagination. These books, in times when there was a vast difference between the educated and the ignorant, became inspired and people bowed down and worshipped them.

I saw a little while ago a Bible with immense oaken covers, with hasps and clasps large enough almost for a penitentiary, and I can imagine how that book would be regarded by barbarians in Europe when not more than one person in a dozen could read and write. In imagination I saw it carried into the cathedral, heard the chant of the priest, saw the swinging of the censer and the smoke rising; and when that Bible was put on the altar I can imagine the barbarians looking at it and wondering what influence that black book could have on their lives and future. I do not wonder that they imagined it was inspired. None of them could write a book, and consequently when they saw it they adored it; they were stricken with awe; and rascals took advantage of that awe.

Now they say that the book is inspired. I do not care whether it is or not; the question is: Is it true? If it is true it don't need to be inspired. Nothing needs inspiration except a falsehood or a mistake. A fact never went into partnership with a miracle. Truth scorns the assistance of wonders. A fact will fit every other fact in the universe, and that is how you can tell whether it is or is not a fact. A lie will not fit anything except another lie made for the express purpose; and, finally, some one gets tired of lying, and the last lie will not fit the next fact, and then there is a chance for inspiration. Right then and there a miracle is needed. The real question is: In the light of science, in the light of the brain and heart of the nineteenth century, is this book true? The gentlemen who wrote it begins by telling us that God made the universe out of nothing. That I cannot conceive; it may be so, but I cannot conceive it. Nothing, regarded in the light of raw material, is, to my mind, a decided and disastrous failure. I cannot imagine of nothing being made into something, any more than I can of something being changed back into nothing. . I cannot conceive of force aside from matter, because force to be force must be active, and unless there is matter there is nothing for force to act upon, and consequently it cannot be active. So I simply say I cannot comprehend it. I cannot believe it. I may roast for this, but it is my honest opinion. The next thing he proceeds to tell us is that God divided the darkness from the light; and right here let me say when I speak about God I simply mean the being described by the Jews. There may be in immensity some being beneath whose wing the universe exists, whose every thought is a glittering star, but I know nothing about Him,—not the slig' test,—and this afternoon I am simply talking about the being described by the Jewish people. When I say God, I mean Him. Moses describes God dividing the light from the darkness. I suppose that at

that time they must have been mixed. You can readily see how light and
darkness can get mixed. They must have been entities. The reason I
think so is because in that same book I find that darkness overspread
Egypt so thick that it could be felt, and they used to have on exhibition
in Rome a bottle of the darkness that once overspread Egypt. The gentleman who wrote this in imagination saw God dividing light from the
darkness. I am sure the man who wrote it, believed darkness to be an
entity, a something, a tangible thing that can be mixed with light.

The next thing that he informs us is that God divided the waters above
the firmanent from those below the firmanent. The man who wrote that
believed the firmanent to be a solid affair. And that is what the gods
did. You recollect the gods came down and made love to the daughters
of men—and I never blamed them for it. I have never read a description
of any heaven I would not leave on the same errand. That is where the
gods lived. That is where they kept the water. It was solid. That is
the reason the people prayed for rain. They believed that an angel could
take a lever, raise a widow and let out the desired quantity. I find in the
Psalms that " He bowed the heavens and came down;" and we read that
the children of men built a tower to reach the heavens and climb into the
abode of the gods. The man who wrote that believed the firmanent to
be solid. He knew nothing about the laws of evaporation. He did not
know that the sun wooed with amorous kiss the waves of the sea, and
that, disappointed, their vaporous sighs changed to tears and fell again
as rain. The next thing he tells us is that the grass began to grow, and
the branches of the trees laughed into blossom, and the grass ran up the
shoulder of the hills, and yet not a solitary ray of light had left the
eternal quiver of the sun. Not a blade of grass had ever been touched
by a gleam of light. And I do not think that grass will grow to
hurt without a gleam of sunshine. I think the man who wrote that
simply made a mistake, and is excusable to a certain degree The next
day he made the sun and moon—the sun to rule the day and the moon to
rule the night. Do you think the man who wrote that knew anything
about the size of the sun? I think he thought it was about three feet in
diameter, because I find in some book that the sun was stopped a whole
day, to give a general named Joshua time to kill a few more Amalekites;
and the moon was stopped also. Now it seems to me that the sun would
give light enough without stopping the moon; but as they were in the
stopping business they did it just for devilment. At another time, we
read, the sun was turned ten degrees backward to convince Hezekiah
that he was not going to die of a boil. How much easier it would have
been to cure the boil. The man who wrote that thought the sun was two
or three feet in diameter, and could be stopped and pulled around like the

sun and moon in a theatre. Do you know that the sun throws out every
second of time as much heat as could be generated by burning eleven
thousand millions tons of coal? I don't believe he knew that, or that he
knew the motion of the earth. I don't believe he knew that it was turning on its axis at the rate of a thousand miles an hour, because if he did,
he would have understood the immensity of heat that would have been
generated by stopping the world. It has been calculated by one of the
best mathematicians and astronomers that to stop the world would cause
as much heat as it would take to burn a lump of solid coal three times as
big as the globe. And yet we find in that book that the sun was not only
stopped, but turned back ten degrees, simply to convince a gentleman
that he was not going to die of a boil. They may say I will be damned
if I do not believe that, and I tell them I will if I do.

Then he gives us the history of astronomy, and he gives it to us in five
words: "He made the stars also." He came very near forgetting the
stars. Do you believe that the man who wrote that knew that there are
stars as much larger than this earth as this earth is larger than the apple
which Adam and Eve are said to have eaten? Do you believe that he
knew that this world is but a speck in the shining, glittering universe of
existence? I would gather from that that he made the stars after he got
the world done. The telescope, in reading the infinite leaves of the
heavens, has ascertained that light travels at the rate of 192,000 miles
per second, and it would require millions of years to come from some of
the stars to this earth. Yet the beams of those stars mingle in our
atmosphere, so that if those distant orbs were fashioned when this world
began, we must have been whirling in space not six thousand, but many
millions of years. Do you believe the man who wrote that as a history
of astronomy really knew that this world was but a speck compared with
millions of sparkling orbs? I do not. He then proceeds to tell us that
God made fish and cattle, and that man and woman were created male
and female. The first account stops at the second verse of the second
chapter. You see, the Bible originally was not divided into chapters;
the first Bible that was ever divided into chapters in our language was
made in the year of grace 1550. The Bible was originally written in the
Hebrew language, and the Hebrew language at that time had no vowels
in writing. It was written entirely with consonants, and without being
divided into chapters or into verses, and there was no system of punctu-
ation whatever. After you go home to-night write an English sentence
or two with only consonants close together, and you will find that it will
take twice as much inspiration to read it as it did to write it. When the
Bible was divided into verses and chapters, the divisions were not always
correct, and so the division between the first and second chapter of Gen-

esis is not in the right place. The second account of the creation com-
mences at the third verse, and it differs from the first in two essential
points. In the first account man is the last made; in the second, man is
made before the beasts. In the first account, man is made "male and
female;" in the second only a man is made, and there is no intention of
making a woman whatever.

You will find by reading that second chapter that God tried to palm
off on Adam a beast as his helpmeet. Everybody talks about the Bible
and nobody reads it; that is the reason it is so generally believed. I am
probably the only man in the United States who has read the Bible
through this year. I have wasted that time, but I had a purpose in
view. Just read it, and you will find, about the twenty-third verse, that
God caused all the animals to walk before Adam in order that he might
name them. And the animals came like a menagerie into town, and as
Adam looked at all the crawlers, jumpers and creepers, this God stood by
to see what he would call them. After this procession passed, it was
pathetically remarked, "Yet was there not found any helpmeet for
Adam." Adam didn't see anything that he could fancy. And I am glad
he didn't. If he had, there would not have been a free-thinker in this
world; we should have all died orthodox. And finding Adam was so particular, God had to make him a helpmeet, and having used up the nothing
he was compelled to take part of the man to make the woman with, and
he took from the man a rib. How did he get it? And then imagine a
God with a bone in his hand, and about to start a woman, trying to make
up his mind whether to make a blonde or a brunette.

Right here it is only proper that I should warn you of the consequences
of laughing at any story in the holy Bible. When you come to die, your
laughing at this story will be a thorn, in your pillow. As you look back
upon the record of your life, no matter how many men you have wrecked
and ruined, and no matter how many women you have deceived and
deserted—all that may be forgiven you; but if you recollect that you have
laughed at God's book you will see through the shadows of death,
the leering looks of fiends and the forked tongues of devils. Let me show
you how it will be: For instance, it is the day of judgment. When the
man is called up by the recording secretary, or whoever does the cross-
examining, he says to his soul: "Where are you from?" "I am from
the world." "Yes, sir. What kind of a man were you?" "Well, I
don't like to talk about myself." "But you have to. What kind of a
man were you?" "Well, I was a good fellow; I loved my wife, I loved
my children. My home was my heaven; my fireside was my paradise,
and to sit there and see the lights and shadows falling on the faces of
those I love, that to me was a perpetual joy. I never gave one of them a

solitary moment of pain. I don't owe a dollar in the world, and I left enough to pay my funeral expenses and keep the wolf of want from the door of the house I loved. That is the kind of a man I am." "Did you belong to any church?" "I did not. They were too narrow for me. They were always expecting to be happy simply because somebody else was to be damned." "Well, did you believe that rib story?" "What rib-story? Do you mean that Adam and Eve business? No, I did not. To tell you the God's truth, that was a little more than I could swallow." "To hell with him! Next. Where are you from?" "I'm from the world, too." "Do you belong to any church?" "Yes, sir, and to the Young Men's Christian Association." "What is your business?" "Cashier in a bank." "Did you ever run off with any of the money?" "I don't like to tell, sir." "Well, but you have to." "Yes, sir; I did." "What kind of a bank did you have?" "A savings bank." "How much did you run off with?" "One hundred thousand dollars." "Did you take anything else along with you?" "Yes, sir." "What?" "I took my neighbor's wife." "Did you have a wife and children of your own?" "Yes, sir." "And you deserted them?" "Oh, yes; bu such was my confidence in God that I believed he would take care of them." "Have you heard of them since?" "No, sir." "Did you believe that rib story?" "Ah, bless your soul, yes! I believe all of it, sir; I often used to be sorry that there were not harder stories yet in the Bible, so that I could show what my faith could do." "You believed it, did you?" "Yes, with all my heart." "Give him a harp."

I simply wanted to show you how important it is to believe these stories. Of all the authors in the world God hates a critic the worst. Having got this woman done he brought her to the man, and they started housekeeping, and a few minutes afterward a snake came through a crack in the fence and commenced to talk with her on the subject of fruit. She was not acquainted in the neighborhood, and she did not know whether snakes talked or not, or whether they knew anything about the apples or not. Well, she was misled, and the husband ate some of those apples and laid it all on his wife; and there is where the mistake was made. God ought to have rubbed him out once. He might have known that no good could come of starting the world with a man like that. They were turned out. Then the trouble commenced, and people got worse and worse. God, you must recollect, was holding the reins of government, but he did nothing for them. He allowed them to live six hundred and sixty-nine years without knowing their A. B. C. He never started a school, not even a Sunday school. He didn't even keep His own boys at home. And the world got worse every day, and finally he concluded to drown them. Yet that same god has the impudence to tell me how to raise my own children. What would you think of a neighbor, who had just killed his babes giving you his views on domestic economy? God found that he could do nothing with them and He said: "I will drown them all, except a few." And He picked out a fellow by the name of Noah, that had been a bachelor for five hundred years. If I had to drown anybody, I would have drowned him. I believe that Noah had then been married something like one hundred years. God told him to build a boat, and he built one five hundred feet long, eighty or ninety feet broad and fifty-five feet high, with one door shutting on the outside, and one window twenty-two inches square. If Noah had any hobby in the world it was vetilation. Then into this ark he put a certain number of all the animals in the world. Naturalists have ascertained that at that time there were at least eleven hundred thousand insects necessary to go into the ark, about forty thousand mammalia, sixteen hundred reptilia, to say nothing about the mastodon, the elephant and the animalculæ, of which thousands live upon a single leaf and which cannot be seen by the naked eye. Noah had no microscope, and yet he had to pick them out by pairs. You have no idea the trouble that man had. Some say that the flood was not universal, that it was partial. Why then did God say: "I will destroy every living thing beneath the heavens." If it was partial why did Noah save the birds? An ordinary bird, tending strictly to business, can beat a partial flood. Why did he put the birds in there—the eagles, the vultures, the condors—if it was only a partial flood? And how did he get them in there? Were they inspired to go there, or did he drive them up? Did the polar bear leave his home of ice and start for the tropics inquiring for Noah; or could the kangaroo come from Australia unless he was inspired, or somebody was behind him? Then there are animals on this hemisphere not on that. How did he get them across? And there are some animals which would be very unpleasant in an ark unless the ventilation was very perfect.

When he got the animals in the ark, God shut the door and Noah pulled down the window. And then it began to rain, and it kept on raining until the water went twenty-nine feet over the highest mountain. Chimborazo, then as now, lifted its head above the clouds, and then as now, there sat the condor. And yet the waters rose and rose over every mountain in the world—twenty-nine feet above the highest peaks, covered with snow and ice. How deep were these waters? About five and a half miles. How long did it rain? Forty days. How much did it have to rain a day? About eight hundred feet. How is that for dampness? No wonder they said the windows of the heavens were open. If I had been there I would have said the whole side of the house was out. How long were they in this ark? A year and ten days, floating around with

no rudder, no sail, nobody on the outside at all. The window was shut,.
and there was no door, except the one that shut on the outside. Who-
ran this ark—who took care of it? Finally it came down on Mount Ararat,
a peak seventeen thousand feet above the level of the sea, with about
three thousand feet of snow, and it stopped there simply to give the animals from the tropics a chance. Then Noah opened the window and got
a breath of fresh air, and he let out all the animals; and then Noah took
a drink, and God made a bargain with him that He would not drown us
any more, and He put a rainbow in the clouds and said: "When I see
that I will recollect that I have promised not to drown you." Because
if it was not for that He is apt to drown us at any moment. Now can
anybody believe that that is the origin of the rainbow? Are you not
all familiar with the natural causes which bring those beautiful arches
before our eyes? Then the people started out again, and they were as
bad as before. Here let me ask why God did not make Noah in the first
place? He knew he would have to drown Adam and Eve and all his
family. Then another thing, why did He want to drown the animals?
What had they done? What crime had they committed? It is very
hard to answer these questions—that is, for a man who has only been
born once. After a while they tried to build a tower to get into heaven,
and the gods heard about it and said: "Let's go down and see what man
is up to." They came, and found things a great deal worse than they
thought, and thereupon they confounded the language to prevent them
succeeding, so that the fellow up above could not shout down "mortar"
or "brick" to the one below, and they had to give it up. Is it possible
that any one believes that that is the reason why we have the variety of
languages in the world? Do you know that language is born of human
experience, and is a physical science? Do you know that every word has
been suggested in some way by the feelings or observations of man—that
there are words as tender as the dawn, as serene as the stars, and others
as wild as the beasts? Do you know that language is dying and being
born continually—that every language has its cemetery and cradle, its
bud and blossom, and withered leaf? Man has loved, enjoyed and suffered, and language is simply the expression he gives those experiences.

  Then the world began to divide, and the Jewish nation was started.
Now I want to say that at one time your ancestors, like mine, were barbarians. If the Jewish people had to write these books now they would be
civilized books, and I do not hold them responsible for what their ancestors
did. We find the Jewish people first in Canaan, and there were seventy
of them, counting Joseph and his children already in Egypt. They lived
two hundred and fifteen years, and they then went down into Egypt and
stayed there two hundred and fifteen years; they were four hundred and-

thirty years in Canaan and Egypt. How many did they have when they went to Egypt? Seventy. How many were they at the end of two hundred and fifteen years? Three millions. That is a good many. We had at the time of the Revolution in this country three millions of people. Since that time there have been four doubles, until we have forty-eight millions to-day. How many would the Jews number at the same ratio in two hundred and fifteen years? Call it eight doubles and we have forty thousand. But instead of forty thousand they had three millions. How do I know they had three millions? Because they had six hundred thousand men of war. For every honest voter in the State of Illinois there will be five other people, and there are always more voters than men of war. They must have had at the lowest possible estimate three millions of people. Is that true? Is there a minister in the city of Chicago that will certify to his own idiocy by claiming that they could have increased to three millions by that time? If there is, let him say so. Do not let him talk about the civilizing influence of a lie.

When they got into the desert they took a census to see how many first-born children there were. They found they had twenty-two thousand two hundred and seventy-three first born males. It is reasonable to suppose there was about the same number of first born girls, or forty-five thousand first born children. There must have been about as many mothers as first-born children. Dividing three millions by forty-five thousand mothers, and you will find that the women in Israel had to have on the average sixty-eight children apiece. Some stories are too thin. This is too thick. Now, we know that among three million people there will be about three hundred births a day; and according to the Old Testament, whenever a child was born the mother had to make a sacrifice—a sin-offering for the crime of having been a mother. If there is in this universe anything that is infinitely pure, it is a mother with her child in her arms. Every woman had to have a sacrifice of a couple of doves, a couple of pigeons, and the priests had to eat those pigeons in the most holy place. At that time there were at least three hundred births a day, and the priests had to cook and eat those pigeons in the most holy place; and at that time there were only three priests. Two hundred birds apiece per day! I look upon them as the champion bird-eaters of the world.

Then where were these Jews? They were upon the desert of Sinai; and Sahara compared to that is a garden. Imagine an ocean of lava, torn by storm and vexed by tempest, suddenly gazed at by a Gorgon and changed to stone. Such was the desert of Sinai. The whole supplies of the world could not maintain three millions of people on the desert of Sinai for forty years. It would cost one hundred thousand millions of dollars, and would bankrupt Christendom. And yet there they were with flocks and herds—so many that they sacrificed over one hundred and fifty thousand first-born lambs at one time. It would require millions of acres to support those flocks, and yet there was no blade of grass, and there is no account of it raining baled hay. They sacrificed one hundred and fifty thousand lambs, and the blood had all to be sprinkled on the altar within two hours, and there were only three priests. They would have to sprinkle the blood of twelve hundred and fifty lambs per minute. Then all the people gathered in front of the tabernacle eighteen feet deep. Three millions of people would make a column six miles long. Some reverend gentlemen say they were ninety feet deep. Well, that would make a column of over a mile.

Where were these people going? They were going to the Holy Land. How large was it? Twelve thousand square miles—one-fifth the size of Illinois—a frightful country, covered with rocks and desolation. There never was a land agent in the city of Chicago that would not have blushed with shame to have described that land as flowing with milk and honey. Do you believe that God Almighty ever went into partnership with hornets? Is it necessary unto salvation? God said to the Jews: "I will send hornets before you, to drive out the Canaanites." How would a hornet know a Canaanite? Is it possible that God inspired the hornets —that he granted letters of marque and reprisal to hornets? I am willing to admit that nothing in the world would be better calculated to make a man leave his native country than a few hornets attending strictly to business. God said "Kill the Canaanites slowly." Why? "Lest the beasts of the field increase upon you." How many Jews were there? Three millions. Going to a country, how large? Twelve thousand square miles. But were there nations already in this Holy Land? Yes, there were seven nations "mightier than the Jews." Say there would be twenty-one millions when they got there, or twenty-four millions with themselves. Yet they were told to kill them slowly, lest the beasts of the field increase upon them. Is there a man in Chicago that believes that! Then what does he teach it to little children for? Let him tell the truth.

So the same God went into partnership with snakes. The children of Israel lived on manna—one account says all the time, and another only a little while. That is the reason there is a chance for commentaries, and you can exercise faith. If the book was reasonable everybody could get to heaven in a moment. But whenever it looks as if it could not be that way and you believe, you are almost a saint, and when you know it is not that way and believe you are a saint. He fed them on manna. Now manna is very peculiar stuff. It would melt in the sun, and yet they used to cook it by seething and baking. I would as soon think of

frying snow or boiling icicles. But this manna had other peculiar qualities. It shrank to an omer, no matter how much they gathered, and
swelled up to an omer, no matter how little they gathered. What a
magnificent thing manna would be for the currency, shrinking and swel-
ling according to the volume of business! There was not a change in the
bill of fare for forty years, and they knew that God could just as well give
them three square meals a day. They remembered about the cucumbers,
and the melons, and the leeks and the onions of Egypt, and they said:
" Our souls abhoreth this light bread." Then this God got mad—you
know cooks are always touchy—and thereupon He sent snakes to bite
the men, women and children. He also sent them quails in wrath and
anger, and while they had the flesh between their teeth, He struck
thousands of them dead. He always acted in that way, all of a sudden.
People had no chance to explain—no chance to move for a new trial—
nothing. I want to know if it is reasonable he should kill people for
asking for one change of diet in forty years. Suppose you had been
boarding with an old lady for forty years, and she never had a solitary
thing on her table but hash, and one morning you said: " My soul abhoreth hash." What would you say if she let a basketful of rattlesnakes
upon you? Now is it possible for people to believe this? The Bible
says that their clothes did not wax old, they did not get shiny at the
knees or elbows; and their shoes did not wear out. They grew right
along with them. The little boy starting out with his first pants grew
up and his pants grew with him. Some commentators have insisted that
angels attended to their wardrobes. I never could believe it. Just think
of one angel hunting another and saying: " There goes another button."
I cannot believe it.

There must be a mistake somewhere or somehow. Do you believe
the real God—if there is one—ever killed a man for making hair-oil?
And yet you find in the Pentateuch that God gave Moses a recipe for
making hair-oil to grease Aaron's beard; and said if anybody made the
same hair-oil he should be killed. And He gave him a formula for
making ointment, and He said if anybody made ointment like that he
should be killed. I think that is carrying patent-laws to excess. There
must be some mistake about it. I cannot imagine the infinite Creator
of all the shining worlds giving a recipe for hair-oil. Do you believe
that the real God came down to Mount Sinai with a lot of patterns for
making a tabernacle—patterns for tongs, for snuffers, and such things?
Do you believe that God came down on that mountain and told Moses
how to cut a coat, and how it should be trimmed? What would an infinite God care on which side he cut the breast, what color the fringe was,
or how the buttons were placed? Do you believe God told Moses to

make curtains of fine linen? Where did they get their flax in the desert? How did they weave it? Did He tell him to make things of gold, silver and precious stones, when they hadn't them? Is it possible that God told them not to eat any fruit until after the fourth year of planting the trees? You see all these things were written hundreds of years afterwards, and the priests, in order to collect the tithes, dated the laws back. They did not say, "This is our law," but, "Thus said God to Moses in the wilderness." Now, can you believe that? Imagine a scene: The eternal God tells Moses, "Here is the way I want you to consecrate my priests. Catch a sheep and cut his throat." I never could understand why God wanted a sheep killed just because a man had done a mean trick; perhaps it was because his priests were fond of mutton. He tells Moses further to take some of the blood and put it on his right thumb, a little on his right ear, and a little on his right big toe? Do you believe God ever gave such instructions for the consecration of His priests? If you should see the South Sea Islanders going through such a performance you could not keep your face straight. And will you tell me that it had to be done in order to consecrate a man to the service of the infinite God? Supposing the blood got on the left toe?

Then we find in his book how God went to work to make the Egyptians let the Israelites go. Suppose we wish to make a treaty with the mikado of Japan, and Mr. Hayes sent a commissioner there; and suppose he should employ Hermann, the wonderful German, to go along with him; and when they came in the presence of the mikado Hermann threw down an umbrella, which changed into a turtle, and the commissioner said: "That is my certificate." You would say the country is disgraced. You would say the president of a republic like this disgraces himself with jugglery. Yet we are told God sent Moses and Aaron before Pharaoh, and when they got there Moses threw down a stick which turned into a snake. That God is a juggler—he is the infinite prestidigitator. Is that possible? Was that really a snake, or was it the appearance of a snake? If it was the appearance of a snake, it was a fraud. Then the necromancers of Egypt were sent for, and they threw down sticks, which turned into snakes, but those were not so large as Moses' snakes, which swallowed them. I maintain that it is just as hard to make small snakes as it is to make large ones; the only difference is that to make large snakes either larger sticks or more practice is required.

Do you believe that God rained hail on the innocent cattle, killing them in the highways and in the field? Why should he inflict punishment on cattle for something their owners had done? I could never have any respect for a God that would so inflict pain upon a brute beast simply on account of the crime of its owner. Is it possible that God worked mira-

cles to convince Pharaoh that slavery was wrong? Why did he not tell
Pharaoh that any nation founded on slavery could not stand? Why did he
not tell him, "Your government is founded on slavery, and it will go down,
and the sands of the desert will hide from the view of man your temples,
your altars, and your fanes?" Why did he not speak about the infamy
of slavery? Because he believed in the infamy of slavery himself. Can
we believe that God will allow a man to give his wife the right of divorcement and make the mother of his children a wanderer and a vagrant.
There is not one word about woman in the Old Testament except the word
of shame and humiliation. The God of the Bible does not think woman
is as good as man. She was never worth mentioning. It did not take
the pains to recount the death of the mother of us all. I have no respect
for any book that does not treat woman as the equal of man. And if
there is any God in this universe who thinks more of me than he thinks
of my wife, he is not well acquainted with both of us. And yet they say
that that was done on account of the hardness of their hearts; and that was
done in a community where the law was so fierce that it stoned a man to
death for picking up sticks on Sunday. Would it not have been better
to stone to death every man who abused his wife and allowed them to
pick up sticks on account of the hardness of their hearts? If God wanted
to take those Jews from Egypt to the land of Canaan, why didn't He do
it instantly? If He was going to do a miracle, why didn't He do one
worth talking about?

After God had killed all the first-born in Egypt, after he had killed all
the cattle, still Egypt could raise an army that could put to flight six hundred thousand men. And because this God overwhelmed the Egyptian
army, he bragged about it for a thousand years, repeatedly calling the
attention of the Jews to the fact that he overthrew Pharaoh and his hosts.
Did he help much with their six hundred thousand men? We find by the
records of the day that the Egyptian standing army at that time was
never more than one hundred thousand men. Must we believe all these
stories in order to get to Heaven when we die? Must we judge of a man's
character by the number of stories he believes? Are we to get to Heaven
by creed or by deed? That is the question. Shall we reason, or shall we
simply believe? Ah, but they say the Bible is not inspired about those
little things. The Bible says the rabbit and the hare chew the cud. But
they do not. They have a tremulous motion of the lip. But the Being
that made them says they chew the cud. The Bible, therefore, is not
inspired in natural history. Is it inspired in its astrology? No. Well,
what is it inspired in? In its law? Thousands of people say that if it
had not been for the ten commandments we would not have known any
better than to rob and steal. Suppose a man planted an acre of potatoes,

hoed them all summer, and dug them in the fall; and suppose a man had sat upon the fence all the time and watched him; do you believe it would be necessary for that man to read the ten commandments to find out who, in his judgment, had a right to take those potatoes? All laws against larceny have been made by industry to protect the fruits of its labor. Why is there a law against murder? Simply because a large majority of people object to being murdered. That is all. And all these laws were in force thousands of years before that time.

One of the commandments said they should not make any graven images, and that was the death of art in Palestine. No sculptor has ever enriched stone with the divine forms of beauty in that country; and any commandment that is the death of art is not a good commandment. But they say the Bible is morally inspired; and they tell me there is no civilization without this Bible. Then God knows that just as well as you do. God always knew it, and if you can't civilize a nation without a Bible, why didn't God give every nation just one Bible to start with? Why did God allow hundreds of thousands and billions of billions to go down to hell just for the lack of a Bible? They say that it is morally inspired. Well, let us examine it. I want to be fair about this thing, because I am willing to stake my salvation or damnation upon this question—whether the Bible is true or not. I say it is not; and upon that I am willing to wager my soul. Is there a woman here who believes in the institution of polygamy? Is there a man here who believes in that infamy? You say: "No. we do not." Then you are better than your God was four thousand years ago. Four thousand years ago he believed in it, taught it and upheld it. I pronounce it and denounce it the infamy of infamies. It robs our language of every sweet and tender word in it. It takes the fireside away forever. It takes the meaning out of the words father, mother, sister, brother, and turns the temple of love into a vile den where crawl the slimy snakes of lust and hatred. I was in Utah a little while ago, and was on the mountain where God used to talk to Brigham Young. He never said anything to me. I said it was just as reasonable that God in the nineteenth century should talk to a polygamist in Utah as it was that four thousand years ago, on Mount Sinai, he talked to Moses upon that hellish and damnable question.

I have no love for any God who believes in polygamy. There is no heaven on this earth save where the one woman loves the one man and the one man loves the one woman. I guess it is not inspired on the polygamy question. Maybe it is inspired about religious liberty. God says that if anybody differs with you about religion, "kill him." He told His peculiar people, "If any one teaches a different religion, kill him!" He did not say, "Try and convince him that he is wrong," but "kill him!" He did not say, "I am in the miracle business, and I will convince him;" but "kill him." He said to every husband, "If your wife, that you love as you love your own soul, says, 'let us go and worship other gods,' then 'thy hand shall be first upon her and she shall be stoned with stones until she dies.'" Well, now, I hate a God of that kind, and I cannot think of being nearer heaven than to be away from Him. A God tells a man to kill his wife simply because she differs with him on religion! If the real God were to tell me to kill my wife, I would not do it. If you had lived in Palestine at that time, and your wife—the mother of your children—had woke up at night and said: "I am tired of Jehovah. He is always turning up that board-bill. He is always telling about whipping the Egyptians. He is always killing somebody. I am tired of Him. Let us worship the sun. The sun has clothed the world in beauty; it has covered the earth with green and flowers; by its divine light I first saw your face; its light has enabled me to look into the eyes of my beautiful babe. Let us worship the sun, father and mother of light and love and joy." Then what would it be your duty to do—kill her? Do you believe any real god ever did that? Your hand should be first upon her, and when you took up some ragged rock and hurled it against the white bosom filled with love for you, and saw running away the red current of her sweet life, then you would look up to heaven and receive the congratulations of the infinite fiend whose commandments you had to obey. I guess the Bible was not inspired about religious liberty. Let me ask you right here: Suppose, as a matter of fact, God gave those laws to the Jews and told them "whenever a man preaches a different religion, kill him," and suppose that afterwards the same God took upon himself flesh, and came to the world and taught and preached a different religion, and the Jews crucified him—did he not reap exactly what he sowed?

May be this book is inspired about war. God told the Israelites to overrun that country, and kill every man, woman and child for defending their native land. Kill the old men? Yes. Kill the women? Certainly. And the little dimpled babes in the cradle, that smile and coo in the face of murder—dash out their brains; that is the will of God. Will you tell me that any god ever commanded such infamy? Kill the men and the women, and the young men and the babes! "What shall we do with the maidens?" "Give them to the rabble murderers!" Do you believe that God ever allowed the roses of love and the violets of modesty that shed their perfume in the heart of a maiden to be trampled beneath the brutal feet of lust? If there is any God, I pray him to write in the book of eternal remembrance opposite to my name, that I denied that lie. Whenever a woman reads a Bible and comes to that passage, she ought

8

to throw the book from her in contempt and scorn. Do you tell me that any decent god would do that? What would the devil have done under the same circumstances? Just think of it; and yet that is the God that we want to get into the Constitution. That is the God we teach our children about, so that they will be sweet and tender, amiable and kind! That monster—that fiend! I guess the Bible is not inspired about religious liberty, nor about war.

Then, if it is not inspired about these things, maybe it is inspired about slavery. God tells the Jews to buy up the children of the heathen round about and they should be servants for them. What is a "servant?" If they struck a "servant" and he died immediately, punishment was to follow; but if the injured man should linger a while, there was no punishment, because the servant represented their money! Do you believe that it is right—that God made one man to work for another and to receive pay in rations? Do you believe God said that a whip on the naked back was the legal tender for labor performed? Is it possible that the real God ever gave such infamous, blood-thirsty laws? What more does he say? When the time of a married slave expired, he could not take his wife and children with him. Then if the slave did not wish to desert his family, he had his ears pierced with an awl, and became his master's property forever. Do you believe that God ever turned the dimpled cheeks of little children into iron chains to hold a man in slavery? Do you know that a God like that would not make a respectable devil? I want none of his mercy. I want no part and no lot in the heaven of such a God. I will go to 'perdition, where there is human sympathy. The only voice we have ever had from either of those other worlds came from hell. There was a rich man who prayed his brothers to attend to Lazarus so that they might "not come to this place." That is the only instance, so far as we know, of souls across the river having any sympathy. And I would rather be in hell, asking for water, than in heaven denying that petition. Well, what is this book inspired about? Where does the inspiration come from? Why was it that so many animals were killed? It was simply to make atonement for man—that is all. They killed something that had not committed a crime, in order that the one who had committed the crime might be acquitted. Based upon that idea is the atonement of the Christian religion. That is the reason I attack this book—because it is the basis of another infamy, viz: that one man can be good for another, or that one man can sin for another. I deny it. You have got to be good for yourself; you have got to sin for yourself. The trouble about the atonement is, that it saves the wrong man. For instance, I kill some one. He is a good man. He loves his wife and children and tries to make them happy; but he is not a Chris-

I

tian, and he goes to hell. Just as soon as I am convicted and cannot get a pardon I get religion, and I go to heaven. The hand of mercy cannot reach down through the shadows of hell to my victim.

There is no atonement for the saint—only for the sinner and the criminal. The atonement saves the wrong man. I have said that I would never make a lecture at all without attacking this doctrine. I did not care what I started out on. I was always going to attack this doctrine. And in my conclusion I want to draw you a few pictures of the Christian heaven. But before I do that I want to say the rest I have to say about Moses. I want you to understand that the Bible was never printed until 1488. I want you to know that up to that time it was in manuscript, in possession of those who could change it if they wished; and they did change it, because no two ever agreed. Much of it was in the waste basket of credulity, in the open mouth of tradition, and in the dull ear of memory. I want you also to know that the Jews themselves never agreed as to what books were inspired, and that there were a lot of books written that were not incorporated in the Old Testament. I want you to know that two or three years before Christ, the Hebrew manuscript was translated into Greek, and that the original from which the translation was made has never been seen since. Some Latin Bibles were found in Africa but no two agreed; and then they translated the Septuagint into the languages of Europe, and no two agreed. Henry VIII. took a little time between murdering his wives to see that the Word of God was translated correctly. You must recollect that we are indebted to murderers for our Bibles and our creeds. Constantine, who helped on the good work in its early stage, murdered his wife and child, mingling their blood with the blood of the Savior.

The Bible that Henry VIII. got up did not suit, and then his daughter, the murderess of Mary, Queen of Scotts, got up another edition, which also did not suit; and finally, that philosophical idiot, King James, prepared the edition which we now have. There are at least one hundred thousand errors in the Old Testament, but everybody sees that it is not enough to invalidate its claim to infallibility. But these errors are gradually being fixed, and hereafter the prophet will be fed by Arabs instead of "ravens," and Samson's three hundred foxes will be three hundred "sheaves" already bound, which were fired and thrown into the standing wheat. I want you all to know that there was no contemporaneous literature at the time the Bible was composed, and that the Jews were infinitely ignorant in their day and generation—that they were isolated by bigotry and wickedness from the rest of the world. I want you to know that there are fourteen hundred millions of people in the world; and that with all the talk and work of the societies, only one hundred and twenty millions have

got Bibles.   I want you to understand that not one person in one hundred
in this world ever read the Bible, and no two ever understood it alike who
did read it, and that no one person probably ever understood it aright.
I want you to understand that where this Bible has been, man has hated
his brother—there have been dungeons, racks, thumbscrews, and the
sword.   I want you to know that the cross has been in partnership with
the sword, and that the religion of Jesus Christ was established by murderers, tyrants and hypocrites.   I want you to know that the church
carried the black flag.   Then talk about the civilizing influence of this
religion!

Now, I want to give an idea or two in regard to the Christian's heaven.
Of all the selfish things in this world, it is one man wanting to get to
heaven, caring nothing what becomes of the rest of mankind.   "If I
can only get my little soul in!"   I have always noticed that the people
who have the smallest souls make the most fuss about getting them saved.
Here is what we are taught by the church to-day.   We are taught by it
that fathers and mothers, brothers and sisters can all be happy in heaven,
no matter who may be in hell; that the husband can be happy there
with the wife that would have died for him at any moment of his life in
hell.   But they say, "We don't believe in fire.   What we believe in now
is remorse."   What will you have remorse for?   For the mean things
you have done when you are in hell?   Will you have any remorse for the
mean things you have done when you are in heaven?   Or will you be so
good then that you won't care how you used to be?   Don't you see what
an infinitely mean belief that is?   I tell you to-day that, no matter in
what heaven you may be, no matter in what star you are spending
the summer, if you meet another man whom you have wronged you
will drop a little behind in the tune.   And, no matter in what part
of hell you are, and you meet some one whom you have succored, whose
nakedness you have clothed, and whose famine you have fed, the fire will
cool up a little.   According to this Christian doctrine, when you are in
heaven you won't care how mean you were once.   What must be the
social condition of a gentleman in heaven who will admit that he never
would have been there if he had not got scared?   What must be the
social position of an angel who will always admit that if another had not
pitied him he ought to have been damned?   Is it a compliment to an infinite God to say that every being He ever made deserved to be damned
the minute He got him done, and that He will damn everybody He has
not had a chance to make over?   Is it possible that somebody else can be
good for me, and that this doctrine of the atonement is the only anchor
for the human soul?

For instance: here is a man seventy years of age, who has been a splendid fellow and lived according to the laws of nature. He has got about him splendid children, whom he has loved and cared for with all his heart. But he did not happen to believe in this Bible; he did not believe in the Pentateuch. He did not believe that because some children made fun of a gentleman who was short of hair, God sent two bears and tore the little darlings to pieces. He had a tender heart, and he thought about the mothers who would take the pieces, the bloody fragments of the children, and press them to their bosom in a frenzy of grief; he thought about their wails and lamentations, and could not believe that God was such an infinite monster. That was all he thought, but he went to Hell. Then, there is another man who made a hell on earth for his wife, who had to be taken to the insane asylum, and his children were driven from home and were wanderers and vagrants in the world. But just between the last sin and the last breath, this fellow got religion, and he never did another thing except to take his medicine. He never did a solitary human being a favor, and he died and went to heaven. Do n't you think he would be astonished to see that other man in hell, and say to himself, "Is it possible that such a splendid character should bear such fruit, and that all my rascality at last has brought me next to God?"

Or, let us put another case. You were once alone in the desert—no provisions, no water, no hope. Just when your life was at its lowest ebb, a man appeared, gave you water and food and brought you safely out. How you would bless that man. Time rolls on. You die and go to heaven; and one day you see through the black night of hell, the friend who saved your life, begging for a drop of water to cool his parched lips. He cries to you, "Remember what I did in the desert—give me to drink." How mean, how contemptible you would feel to see his suffering and be unable to relieve him. But this is the Christian heaven. We sit by the fireside and see the flames and the sparks fly up the chimney—everybody happy, and the cold wind and sleet are beating on the window, and out on the doorstep is a mother with a child on her breast freezing. How happy it makes a fireside, that beautiful contrast. And we say "God is good," and there we sit, and she sits and moans, not one night but forever. Or we are sitting at the table with our wives and children, everybody eating, happy and delighted, and Famine comes and pushes out its shriveled palms, and, with hungry eyes, implores us for a crust. How that would increase the appetite! And yet that is the Christian heaven. Don't you see that these infamous doctrines petrify the human heart? And I would have every one who hears me, swear that he will never contribute another dollar to build another church, in which is taught such infamous lies. I want every one of you to say that you never will, directly or indirectly, give a dollar to any man to preach that falsehood. It has done harm enough. It has covered the world with blood. It has filled the asylums for the insane. It has cast a shadow in the heart, in the sunlight of every good and tender man and woman. I say let us rid the heavens of this monster, and write upon the dome "Liberty, love and law."

No matter what may come to me or what may come to you, let us do exactly what we believe to be right, and let us give the exact thought in our brains. Rather than have this Christianity true, I would rather all the gods would destroy themselves this morning. I would rather the whole universe would go to nothing, if such a thing were possible, this instant. Rather than have the glittering dome of pleasure reared on the eternal abyss of pain, I would see the utter and eternal destruction of this universe. I would rather see the shining fabric of our universe crumble to unmeaning chaos, and take itself where oblivion broods and memory forgets. I would rather the blind Samson of some imprisoned force, released by thoughtless chance, should so rack and strain this world that man in stress and straint, in astonishment and fear, should suddenly fall back to savagery and barbarity. I would rather that this thrilled and thrilling globe, shorn of all life, should in its cycles rub the wheel, the parent star, on which the light should fall as fruitlessly as falls the gaze of love on death, than to have this infamous doctrine of eternal punishment true; rather than have this infamous selfishness of a heaven for a few and a hell for the many established as the word of God!

One world at a time is my doctrine. Let us make some one happy here. Happiness is the interest that a decent action draws, and the more decent actions you do, the larger your income will be. Let every man try to make his wife happy, his children happy. Let every man try to make every day a joy, and God cannot afford to damn such a man. I cannot help God; I cannot injure God. I can help people; I can injure people. Consequently humanity is the only real religion.

I cannot better close this lecture than by quoting four lines from Robert Burns:

> " To make a happy fireside clime
> To weans and wife— •
> That's the true pathos and sublime
> Of human life."

MISTAKES

OF

INGERSOLL

AS SHOWN BY

REV. W. F. CRAFTS, BISHOP CHARLES E. CHENEY, CHAPLAIN C. C
McCABE, D.D., ARTHUR SWAZEY, D.D., ROBERT COLLYER, D.D.,
FRED. PERRY POWERS, AND OTHERS.

INCLUDING INGERSOLL'S LECTURE

ON

SKULLS, AND HIS ANSWER

TO

PROF. SWING, DR. RYDER, DR. HERFORD, DR. COLLYER,
DR. THOMAS, DR. KOEHLER, AND OTHER CRITICS.

ALSO

INGERSOLL'S ORATION AT HIS BROTHER'S GRAVE,

TOGETHER WITH

HENRY WARD BEECHER'S AND HON. ISAAC N. ARNOLD'S

COMMENTS ON THE SAME.

EDITED BY

J. B. McCLURE.

CHICAGO:
RHODES & McCLURE, PUBLISHERS.
1879.

Not satisfied with his recent parade of the "Mistakes of Moses" before the Chicago public (which called forth our first book, entitled the "Mistakes of Ingersoll, as Shown By Prof. Swing and Others"), Mr. I. has since returned and delivered another lecture against the Bible and against his critics, Prof. Swing. Dr. Ryder, Dr. Herford and Dr. Collyer. These last efforts of Mr. Ingersoll have called forth the present volume, in which will be found additional "Mistakes," as shown by Rev. W. F. Crafts, who is the well-known successor of Dr. Tiffany in Trinity Methodist Episcopal Church; by Chaplain C. C. McCabe, Bishop Cheney, Arthur Swazey, D.D., Robert Collyer, D.D., whose names are all familar to the public; and by Fred Perry Powers, who is favorably identified with Chicago journalism. The "commendable fairness," mentioned by the press, in printing both the "text and replies" in the former volume, requires in this instance, also the text, which is given at the close and which includes Mr. Ingersoll's replies to Prof. Swing, Dr. Ryder, Brooke Herford and others.

J. B. McCLURE.

CHICAGO, May 17, 1879.

Entered according to Act of Congress, in the year 1879, by J. B. McCLURE & R. S. RHODES, in the Office of the Librarian of Congress, at Washington, D. C.

OTTAWAY & COMPANY,
Printers.

DONOHUE & HENNEBERRY,
Binders.

CONTENTS.

W. P. Crafts.

MISTAKES OF INGERSOLL

AS SHOWN BY

W. F. CRAFTS,	ROBERT COLLYER, D. D.
CHAPLAIN McCABE,	F. P. POWERS,
ARTHUR SWAZEY, D. D.	BISHOP CHENEY,
	AND OTHERS.

ALSO INCLUDING

INGERSOLL'S LECTURE IN FULL ON "SKULLS," AND HIS RE-
PLIES TO PROF. SWING, W. H. RYDER, BROOKE
HERFORD, AND OTHER CRITICS.

W. F. CRAFTS' REPLY.

Ingersollism Outlined—"Ten Points" instead of "Five"—Infidel Protoplasm.

"I WAR with principles, not with men"—the motto of Webster in political debates—should be the law in all conflicts of ideas, especially in the realm of religion. It is not of the person, Mr. Ingersoll, that I speak, but rather of the principles of which he is the most popular spokesman, and which make up that shallowest, but loudest, Jericho book of infidelity's bitter waters which begins in a few tears of pretended martyrdom to love of truth; spatters the mud of epithets upon Christians, while condemning that very vice in a part of the Church in less advanced

7

ages; babbles shallowly along its little channel about law as an almighty executive, as if the rails that give direction to a train took the place of the engine that draws it; winds very crookedly through the Old Testament, avoiding every passage except those few that can be used for ridicule; plows still more crookedly through church history, shunning every part except the unchristian swamps of bigotry and superstition; keeps up the same snaky crookedness in its passage through religion of to-day, hurrying noisily among only the few rocky and marshy places, where it can find the reptiles of superstition and error; passes with great dash of spray along the audacious theory that Christian civilization is the result of anti-Christian forces; plunges with loud roar of waters down its claim that infidelity is the only liberator of man, woman, and child; and still flowing within its narrow little channel babbles of itself as an emancipated ocean of untrammeled thought.

These characteristics of the brook are the ten points of Ingersollism. I have read and re-read, carefully, the nine published lectures of Mr. Ingersoll on religious themes, besides hearing the one entitled " Skulls," and every one of them has something on each of these ten points of his fixed and unchanging creed, and not one or all has anything beyond these ten " doctrines "—for he often uses the words, " That is my doctrine." While attacking creeds of the Church he holds and urges all to believe his own unformulated but distinct creed, offering in place of the " five points of Calvinism " the ten points of Ingersollism, the latter occurring as regularly in every one of his lectures in this age as the former did a century ago in the sermons of Calvinists, which he ridicules for their sameness.

What is this frightful monster that we call " a creed?" Simply a statement of what one believes. Every man, unless he is an idiot, has a creed in which he agrees with somebody. The only question is to find by " reason, observation, and experience," which is the best. It would hardly be considered bigotry for a scientist to believe a few things as a creed of fixed scientific truths which no progress can ever erase, for instance, the rotundity and revolution of the earth, the attraction of the planets upon each other, and scores of other things which every scientist has held for many years unchanged, and is sure are unchangeable because proved conclusively. There are some certainties in the science of religion, such as are referred to in the Apostles' Creed, which may, without any greater bigotry, be considered as proved and established. The Christian Church of to-day does not generally insist upon anything further than these few concrete facts of the Apostles' Creed " as essentials " in Christian belief. When Evangelical churches shout their watchword, " In essentials, unity; in non-essentials, liberty; in all things, charity," it is as if a company of scientists should say, " On proved facts we will all agree, but in the realms of hypothesis and opinion, we will agree to disagree."

But the special point we wish to notice is, that Mr. Ingersoll attacks creed with creed. He is as bigoted a partisan of his own creed as ever called hard names. The very heart of his creed seems to be the belief that his mission is to destroy the creed of everybody else.

It is a suggestive fact that the naturally-gifted mind of Mr. Ingersoll, who declares that godless and soulless materialism is the emancipator and inspirer of thought, should be able, in all the years which these ten lectures represent, to produce but ten ideas, the same ten ideas which made up his earliest lecture, years ago, appearing successively in each of the succeeding lectures, including that of to-day, there being no change save in the cap and bells of his jokes. Reading these ten ideas over and over for as many

hours in going through these lectures, brought back a
ludicrous scene in our college burial of mathematics when
fifteen notes of Pleyel's hymn were played dolefully over
and over again for nearly an hour, as marching music.

In reading these lectures, which are but ten combinations
and permutations of ten ideas, one is reminded also of the
lecturer's own illustration of the boarding house keeper,
who, for years, had no change of diet from hash, for every
lecture is the same hash of ten ideas, changed only in
the name and in the order of putting in the ten elements.

ARTICLE I.

First Point in the Ten—Sepulchral Hoots of the Ingersoll Owl—A Theological Rip Van Winkle.

As in the beet hash of New England the blood red beet
predominates and gives color to the whole, so the principal
element in these lectures against Christianity is the blood
of past persecutions by a corrupt part of the Church, for
which true Christianity has no more responsibility than a
loyal colonel in our war of 1776, or 1861, for the robberies
and crimes of camp-followers or traitors. In every published
lecture on religion, Mr. Ingersoll deliberately cites the acts
of the Benedict Arnolds of the Christian army as representing the Washingtons and Grants. He describes past
counterfeits of religion as specimens of its accepted currency. It is as if one should attack present astronomers by
relating ridiculous stories of the old astrologers, or assail
present physicians by quoting the strange practices of the
ancient alchemists.

In one lecture—a fair representative of all in this respect
—I found that in forty-three pages only two did not contain these stale references to past persecutions, except a few
pages given to the trial of Professor Swing, which were
equally stale as assailing chiefly abandoned features of

human Calvinism. Past errors and follies of the human Calvinism, human Catholicism, and heathen religions are constantly spoken of as if vital elements of Christianity.

Mr. Ingersoll ought to have a hymn to sing at the opening and close of his lectures, made on the pattern of that one whose first verse is:

> Go on, go on, go on, go on,
> Go on, go on, go on,
> Go on, go on, go on, go on,
> Go on, go on, go on,

with forty-two verses more of the same, substituting " past persecutions," instead of " go on," which is too progressive for a " go-back " lecture.

Mr. Ingersoll is a Rip Van Winkle in theology, who seems to have slept ever since the days of persecution. He is a Sancho Panza who assails imaginary foes of his own making, and thinks he has captured the golden helmet of Christianity when he has only secured the abandoned brass kettle of old traditions and discarded superstitions. He is a Falstaff killing the dead Percy of past follies. His lectures bustle with the antiquated and misused words "priests," " dark ages," "witches," " fagots," " religious wars," "church fathers," " damned infants," " martyrs," " gods," etc., as if he were speaking in a heathen land, and also in some dead century. And he uses the past tense so exclusively in his " progressive " lectures that one would suppose English as well as Hebrew had no present tense. It must have been Mr. Ingersoll, in his boyhood, that came from his first hunt crying, " I've shot a cherub," having mistaken an owl for a cherub, because of the wretched pictures of the latter on the old grave stones. Mr. Ingersoll logically destroys some Church owl of the dark ages, and because it corresponds with his own caricature of the Church thinks he has dethroned Christianity

itself. Like Poe's " raven " who had but one word, " Never-
more," Mr. Ingersoll is continually crying in the ears of
the present that worn-out strain about abuses which we all
condemn, " Galileo-Servetus, Galileo-Servetus."

This ten-idea champion of popular materialism, while
talking of progress and condemning those who hold fast to
things of the past, is nevertheless so largely devoted to
showing his carefully preserved martyr-mummies from the
long-past ages of persecution, that we find Mark Twain's
question constantly arising at each new charge against
Christianity: " Is he—is he dead? " and we are also
tempted to cry out for a " fresh corpse " in place of
these very dry and dead mummies of past abuses. To
paraphrase the lecturer's own words, we want one present fact. We pass our hats through the lectures in vain
for some present facts against pure Christianity, which he
assumes to assail and overthrow. There is far more excuse
for Thomas Paine, in an age when the old Calvinistic errors
were largely held, and for Voltaire, surrounded by the
superstitions of Romanism, misunderstanding Christianity,
than for this modern lecturer, who very well knows that
the caricatures which he represents as Christianity are
very old pictures of its ancient camp-followers.

ARTICLE II.

Ingersoll Mistakes a Part for the Whole—Gross Misrepresen-
tations.

Article Second of Ingersollism, like unto the first, but
with present instead of past tense, is about as follows:
Christianity to-day is proved to be false by the present
errors and abuses that are found in some of the churches.

Romish superstitions and the errors of those who have
grossly misinterpreted the Bible as a support of slavery,
polygamy, etc., are continually used by this champion of

"liberty of thought," and "charity" and "brotherhood," as representing true Christianity to-day, which is quite as honorable as if a man should attack the principles of medicine by citing the tricks of quacks. An examination of the hull of the Great Eastern found adhering to the iron-plates of the bottom an enormous multitude of mussels, whose weight is estimated at three hundred tons. The great ship has been carrying on her hull a burden equal to full cargoes for six or eight sailing ships.

Suppose I should show you a few of those barnacles as specimens of what the Great Eastern is made of, and then denounce its builders as fools? Mr. Ingersoll is constantly confounding barnacles of some "church" with Christianity. Suppose I should take the belts and whips of torture that are used by Romanists in Mexico and show them in lectures as specimens of the barbarism of Congregationalists and Methodists? It is certainly most palpable unfairness for Mr. Ingersoll to use the word "gods" indiscriminately of heathen and Christian objects of worship, and to employ the words, "The Church," as if there were no false or true, past or present in connection with it, and as if its meaning were as much a unit as "The Moon." So also he unfairly classes all ministers as "priests." It would be quite as fair to speak of all "medicine men," past and present, savage and civilized, under the words, "The Doctors."

ARTICLE III.

The Great Ingersoll Boomerang—How it Works—Further Misrepresentations Carefully Examined.

Far less prominent, but ever present, is the third element in Ingersollism—an oft-recurring moan—"Infidels to-day are martyrs at whom men cast epithets, but not ballots."

The defeated infidel politician appears as regularly and

revengefully in every lecture (indirectly, of course) as the misanthropic Byron shows himself in each of his poems as the real hero under the various names of "Childe Harold" "Don Juan," "Corsair," etc. He who cries out against the past for calling infidels by hard names hurls in the more kindly present more anathemas than any other Pope.

"You are an infidel."

"You're a bigot! Arn't you ashamed to be calling names, you old hypocrite?"

In this debate of Mr. Ingersoll's bigotry with the bigotry of the past, a printer might fitly misprint the "pros and cons," "pigs and cows." It is like the English lady who criticised an American friend for saying, at a mistake in croquet, "What a horrid scratch," and when asked what would have been better, replied, "You might have said, 'What a beastly fluke.'" It is not strange that the people will not elect to represent them in politics, one who so audaciously misrepresents them, as does Mr. Ingersoll in nearly every attempt to declare the belief of Christians.

Misrepresenting Bible Passages.

Dr. Ryder, Prof. Swing, and Dr. Herford, have abundantly shown his numerous and inexcusable misrepresentations of Bible passages, to which may be added another more atrocious, if possible, the implication that the persecutions of Saul of Tarsus, and the adulteries of Solomon, are a part of the Christian system, and also that Jephthah really killed his daughter as a sacrifice, which the Bible does not declare, nor any Christian believe, and the misinterpretation of the passage about women keeping silence in the churches, which the Christian Church of to-day considers of only temporary force, a command to Corinth, and not to Christendom, no more binding upon us than Paul's request that Timothy should bring his cloak that was left at Troas. It is a kindred misrepresentation to say the assertion that those who tortured the martyrs were the same ones who made the Bible—an assertion which history clearly refutes, as the Old Testament was arranged in its present form 388 B. C., and the New Testament was collected as it is at present before the days of persecution by the church began.

It is also a misrepresentation, not only of the Bible, but of the common principles of interpretation in every department of literature, to intimate that an explanation of passages as poetic and figurative, is unfair and begging the question. Suppose we should put a literal interpretation upon the tropical figures of Mr. Ingersoll's eloquence, and when he speaks of the sun's rays "as arrows from the quiver of the sun," declare him an ignorant idolator, who thinks the sun an intelligent being who has caught the passion for archery.

Sun and Moon Standing Still.

It is equally absurd for him to interpret the poem about the sun and moon standing still by the rules of prose. Mr. Ingersoll also says, poetically: "Think of that wonderful chemistry by which bread was changed into the divine tragedy of Hamlet." Suppose we should interpret that sentence as fact rather than figure, and say that Mr. Ingersoll believes that by the combination of certain liquids and solids in the chemist's retort this marvelous literary production was created! It would be quite as reasonable as to insist upon absolute literalness in the bold figures of Oriental eloquence and poetry.

Mr. Ingersoll also misrepresents the Christian's Sunday in the home, speaking of it as "a day too good for a child to be happy in," saying: "The idea, that any God would hate to hear a child laugh." We all know (?) that in the

Christian homes of to-day the smiles and laughter of childhood are strictly forbidden, and any one who smiles in church is carried out by the police (?).

Hell.

Especially does Mr. Ingersoll continually and grossly misrepresent Christianity in regard to the conditions by which men are believed to bring themselves to Hell. Hear him: " It is infinitely absurd to suppose that a God would address a communication to intelligent beings, and yet make it a crime, to be punished in eternal flames, for them to use their intelligence for the purpose of understanding His communication. Neither can they show why any one should be punished, either in this world or another, for acting honestly in accordance with reason; and yet a doctrine with every possible argument against it has been, and still is, believed and defended by the entire orthodox world. If I should say ninety-nine in a hundred go down to Hell, I should have the support of the entire orthodox world. You can see for yourselves the justice of damning a man if his parents happened to baptize him in the wrong way. Think of a God who will damn his children for the expression of an honest thought!"

Few, if any, intelligent Christians teach that a man must accept their denominational creed in all its details in order to be saved, as the careless critics of Christianity so often assert, but rather all evangelical Christians repeat the New Testament conditions of salvation, " Believe on the Lord Jesus Christ and thou shalt be saved," and declare negatively, not as has been said by Mr. Ingersoll, said by infidels, that all who do not believe will not be saved, but rather in the words of Martin Luther, " No man shall die in his sins, except him who, through disbelief, thrusts from him the forgiveness of sin, which in the name of Jesus is offered him." It is the firm of Ignorance and Bigotry that declare that evangelical Christianity teaches that a man can not be saved who does not believe in its statement of the Trinity and its interpretations of the Bible.

He also utterly misrepresents the Christian conception of saving faith as ignoring reason and action, both of which it includes, and as resting chiefly on a book or a creed as its end, rather than on the person, Christ. Every church teaches that intelligent faith and faithfulness toward Christ (not creeds in detail) is the condition of salvation. "Faith," says Bishop Wightman, "believes on competent testimony what it could not otherwise know." Or, as Dr. Arnold says: "Faith is reason leaning on God." Reason is the foundation of belief.

The Present vs. the Future.

Another of the almost countless misrepresentations of religion by Mr. Ingersoll, is the frequent statement that Christianity is wholly devoted to the future, and ignores man's present needs, which reminds us that it was Thomas Paine (?) and not the Bible that said, "Pure religion and undefiled before God the Father, is this, to visit the fatherless and the widows in their affliction, and to keep himself unspotted from the world." And you have all observed that the organized societies and benevolences, by which orphans, and the aged, and the helpless, are aided in asylums and refuges, were not (?) established by this Christianity which "ignores man's present needs, and devotes itself exclusively to the future." Christian ministers never preach on combining works with faith, or showing character by conduct, or loving their neighbors as themselves. Mr. Ingersoll declares that a little restitution is better than a great deal of repentance, and we have noticed that when Ingersoll has delivered a lecture or two in our large cities.

those among his hearers who have defrauded others have, at once, begun the work of restitution (?) by sending back the money they had stolen from employers, creditors and customers. (?) Mr. Moody, who preaches repentance as well as restitution, of course (?) has no such results following his work, as he proclaims the Christianity whose entire interest is in the future life. (?) You smile at this practical test of Mr. Ingersoll's theory, in view of the fact that we have no record of a single instance where one of his lectures has led to the restitution of stolen property; while such cases are constantly occurring in connection with the work of Mr. Moody and other Christians. Several very notable ones have come under my own immediate notice.

It is an equally astounding, barefaced misrepresentation, or to put it in fewer letters, false, when he states that all of the orthodox religion of the day is Calvinistic. Part of the so-called Calvinistic churches are not Calvinistic in the usual sense of the word, and we had fondly dreamed that there was such a body of Christians as Methodists who are distinctly anti-Calvinistic, and hold the first place in numbers among Protestant Churches in America.

It is also a misrepresentation to say, " Whoever thinks he has found it all out, he is orthodox," for every orthodox pulpit constantly preaches the duty of growth, intellectual and spiritual. Mr. Ingersoll declares that Protestants to-day would persecute, as in the past, if they had the power, a statement in which he assumes the role of the prophet, and shows the profundity of his insight into the spirit of Christianity to-day, which binds up the broken-hearted and ministers to the troubled and sorrowing. It is cunning sophistry to say that every one is opposed to the union of Church and state, because they know that the Church could not be trusted with power, a statement which obtains its force by suppressing the very important fact that the

Church when united with political power draws into itself unprincipled politicians, and becomes entirely a different body through the opportunities it offers to selfishness and ambition. It is also a misrepresentation to say that " Protestants stand up for Protestant persecutors of the past," for all Protestant churches of to-day condemn the burning of Servetus and such acts as much as any one. It is also a misrepresentation by holding back half the truth to tell us of that base or mistaken element of the Church that made the rack and not of that other noble element of the Church that was upon the rack, for the martyrs were seldom if ever infidels.

Ingersoll's Horrible Estimate of Truth.

Mr. Ingersoll, in his recent lecture on " Skulls," twice said that truth was not worth a little suffering, that one had better lie or recant than suffer a little pain, or lose a drop of blood. He would " turn Judas Iscariot to his own soul " to save a thumb. This significant item as to his whole estimate of truth helps us to account for the wholesale manufacture of falsehoods in his lectures.

Mr. Ingersoll's most gross misrepresentation is the habitual custom of telling only one side of a fact, quoting difficult Bible passages but never sublime ones, bad customs of the Church but never good ones, defects in Christians but never excellences. When Mr. Ingersoll speaks of " a lawyer whipping his child for holding back part of the truth," he describes his own partisan and one-sided method, as Professor Swing has shown, attacking Christianity as the hired attorney of infidelity, or the hired campaigner of the anti-Christian party who is to present only one side. This, too, from a man who claims that infidelity unfetters thought and broadens mind.

The Bible the Best of Books, and Christ the Best of Men.

Mr. Ingersoll also misrepresents the differences among the various forms of Christianity. All men of broad scholarship of the last and best century who have written on religion, both skeptics and Christians, agree on two things—the Bible as the best of books, and Christ as the best of men. So much at least may be said to be indorsed by all scholarship, and when a man rests down upon these two truths as proved and established, and follows them out into the truths to which they lead, he will not be likely to go far astray, for if Christ is confessedly the greatest and best of men, the "Teacher sent from God," then His teachings are to be accepted, and those teachings are the foundations of all essential Christianity; and if the Bible is the best of books, the moral and spiritual guide of man, then its teachings are to be carefully read and deeply regarded, and all who take this book as life's guide book will be led into all truths of Christianity that are funda-mental and important.

All Christians, Romanists and Protestants, agree that Christ is the living embodiment and pattern of Christian manhood, and that the Bible, at least, contains the "Word of God." All evangelical Christians agree on that broad and simple platform of the Apostles Creed, and declare not "many," but one way to Heaven, and that not by "believing an incomprehensible creed," but by faith and faithfulness of intellect, will, heart and life, toward the person, Jesus Christ. Two quotations fairly represent all the evangelical churches on this matter. Bishop Whipple, an Episcopalian, recently remarked, "As the grave grows nearer, my theology is growing strangely simple, and it begins and ends with Christ, as the only refuge for the lost." Dr. Alexander, of Princeton, a Presbyterian, when dying said; "All my theology is reduced to this narrow compass, 'Jesus Christ came into the world to save sinners.'" Mr. Ingersoll, misrepresents the most familiar facts when he says, "Just in proportion as the human race has advanced, the church has lost power. There is no exception to this rule." It is a fact so familiar that every intelligent child knows it, that Christianity was never so powerful in the world, as to-day—never had so many followers. By the multiplied agencies of church work, six thousand are converted per day—two Pentecosts every twenty-four hours.

Mr. Ingersoll misrepresents not only the Bible and church history, by leaving out all that would not help his theories, and stating one half the truth, but he also misrepresents the Declaration of Independence as "retiring God from politics," as if the words were not there, "the station to which the laws of nature, and nature's God entitle them," "All men are endowed by their Creator with certain inalienable rights"—"and for the support of this declaration, and in a firm reliance upon Divine Providence, we mutually pledge to each other our lives, our fortunes, and our sacred honor." It is surely infinitely absurd to expect a man broadly and truly to represent us in politics, who so inexcusably and grossly misrepresents us in religion.

ARTICLE IV.

Something New if True—Infidelity the Essential Factor in Progressive Civilization—But Coleridge, Wm. H. Seward, Bismarck, and other great Statesmen can not see it—Civilization goes only with Christianity.

The fourth article in Ingersollism is as follows: "The civilization of this country is not the child of faith, but of unbelief—the result of free thought. But for the efforts of a few brave infidels, the church would have taken the

world back to the midnight of barbarism." How ignorant
we have all been! Luther, who led Europe out of the
Dark Ages, was not, it seems, a child of faith, but of free
thought (?) and Paul also, who brought civilization into
barbarous Europe, peopled with savage tribes, as
described by Julius Cæsar in his Commentaries. The
transformation of savage Gaul and Britain into civilized
France and England was accomplished by the efforts of
" unbelief." (?)

Long ago, Christianity had a contest with Atheism, Pantheism, and Culture, as to which was the best civilizer.
Christianity selected Europe, and gave the other three con-
testants Asia, with several centuries the start. Atheism,
or Buddhism, which ignores all spiritual things and devotes
itself to the present life, has operated for thousands of
years in India. Pantheism, or Brahminism, made its
experiment in the same country; and Culture obtained
exclusive control of China, ruling both church and state.
As a result, in accordance with Mr. Ingersoll's theory, these
elements of Ingersollism have developed a lofty civilization (?) in China and India, given education to woman,
torn away the veil of her slavish seclusion, made her the
equal of man, treated female infants as honorably as the
boys, developed a high morality in the community,
and supplied the world with its standard literature, its
foremost science, and its chief inventions.(?) On the other
hand, Christianity came into barbarous Europe a dozen
centuries later, caused the degradation and enslavement of
women and children, (?) repressed scientific investigation, (?)
prevented invention, (?) checked thought, (?) and thus hin-
dered literary activity, and, by the barbarism of the Bible,
" brought bondage to man, woman, and child " in body and
brain.(?) If the facts do not correspond to these legitimate
deductions from Mr. Ingersoll's theories as to the effect of

atheistic culture, on the one hand, and Christianity, on the other, upon national life, so much the worse for the facts.

Mr. Ingersoll says much against the wars of Christian nations. He forgets that peace societies and arbitration were never known outside of Christianity, and that wars in Christian lands are the gradually disappearing remains of previous barbarism. He talks of science and invention as opening up this era! How does it happen that all this is in Christian rather than in heathen lands? He talks of charity and benevolence of infidels! Why is it that all benevolent societies are Christian, and that Thomas Paine halls can not be supported? He talks of liberty of speech and thought and government! Why is it that such liberty is only found in Christian countries? He has much to say of the barbarous age of dug-outs, tom-toms, and wooden plows! Has he not seen in the World's Expositions these very things as representing nations to-day, that have not risen from their primitive degradation and ignorance because Christianity has not yet reached them?

As to the relation of the Bible to civilization, Samuel Taylor Coleridge declares that " for more than a thousand years the Bible, collectively taken, has gone hand in hand with civilization, science, law, in short, with moral and intellectual cultivation, always supporting, and often leading the way."

William H. Seward says, "The whole hope of human progress is suspended on the ever-growing influence of the Bible."

Bismarck utters a similar sentiment, as quoted in his recent biography: " How, without faith in a revealed religion, in a God who wills what is good, in a Supreme Judge, and a future life, men can live together harmoniously —each doing his duty and letting every one else to do his— I do not understand." Similar sentiments are uttered by

the leading statesmen of all lands. the unanimous verdict
of statesmanship being that civilization can not be carried
forward without Christianity.

ARTICLE V.

**Marvelous Power of Time and Circumstance—Tragic Effect of
Iso-thermal Lines—Peoria Mud Necessarily the Seventh
Heaven as Ingersoll Sees it.**

The fifth article of Ingersollism is, that gods and men
are but evolutions of matter and circumstance, the difference between heathen gods and the Christian's God being
the result of a difference in their worshippers, and the difference in men being the result of varying soils and surroundings. He says : " No god was ever in advance of the
nation that created him." In answer to this last statement,
which is true, of course, of all imaginary deities, but not of
the One True God, it is only necessary to ask any candid
and intelligent man to read the description of God given
in the Bible, where both Testaments declare Him to be
"merciful and gracious, long suffering and abundant in
goodness and truth, but will by no means spare the guilty,"
and then say whether this God is nothing more than the reflection of the stiff-necked and perverse people who held to this
conception of Deity. The fact is, God as described in the
Bible is infinitely loftier and purer than the Jewish people,
or any people of any age. It is still more absurd, if possible, for Mr. Ingersoll to assert that " men are but the
creatures of their surroundings, made what they are wholly
by material causes, such as soil and climate." It is one of
the characteristic contradictions of history, such as are found
so frequently in Mr. Ingersoll's lectures, when he asserts
that great minds have never been found except in the "lands
of respectable winters," with the intimation that no great
achievements in art or literature are possible in warm

Oriental lands. As if Babylon, and Nineveh, and Egypt had not been in early ages the universities of the world. Carlyle must have been very much deceived when he declared Job of the Oriental land of Uz to be the greatest poet the world has known. Mohammed of those warm lands was certainly great, even though wrong, and scores of others, equally eminent, might be mentioned, although, of course, it is evident that greatness of men or peoples in tropical lands is rather in spite of circumstances than by their help.

Mr. Ingersoll in his lecture on "Man, Woman, and Child," speaking of one of these warm countries as the representative of all, says: "You might go there with five thousand Congregational preachers, five thousand deacons, five thousand professors in colleges, five thousand of the solid men of Boston and their wives, settle them all, and you will see the second generation riding upon a mule bareback, no shoes, a grapevine whip, with a rooster under each arm going to a cock fight on Sunday. Such is the influence of climate." But like most of Mr. Ingersoll's theories, this one is unfortunately the direct opposite of facts. The Sandwich Islands have all these disadvantages of climate, and fifty years ago were plunged in the deepest barbarism, with all the vices of savage life; but to-day, as all well-informed persons know, they are as truly civilized as any land, with industries, education, protection of life and property, equal to what is found in our own favored country. And this is all due, as King Kalikua said in New York, to the Christianizing of his people. Indeed, Mr. Ingersoll contradicts his own theory as to the dependence of the individual upon surroundings in his lectures on Humboldt and Paine, both of whom he represents as becoming great in spite of surroundings that would naturally have led in the opposite direction, thus involuntarily recognizing something in man deeper than mere physical evolution.

The whole absurd theory of individuals and nations being wholly dependent upon soil, and climate, and surroundings for their character, is fairly represented in the following incident:

" Pa," said a little six-year old, " what makes me grow ?"

" Why, the bread and potato I feed you with."

" Does potatoes make our pig grow, too?"

" Yes."

" Then, what makes him be a pig and me be a boy?"

That boy's simple question explodes all the theories of evolution.

ARTICLE VI.

Law is Ingersoll's God.

The sixth article of Ingersollism is, " I believe in law, the Almighty maker of Heaven and earth." One might as well say that the United States Constitution made our country, or try to rule the land by laws without enforcers.

That the universe is governed according to a system of law is recognized by Christians as much as by any one, and the laws of the Bible are not new arbitrary enactments, but recognitions and proclamations of that part of the law-system of the universe that relates to religion and morality. Laws of spirit are as eternal as laws of matter. Natural science proclaims the latter, religious science the former.

ARTICLE VII.

Liberty and Infidelity—What De Tocqueville Says About it.

The seventh article is made up of the following statements: " All religions are inconsistent with mental freedom. The doubter, the investigator, the infidel, have been the saviours of liberty."

Mr. Ingersoll, when talking of liberty contradicts what he himself has said of law, and fails to remind his hearers and readers that the circle of law bounds on every side the privileges of liberty, that one has liberty only within the range of propriety, and that all beyond that is license. He also forgets the very evident fact that the prevailing ideas of personal liberty in the world are due to the general dissemination, by Christianity, of the truth that a man is a soul as well as a body. Wherever men are regarded as mere physical beings, with no life deeper than the bodily life, the stronger will enslave the weaker—woman, child and captive. When the idea that each man is an immortal soul takes hold upon man, with it there comes the idea of individual rights. If Ingersollism should ever persuade a civilized people that man has no soul, this form of bondage of the weaker to the stronger will be resumed. Not soil, but soul, is the secret of liberty.

Even Mr. Frothingham recently declared that the Bible is a democratic book, and that we get out of it our ideas of equality. He remembered what Mr. Ingersoll seems to forget, that all through the Bible, the idea of personal and religious liberty is found, especially in those words of the Apostles to the rulers who attempted to tyrannize over their consciences, " We ought to obey God rather than man," which has fitly been termed the concisest of all statements of the principles of personal liberty. We may show this relation of religion to liberty in the words of the greatest modern writer upon such questions, De Tocqueville, who says, " Bible Christianity is the companion of liberty in all its conflicts, the cradle of its infancy, and the divine source of its claims."

ARTICLE VIII.

Woman—Ingersoll's Theory at Variance with Facts.

The eighth article of Ingersollism, is in regard to woman, and is as follows: " As long as woman regards the Bible as the charter of her rights, she will be the slave of man.

The Bible was not written by a woman. Within its lids there is nothing but humiliation and shame for her."

You have all doubtless observed that in heathen countries, where the Bible has not yet come with its enslaving (?) influence woman has (?) liberty and honor, and education, and opportunities of public activity and benevolence (?), but in Christian lands she is veiled, degraded, shut out of sight and restrained from education (?). I have always observed, as a pastor, that it is the religious, and church-going husbands that tyrannize over their wives as "bosses," and deny them their liberties of conscience, and other rights. (?)

You smile at the absurd statement, knowing that the "heathen at home," who as husbands are harsh and brutal to the wives they have promised to cherish, are frequently ardent believers in Ingersollism, and seldom in any way connected with even nominal Christianity, while every school boy is familiar with the fact that woman, in all except Christian lands, is hardly better than a slave, notably so, in that land where Ingersollism under the name of Buddhism has the controlling influence. Mr. Ingersoll utters many true sentiments about the family, but all of these he learned of Christianity, not from China, or Egypt.

ARTICLE IX.

Ingersoll's Theory of Childhood—Some of His Little Stories—The Whole Subject Carefully Examined—Significant Incident in the Life of Abraham Lincoln.

The ninth article of Ingersollism is a theory of childhood which attacks the principles of sound government and health even more than religion: " Do not have it in your mind that you must govern them; that they (children) must obey. Let your children eat what they desire. They know what they wish to eat. Let them begin at which end of the dinner they please."

Such a theory is worthy of nothing more than the smile with which you hear it. It is all answered in the following representative fact of childhood: A little bit of a girl wanted more and more buttered toast, till she was told that too much would make her sick. Looking wistfully at the dish for a moment, she thought she saw a way out of her difficulty, and exclaimed, "Well, give me annuzer piece, and send for the doctor!"

Mr. Ingersoll, in connection with his theory of childhood, often refers to the fact, that he leaves his pocketbook around where his children can help themselves to whatever they wish, and urges the same course upon all parents. It is said that one of the lecturer's admirers, being convinced that this was the correct theory, determined to give up punishing his child, and try the new plan. Accordingly, he said to his boy, "John, I am convinced I have been taking the wrong course to try to make you a better boy. I am going to trust you more, and give up whippings. I am going away for a few days, and I have left my pocket-book in the top drawer of the bureau. Help yourself to money whenever you need it." After a few days the father returned to his home, late at night. As he opened the door he stumbled over a large canoe in the entry, and was then attacked by a large bull-dog that his boy had bought. Entering the boy's room, he found it hung round with guns, and fishing poles, and daggers, with another canoe, and several small dogs—his pocket-book lying empty on the top of the bureau. He is now less enthusiastic in regard to Ingersoll's knowledge of domestic government.

The leading point which Mr. Ingersoll endeavors to make in connection with his lecture on Thomas Paine is that the Bible shocks a child, and, therefore, can't be true. You have all observed how much children are shocked as they gather about the mother's knees in the twilight, and hear her tell the stories of Jesus, and Joseph, and Moses, and Samuel, and Daniel (?). As to the relation of the Bible to childhood and home life, let me quote the opinion of several eminent men, mostly skeptics, for whom even Mr. Ingersoll cherishes the highest regard:

Thomas Jefferson, speaking of the Bible and home life, says: " I have always said, and always will say, that the studious perusal of the sacred volume will make better citizens, better fathers, and better husbands."

John Quincy Adams says: " So great is my veneration for the Bible, that the earlier my children begin to read it, the more confident will be my hopes that they will prove useful citizens to their country and respectable members of society."

Theodore Parker says: " There is not a boy on the hills of New England, not a girl born in the filthiest cellar which disgraces a capital in Europe, and cries to God against the barbarism of modern civilization; not a boy nor a girl all Christendom through, but their lot is made better by that great book."

Diderot, the French philosopher and skeptic, was wont to make this confession: " No better lessons than those of the Bible can I teach my child."

Huxley, in an address upon education, says: " I have always been strongly in favor of secular education, in the sense of education without theology; but I must confess I have been no less seriously perplexed to know by what practical measures the religious feeling, which is the essential basis of conduct, was to be kept up, in the present utterly chaotic state of opinion on these matters, without the use of the Bible. The pagan moralists lack life and color, and even the noble stoic, Marcus Aurelius, is too high and refined for an ordinary child. Take the Bible as a whole, make the severest deductions which fair criticism can dictate, and there still remains in this old literature a vast residuum of moral beauty and grandeur. By the study of what other book could children be so humanized? If Bible reading is not accompanied by constraint and solemnity, I do not believe there is anything in which children take more pleasure."

What would "shock the mind of a child" would be to hear Mr. Ingersoll excuse them for telling a lie, in order to escape a whipping. What would shock a child would be to hear Mr. Ingersoll uttering profanity ·   ·

·   ·   ·   ·   ·   ·

What would shock the mind of a child would be to hear Mr. Ingersoll telling to a crowded audience with a smile of approval the story of a boy's oath. ·   ·

·   ·   ·   ·   ·   ·

·   ·   ·   ·   ·   ·

·   ·   ·   ·   ·   ·

Speaking of swearing reminds me of that incident of Abraham Lincoln, whom Mr. Ingersoll calls "the grandest man ever President of the United States," who said to a person sent to him by one of the Senators, and who, in conversation, uttered an oath, "I thought the Senator had sent me a gentleman; I see I was mistaken. There is the door, and I bid you good-day." I hold in my hand the last report of the New York Society for the Prevention of Cruelty to Children. Of course, the bruised and beaten little ones, here described, were the victims of cruelty in Christian homes (?). Their fathers and mothers had taken too much religion (?), had become brutalized by reading the Bible (?), and hence abused the children by their own fireside until the law was compelled to interfere for their defense (?).

In my work as a member of the Citizen's League for the suppression of the sale of liquors to minors, I have noticed that this supreme cruelty to children—selling them in their immature years the liquors that make them self-destroyers, violators of the public peace, and candidates for drunkards' graves—is perpetrated by Christian men, not by the infidels who applaud so lustily at Mr. Ingersoll's lectures (?). Here I am reminded of the published report, which seems well authenticated, that Mr. Ingersoll in his childhood lived in one of those exceptional homes where nominal Christianity was combined with harshness, cruelty and bigotry. If so, this would be some slight excuse for his present conduct, were it not for the fact that maturer years have given him abundant opportunity to see the bright and sunny side of Christian gentleness in other homes. And there are no true homes that do not owe their existence to the influence of Christianity upon the family relation.

Having myself made childhood a special study for several years, I find that the degree of recognition given to the opinions and importance of childhood in various ages and countries, is exactly in proportion to the degree of Christianity there, children being scarcely noticed in heathen lands, either in poetry, or history, or ethics, while the Bible religion has always given childhood an exceedingly prominent place. All the attention given to the education and development of the little ones is but the starlight that shines down upon us from the manger of the God-child.

ARTICLE X.

Ingersoll Says Christianity Fetters Thought—The Bible and a Host of Distinguished Men Say Otherwise.

The tenth article of Ingersollism is the frequent assertion that Christianity fetters thought, while infidelity emancipates it, in such passages as these: "In all ages, reason has been regarded as the enemy of religion." "The gods dreaded education and knowledge then (in the time of the Garden of Eden) just as they do now." "For ages a deadly conflict has been waged by a few brave men of thought and genius, on the one side, and the great, ignorant, religious mass, on the other. The few have said: 'Think.' The many have said: 'Believe.'"

In order to ascertain what freedom and power of thought materialism had given to the mind of Mr. Ingersoll, I made special examination of the logic in the lecture on "The Gods," and found there, in a very short time, one or more specimens of all the fallacies laid down in the text-books of logic. "Waiter," said John Randolph, at a certain hotel, "if this is coffee, bring me tea; if this is tea, bring me coffee." And so we say, if this is the "power of thought," give us weakness.

Instead of the Bible forbidding us to think, as Ingersollism so often declares, it is full of ringing appeals to "reason," "think," "consider," "ponder," "prove all things."

Prov. 26:16: "The sluggard is wiser in his own conceit than seven men that can render a *reason.*"

Eccl. 7:25: "I applied mine heart to know, and to search, and to seek out wisdom, and the *reason* of things, and to know the wickedness of folly, even of foolishness and madness."

Isa. 1:18: "Come now and let us *reason* together, saith the Lord; though your sins be as scarlet, they shall be as white as snow; though they be red like crimson, they shall be as wool."

Matt. 22:42: "What *think* ye of Christ?"

Acts 17:2: "Paul, as his manner was, went in unto them, and three Sabbath days *reasoned* with them out of the Scriptures."

Acts 18:4: "He *reasoned* in the synagogue every Sabbath, and persuaded the Jews and the Greeks."

Acts 18:19: "And he came to Ephesus, and left them there; but he himself entered into the synagogue and *reasoned* with the Jews."

Acts 24:25: "And as he *reasoned* of righteousness, temperance, and judgment to come, Felix trembled."

Rom. 12:1: "I beseech you therefore, brethren, by the mercies of God, that you present your bodies a living sacrifice, holy, acceptable unto God, which is your *reasonable* service."

Phil. 4:8: "Finally, brethren, whatsoever things are true, whatsoever things are honest, whatsoever things are just, whatsoever things are pure, whatsoever things are lovely, whatsoever things are of good report, if there be any virtue, and if there be any praise, *think on these things.*"

1 Thess. 5:21: "Prove all things; hold fast that which is good."

Let us look into biography, and make a practical test of this theory that the Bible fetters thought. If so, those who believe and love it will not be strong and leading thinkers. Let us apply the test in the ranks of science.

A Cloud of Witnesses.

Professor Benjamin Pierce, of Harvard College, has recently completed a very remarkable course of lectures at the Lowell Institute, Boston, on "Ideality in Science." Professor Pierce, who is now in his seventieth year, is, perhaps, the most eminent mathematical scholar in this country, and the author of some of the most profound investigations and speculations that have been made in the realm of astronomical science. This man of mighty thought must have been emancipated and inspired by infidelity (?). This scholar, whose mind may be supposed to feed on fact, holds an unquestioning faith in a personal God and the immortal life.

The late Professor Henry, of the Smithsonian Institute, was one of the broadest and best of scientific thinkers because infidelity gave him freedom of thought (?). No, he was a sweet-spirited Christian in his daily life.

Sir David Brewster, another eminent scientist, said of his Christian experience: "I have had this light for many years, and oh! how bright it is to me."

Professor Silliman, who is unsurpassed in his scientific

department, must also be classed under the head of "the ignorant religious mass," for he was another of the very many Christian scientists, whom the world has ignorantly(?) supposed a thinker, in spite of Mr. Ingersoll's theory of faith as being a mental bondage. He says: "I can truly declare that, in the study and exhibition of science to my pupils and fellow men, I have never forgotten to give all honor and glory to the infinite Creator—happy if I might be the honored interpreter of a portion of his works, and of the beautiful structure and beneficent laws discovered therein by the labors of many illustrious predecessors." We might add scores of others in each department of science, who have found no discord between the Word and world of God.

Who are the four greatest thinkers in the realm of statesmanship of this century? Daniel Webster, Gladstone, Thiers, and Bismarck. All of them, of course, are enabled to be thus broad and prominent as national thinkers by the power of infidelity (?). No, each one of them is most positive in his Christian belief.

Webster declares the grandest thought which ever entered his mind was that of "personal accountability to God."

Gladstone gives much of time and attention to religious writing.

Thiers says, in his last days: "I often invoke that God in whom I am happy to believe, who is denied by fools and ignorant people, but in whom the enlightened man finds his consolation and hope."

Bismarck is called, in derision, "the God-fearing man," in reference to his well-known religious principles. (Busch's Bismarck, p. 200).

We might add to these Charles Sumner, who called Christianity the "true religion" and "our faith," and whose speeches constantly recognize God and Christianity.

Who are the leading literary characters of the century?
Victor Hugo, what of him? Did you ever read his chapter
on prayer in Les Miserables, and his grand tribute to
immortality, uttered as a rebuke to a company of French
physicians, a few years ago? Moore—have you read his
"Paradise and the Peri," the Gospel of repentance, and do
you know him as the author of the hymn, "Come, ye Dis-
consolate?" Walter Scott—have you read his translation
of "Dies Iræ," uttered so devoutly in his last days:

> " Oh! in that day, that dreadful day,
> When Heaven and earth shall pass away,
> Be Thou, oh Christ, the sinner's st iy,
> When Heaven and earth shall pass away."

And Shakspeare, whom Mr. Ingersoll accounts one of
the grandest of human minds, was great enough to believe
in the Bible. And so Thackeray, Whittier, Dickens, Gold-
smith, Longfellow, and Irving were intellectual believers in
Christianity.

The following men, also lacking the freedom and power
of thought that comes by materialism (?) became mentally
so weak (?) that they declared, in varying terms, after reading largely in all departments of literature, that the Bible
is the best book in the world: Sir Walter Scott, Sir William Jones, George Gilfillan, Milton, Pollok, Coleridge,
Collins, Bacon, John Adams, Napoleon, James Freeman
Clarke, Lange, Kitto, Robertson. And Channing put the
Gospels where these others place the whole Bible—above
all other literature.

The following persons strongly commend the Bible as a
whole: Dr. Samuel Johnson, Carlyle, Dryden, Young,
Cowper, Locke, Newton, Seward, Dawson, Franklin, John
Quincy Adams, Bellows, Bartol, Theodore Parker, Rous-
seau, Guizot, Bunsen, Story, Webster, Diderot, Matthew
Arnold, and Huxley.

The following persons among many others declare that they found in the Bible, not fetters for thought, but their strongest inspiration to thought : Daniel Webster, Fisher Ames, Mitchell, the Astronomer, Ruskin and Göethe.

It is evident that very many others might truly have said the same, including Theodore Parker and Mr. Frothingham and other skeptics, whose writings show plainly that they owe their beauties of style to a familiarity with the Bible.

Jesus Christ.

With these great men who have commended the Bible should be mentioned one who is confessed by Christians and skeptics the greatest and best of men, JESUS CHRIST, who used the Psalms as His prayer and hymn book, and always spoke of the whole Old Testament as the Eternal Law Book of humanity. There is not time, nor is it necessary now to answer in detail all the hard questions that can be asked about single Bible passages. But these great men and Christ saw all these points of difficulty, and yet accepted the Bible as the pre-eminent book, commending it to the perusal of all as the source of the mind's grandest inspirations. Side by side with these scores of the world's foremost men who declare the Bible the best of books, or strongly commend it, or point to it as the source of their grandest thoughts, put the opinion of that more learned (?), more profound (?), more unprejudiced (?) scholar and philosopher, Colonel Ingersoll, who stands almost alone among educated men in strongly condemning the Bible, which his bigotry prints with a small " b " in spite of the rules of grammar, and describes it as about the worst book of the world, in these words among others: " If men will read the Bible as they read other books, they will be amazed that they ever, for one moment, supposed a being of infinite wisdom to be the author of such ignorance and of such

atrocity.   The Bible burned heretics, built dungeons,
founded the inquisition, and trampled upon all the liberties
of men.   All the philosophy of the Bible would not make
one scene in Hamlet.   I could write a better book than the
Bible, which is full of barbarism."

Amazing Ignorance of Infidels Concerning the Scriptures—Hume's Ignorance of the New Testament — Tom Paine Without a Bible.

" But some one asks, Are there not other eminent men
who have despised and condemned the Bible?   Most certainly, as there are those who have entered their protest
against almost any and everything mentionable.   It is,
nevertheless, worthy of note that, in most instances, those
who have sought the more resolutely to defame the Holy
Scriptures are those who are comparatively unacquainted
with them.   David Hume, distinguished both as essayist
and historian, standing among the most noted of modern
skeptical philosophers, was a resolute objector of the Bible,
but was notoriously ignorant of its contents.   Dr. Johnson,
in conversation with several literary friends, once observed,
in his usual, direct, and unequivocal manner, that no honest man could be a deist, because no man could be so after
a fair examination of the truths of Christianity.   When
the name of Hume was mentioned to him as an exception
to his remark, he replied: 'No, sir; Hume once owned to
a clergyman in the bishopric of Durham, that he had never
read even the New Testament with attention.'"*

Let us cross-question another important witness as to his
knowledge of the book against which he offers testimony.
We ask Thomas Paine as to his familiarity with the Bible,
which he so bitterly condemns, and he replies, "I keep no
Bible."   I hold in my hand a sermon preached in New

---

* From " What Noted Men Think of the Bible."

York City, by Rev. W. F. Hatfield, in reply to Mr. Ingersoll's lecture on Thomas Paine, in which reply, with abundant facts, such as would convince a court, it is shown conclusively that Thomas Paine was vicious and corrupt in life,
and miserable and remorseful in death. As to the value of
Voltaire's testimony against Christianity, Carlyle declares it
worthless on the ground of lack of knowledge on the subject of which he testifies. He says: "It is a serious
ground of offense against Voltaire that he intermeddled in
religion without being himself, in any measure, religious;
that, in a word, he ardently, and with long-continued effort,
warred against Christianity, without understanding, beyond
the mere superfices, what Christianity was."

There are also a class of specialists who are quoted against
the Bible, and who manifest a hostility to it, whose testimony is of little value because of the narrow range in
which they have studied, making them authorities only in
their special department. Halley, the astronomer, once
avowed his skepticism in presence of Sir Isaac Newton.
The venerable man replied: "Sir, you have never studied
these subjects and I have. Do not disgrace yourself as a
philosopher by presuming to judge on questions you have
never examined."

Distributed Ignorance and Concentrated Hatred—Probable Cause of Ingersoll's Infidelity.

The largest proportion of skeptics, however, are mere
sophomores, spoiled with a little learning which is only
"distributed ignorance," well represented by a precocious
boy of fourteen, whom I found writing an essay on "Matrimony," and who left it during my call to argue in favor
of Ingersollism and against the Bible (of which he knew
as little as of matrimony), which he admitted he had never
read, as do nearly all skeptics when questioned on this

matter. The bitterness of the opposition to Christianity of Mr. Ingersoll and other infidels is explained by the Earl of Rochester, who was converted from infidelity and said, in explanation of his former course and that of others: "A bad heart, a bad heart is the great objection against the Holy Book." "The fool hath said in his *heart*" (not his head) "there is no God." The bad heart is father to the infidel thought. It is like the case of the old woman who broke her looking-glass because it showed the wrinkles creeping into her fading face. Men strive to break the Bible glass that shows the wrinkles and defects of character. The whole appearance and tone and spirit of Mr. Ingersoll in his lectures is suggestive of this heart hatred against the book which he attacks, "kicks," "hates," not with the calmness of logic, but with the bitterness of a heart-hostility. Those infidels who have faithfully examined the Bible have usually been convinced of its truth and converted to Christianity. Among them, such distinguished names as Lord Lyttleton, Gilbert West, Soame Jenyus, Bishop Thompson, and at least a score of notable cases in connection with Mr. Moody's revival meetings in England. "What comparison, let us ask, will the number of celebrated skeptics, even when the best possible showing is made, hold with the distinguished men who have ranked the sacred volume above all others? Remember that your mother's love for the Bible and your own early reverence for it, have the indorsement of the grandest and profoundest minds which have been known and honored among humanity."

The Truth of the Whole Matter.

But salvation is not by belief in a book, or a creed, or a Church, but by belief in the person of Jesus Christ. Mr. Ingersoll skips this hard problem, "What think ye of

Christ?" He hardly refers to this citadel of Christianity half a dozen times in all his lectures, making his attacks chiefly on human outposts and then claiming to have overborne the citadel of Christianity. Even Strauss, Renan, Rousseau, Theodore Parker, Napoleon, and Richter—none of them experimental Christians—unite as a jury in the verdict expressed by Richter in regard to Christ, " He is the purest among the mighty, the mightiest among the pure." We have, then, two facts as a sure anchorage of our Christianity to-day. All scholarly skepticism agrees with Christianity that the Bible is the best of books and that Christ is the best of men. He who thus accepts the Bible and Christ can not logically or consistently stop short of a Christian life, following Christ as his pattern, and walking by the Bible as his rule.

We may differ about creeds, and Church forms, and Bible interpretation, but he who has faith and faithfulness toward the person, Jesus Christ shall be saved. Let us then devoutly utter the creed of Daniel Webster, as inscribed by his own request on his tombstone at Marshfield:

" LORD, I
BELIEVE, HELP
THOU MINE UNBELIEF.
PHILOSOPHICAL ARGUMENT
ESPECIALLY THAT DRAWN FROM
THE VASTNESS OF THE UNIVERSE IN COM-
PARISON WITH THE APPARENT INSIGNIFICANCE
OF THIS GLOBE, HAS SOMETIMES SHAKEN MY REASON
FOR THE FAITH THAT IS IN ME; BUT MY HEART HAS
ASSURED ME THAT THE GOSPEL OF JESUS CHRIST MUST
BE A DIVINE REALITY. THE SERMON ON THE
MOUNT CAN NOT BE A MERELY HUMAN
PRODUCTION. THIS BELIEF ENTERS
INTO THE VERY DEPTH OF MY
CONSCIENCE. THE WHOLE
HISTORY OF MAN
PROVES IT."

CHAPLAIN M'CABE'S REPLY.

The Famous Chaplain has a Remarkable Dream—He Sees the Great City of Ingersollville—Which Ingersoll and the Infidel Host Enter—And are Shut in for Six Months—Remarkable Condition of Things Outside and Inside—Happiness and Misery—Ingersoll Finally Petitions for a Church and sends for a Lot of Preachers.

I had a dream which was not all a dream. I thought I was on a long journey through a beautiful country, when suddenly I came to a great city with walls fifteen feet high. At the gate stood a sentinel, whose shining armor reflected back the rays of the morning sun. As I was about to salute him and pass into the city, he stopped me and said:

"Do you believe in the Lord Jesus Christ?"

I answered: "Yes, with all my heart."

"Then," said he, "you can not enter here. No man or woman who acknowledges that name can pass in here Stand aside!" said he, "they are coming."

I looked down the road, and saw a vast multitude approaching. It was led by a military officer.

"Who is that?" I asked of the sentinel.

"That," he replied, "is the great Colonel Robert I——, the founder of the City of Ingersollville."

"Who is he?" I ventured to inquire.

"He is a great and mighty warrior, who fought in many bloody battles for the Union during the great war."

I felt ashamed of my ignorance of history, and stood silently watching the procession. I had heard of a Colonel

I——,   *   *   *   *   *   *   but, of
course, this could not be the man.

The procession came near enough for me to recognize
some of the faces.   I noted two infidel editors of national
celebrity, followed by great wagons containing steam presses.
There were also five members of Congress.

All the noted infidels and scoffers of the country seemed
to be there.   Most of them passed in unchallenged by the
sentinel, but at last a meek-looking individual with a white
necktie approached, and he was stopped.   I saw at a glance
it was a well-known " liberal " preacher of New York.

" Do you believe in the Lord Jesus?" said the sentinel.

" Not much!" said the doctor.

Everybody laughed, and he was allowed to pass in.

There were artists there, with glorious pictures; singers,
with ravishing voices; tragedians and comedians, whose
names have a world-wide fame.

Then came another division of the infidel host—saloon-
keepers by thousands, proprietors of gambling hells, brothels,
and theatres.

Still another division swept by: burglars, thieves, thugs,
incendiaries, highwaymen, murderers — all—all marching
in.   My vision grew keener.   I beheld, and lo! Satan himself brought up the rear.

High afloat above the mass was a banner on which was
inscribed: " What has Christianity done for the country?"
and another on which was inscribed: " Down with the
churches!   Away with Christianity—it interferes with our
happiness!"   And then came a murmur of voices, that
grew louder and louder until a shout went up like the roar
of Niagara: "Away with Him!   Crucify Him, crucify
Him!"   I felt no desire now to enter Ingersollville.

As the last of the procession entered, a few men and
women, with broad-brimmed hats and plain bonnets, made

their appearance, and wanted to go in as missionaries, but they were turned rudely away. A zealous young Metho- dist exhorter, with a Bible under his arm, asked permission to enter, but the sentinel swore at him awfully. Then I thought I saw Brother Moody applying for admission, but he was refused. I could not help smiling to hear Moody say, as he turned sadly away:

" Well! they let me live and work in Chicago; it is very strange they won't let me into Ingersollville."

The sentinel went inside the gate and shut it with a bang; and I thought, as soon as it was closed, a mighty angel came down with a great iron bar, and barred the gate on the outside, and wrote upon it in letters of fire, " Doomed to live together six months." Then he went away, and all was silent, except the noise of the revelry and shouting that came from within the city walls.

I went away, and as I journeyed through the land I could not believe my eyes. Peace and plenty smiled everywhere. The jails were all empty, the penitentiaries were without occupants. The police of great cities were idle. Judges sat in court-rooms with nothing to do. Business was brisk. Many great buildings, formerly crowded with criminals, were turned into manufacturing establishments. Just about this time the President of the United States called for a Day of Thanksgiving. I attended services in a Presby- terian Church. The preacher dwelt upon the changed con- dition of affairs. As he went on, and depicted the great prosperity that had come to the country, and gave reasons for devout thanksgiving, I saw one old deacon clap his handkerchief over his mouth to keep from shouting right out. An ancient spinster, who never did like the "noisy" Methodists—a regular old blue-stocking Presbyterian— couldn't hold in. She expressed the thought of every heart by shouting with all her might, "Glory to God for Ingersollville!" A young theological student lifted up his hand and devoutly added, " *Esto perpetua.*" Everybody smiled. The country was almost delirious with joy. Great processions of children swept along the highways, singing,

> " We'll not give up the Bible,
> God's blessed Word of Truth."

Vast assemblies of reformed inebriates, with their wives and children, gathered in the open air. No building would hold them. I thought I was in one meeting where Bishop Simpson made an address, and as he closed it a mighty shout went up till the earth rang again. O, it was wonderful ! and then we all stood up and sang with tears of joy,

> " All hail the power of Jesus' name !
> Let angels prostrate fall ;
> Bring forth the royal diadem,
> And crown him Lord of all."

The six months had well-nigh gone. I made my way back again to the gate of Ingersollville. A dreadful silence reigned over the city, broken only by the sharp crack of a revolver now and then. I saw a man trying to get in at the gate, and I said to him, " My friend, where are you from ?"

" I live in Chicago," said he, " and they've taxed us to death there; and I've heard of this city, and I want to go in to buy some real estate in this new and growing place."

He failed utterly to remove the bar, but by some means he got a ladder about twelve feet long, and with its aid, he climbed up upon the wall. With an eye to business, he shouted to the first person he saw:

" Hallo, there !—what's the price of real estate in Ingersollville ?"

" Nothing !" shouted a voice; " you can have all you want if you'll just take it and pay the taxes."

" What made your taxes so high?" said the Chicago man. I noted the answer carefully; I shall never forget it.

" We've had to build forty new jails and fourteen penitentiaries—a lunatic asylum and an orphan asylum in
every ward; we've had to disband the public schools, and
it takes all the city revenue to keep up the police force."

" Where's my old friend, I——?" said the Chicago man.

" O, he is going about to-day with a subscription paper
to build a church. They have gotten up a petition to send
out for a lot of preachers to come and hold revival services.
If we can only get them over the wall, we hope there's a
future for Ingersollville yet."

The six months ended. Instead of opening the door,
however, a tunnel was dug under the wall big enough for
one person to crawl through at a time. First came two
bankrupt editors, followed by Colonel I—— himself; and
then the whole population crawled through. Then I
thought, somehow, great crowds of Christians surrounded
the city. There was Moody, and Hammond, and Earle,
and hundreds of Methodist preachers and exhorters, and
they struck up, singing together,

> " Come, ye sinners, poor and needy."

A needier crowd never was seen on earth before.

I conversed with some of the inhabitants of the abandoned city, and asked a few of them this question:

" Do you believe in Hell?"

I can not record the answers; they were terribly orthodox.

One old man said, " I've been there on probation for six
months, and I don't want to join."

I knew by that he was an old Methodist backslider. The
sequel of it all was a great revival, that gathered in a
mighty harvest from the ruined City of Ingersollville.

[Photographed by Mosher.]

DR. SWAZEY'S REPLY.

**Momentary View of Col. Ingersoll Through the Doctor's Glass—
The Bible on the Meridian—What the Doctor Sees in
the Great Book.**

THE genial, eloquent, sensational, unfair, evasive Colonel
Ingersoll has come and gone.   Nobody has been alarmed.
But out of 400,000 people a large audience was found to
laugh with him at Moses and the Bible.   He eschewed
argument altogether.   He did not attempt to instruct anybody.   He had only a campaign speech to make against—
God.   This article is simply an invitation to any fair-
minded doubter to consider the reasonableness of a laugh
at the Christian's Bible.   Is this book a bad book, or a
silly book, just fit for jeer and sarcasm ?   Take a common-
sense view.   In order to do so, it is necessary to take a
common-place view, to bring to the foreground that which
all assailants like to leave in the background, namely, that
the Bible teaches by commandment and precept only that
which is pure and good.

Relating to man's duty to himself, it teaches personal
purity, sexual and otherwise; temperance in meats, drinks,
opinions and ambition, responsibleness for inclinations,
thoughts and actions; a paramount love for the truth;
courage and hopefulness in all lawful purposes; self-im-
provement, and a cheerful enjoyment of the good things of
life.   Relating to man's duty to others, the Bible teaches
honesty between man and man; restitution when wrong
has been done, wittingly or unwittingly; the damnableness

4

of adultery, seduction, and everything that violates the purity of a family or a person; the forgiveness of injuries; a charitable view of human actions, including patience and forbearance, mercy; the duty of life-long usefulness, kindness and helpfulness; a genial temper in social and business life; obedience to magistrates; and a multitude of minor virtues. Relating to the moral order of things, the Bible teaches that wrong-doing is unavoidably the way of sorrow, and right-doing the way of happiness.

These teachings, given not in bald outline, but in fresh and animated pictures and discourses, make up the ethical system of the Bible from the first lesson of the antediluvian age to the last words of the book, which are against whoremongers, and all makers and lovers of a lie, and in praise of all who are just and good. And, still further, in no instance is there left on record an immoral precept, or one which impurity, or injustice, or dishonesty, or unkindness, or selfishness in any form are proposed. There is no mistake in that direction. Still further, we challenge any assailant to name a virtue, acknowledged to be such by the mass of mankind, which is wanting in the catalogue of Bible virtues. The ethical system is as complete as it is pure, as comprehensive as it is sound and true, absolutely covering the whole area of man's duty to himself and to his fellow-man; a system sounding all depths, touching the most delicate fibres of life, and without a flaw or an omission. Its precepts and laws come in their own order, but they all appear in the record first or last. The Buddhistic "decalogue" seems to have been in advance of the Mosaic in this—that it had two commandments wanting in the latter—"Thou shalt not lie," "Thou shalt not get drunk." But these commandments, although not in our own decalogue, are written over and over again in the Old Testament as well as the New. And yet once more the moral requirements of the Bible, are as clear of puerilities as they are of impurity or oblique vision. The Buddhistic decalogue steps right down to a moral weakness of which the Bible is never guilty. "Thou shalt not visit dances nor theatrical representations." "Thou shalt not use ornaments nor perfumery in dress."

Occultation of Ingersoll's Good Sense—General Survey of Deities —Scope of Divine Revelation.

Now the common-sense question occurs whether a book containing such a system, always teaching men what is good and pure, always warning him against evil, and encouraging him to be a strong, sound, pure, complete man in everything, is worthy of sneers, ribaldry and irreverence, even though it were full of unbelievable fables and fantastic ideas of immortality. In what spirit can a company of people shout their applause when a book whose lines of thought are always leading a man above himself is made the target of sarcasm and ridicule, and the cry is almost in so many words, "Down with the Bible!" Let us go a little beyond the strictly ethical. The general ideas of our Bible about God commend themselves to the best wisdom of mankind. We make no reference now to any sect of theologies, but to the theological atmosphere both of the Old and New Testaments, namely, that God is, and being the Creator, the life and force of all things, in other words, as our Bible has it, the Living God, superintends all human affairs. As a Creator He has not forgotten His work; as a Father He is always mindful of His offsprings; and caring for man is leading him on by a great hope to a great inheritance; that His face is against evil doing, that He smiles on all who strive to be just and good, and that in sorrow and want and temptation He folds to His great heart a righteous and even a repentant man; and

as the shuttle goes back and forth, knitting into each other
the soiled and blood-stained threads, He is weaving there-
from a garment of light for mankind: that superstition,
despotism, slavery and war are only other names for His
patience, while man is learning the great lesson. This is
the Bible interpretation of the incomprehensible Cause and
Spirit of the universe, that He is alive, and the Father and
Friend of man now, and will have some more for him after
the years have rolled by.

Suppose, now, it be all untrue, is there not something in
this dream or conceit that should bring a sigh rather than
a sneer from the heart of the unbeliever? The god of
Brahmanism is an abstraction without attributes, the great
nothing of the universe. Much the same is true of Buddhism, only in another way. It has law and virtue, but no
God of love, and asks no trust or faith. The same is true
in the unchanging round which knows no spirit above and
no hope below, taught by Confucius to his disciples. The
religion of the Persians presented a god who had a devil-
god for a yokefellow, keeping up the eternal and never-to-
be-ended quarrel of good and evil. Our Bible begins with
the idea that God is one God, the only and the Supreme,
and ends with this one God sending angels down to say to
the weary world, "Peace on earth good will to men."
Away beyond all the faiths and all the Bibles held sacred
by mankind, ours alone declares that man is not an orphan,
that good and evil are not eternal antagonisms, in other
words, that the Great Supreme is our Father in Heaven.
True or false, wisdom has taught nothing more inspiriting or
helpful to man. Neither imagination nor credulity has else-
where painted a vision so attractive, or out of the "silences"
and "eternities," and mysteries, whispered so good a word
in the ears of mortals. This idea of lordship and father-
hood is not incidental. It runs through every narration,

is implied in every precept, and re-affirmed in every promise. And even if it be beyond proof it makes the whole
Bible at least a golden dream.

Suppose now one does not take as absolutely and historically true the story of Adam's rib and the woman, or of
the fish swallowing a man and throwing him unhurt on the
shore, does not the high moral tone of every command
and every precept everywhere illumined by 'this pure and
golden dream, entitle this book to the reverence of mankind? And especially since by the common consent the idea
of virtue in our Bible goes beyond the many excellent
things of Confucius, Zoroaster and the other sacred writers
of other religions, and its idea of the "living God" sur-
passes in purity and attractiveness, and in consolation and
hope, all other religions, is not this purest blossom of the
instinct, if you please to call it so, of duty and faith, of
inestimable value as the guide and hope of man, even
though it were overlaid with ten-fold more difficulties than
the most ingenious scoffer can present? Or, if it is not
reliable as a guide, is it not worthy of reverence as the
proudest achievement of the hungry mind of man?

The Great Central Figure—Absolute Unity of the Bible System.

Still further, this Bible has for its central, or rather ter-
minal, figure a name so remarkable that none but the
obscene and profane use it lightly, a man so remarkable
that whatever the skeptic may say of Moses or Paul, his
tongue would refuse its office should he attempt to catalogue
the mistakes of Jesus of Nazareth. Voltaire, Diderot,
Bolingbroke, Strauss, Renan, all speak reverently of this
One Man of history. And yet the whole New Testament
is built up on the sayings and doings of this Man. And
not the New Testament only. The Jewish scriptures, full
of errors or not, were full of the ideas of a Messiah, from

Moses to Malachi. And this marvelous man claimed that He was that Messiah. So that the Old Testament, as well, is a record of various forms pointing to this Man. I raise here no question of the truth of prophecy; I simply affirm that this Man. whose purity and wisdom are so singularly impressive, claimed to be the fulfillment of those old writings, identified Himself with Moses and David and Isaiah, and sanctified the great current of thought which from the mouths of these men flowed along the shores of that elder world. So that to revile the old Bible of the Jews is to revile Him. There is no scholar, orthodox or liberal, believing or skeptical, who does not identify the phenomenon of Christianity with the phenomenon of Judaism. Out of the soil of Judaic history sprung this purer growth—Jesus and the things He taught.

I suggest, therefore, that before one joins in the laugh against a religion which was founded long anterior to any other historical records than its own, he pause a little, remembering that this remarkable Man, who has not yet become antiquated, quoted those old books as His Bible, and doubtless had a tolerable understanding of their meaning and worth. And, perhaps, if He whose sermon on the mount is yet as fresh in the nineteenth century as though it were uttered to-day, found a vein of precious ore in those books, those same veins may be yet visible in our time.

The Bible Law of Development vs. Infidel Philosophy.

I have given, you will perceive, room for a large amount of the unaccountable and incredible in a Bible worthy of reverence. In fact, there is no occasion, except in the peculiarity of some men's minds, to allow so much. There is a passage in the Bible that is descriptive of the kingdom of Heaven, and reads thus: " First the blade and then the

ear, and after that the full corn in the ear." The Bible
here gives the key to itself. It is a statement of the law of
development, intellectual and moral. An observation of
the Bible from the standpoint of this law discovers an
answer to the objections that are just now brought against
our sacred Book. Col. Ingersoll and men of his style of
criticism (and, I am sorry to say, some preachers, also,)
quote a verse from Genesis precisely as though the same
words, or the same event, were found in the Gospels.
They judge an act or a usage recorded in the Pentateuch
precisely as though it were found in the Acts of the Apostles. They make no allowance for the stage of human
progress. They would teach a child surveying before he
had learned the multiplication table. They talk about
" skulls " as indicating progress, but God must needs put
the same ideas into a skull of the Laurentian period that
He does into a skull of to-day. Otherwise, God is worthy
of hate. They would preach the doctrine of equality on
the deck of a man-of-war. They utterly ignore the drill
that men and nations need in coming up to their majority.
They would suffer the rabble in a court-room to vote down
the decision of a judge on the bench. The men who are
historically connected with God's order of things must dis-
pense with the great schoolmaster—experience. Ideas
must spring forth complete, like Minerva. Rafters and
dome must touch the skies the same day the foundation
stones were laid. Those are the ideas with which a certain
class of critics approach the Old Testament. If a people
are not ripe for a commonwealth, and God gives them a
king, God is all wrong. If a people are become a great
military camp and Moses proclaims martial law, Moses and
his God are monsters of cruelty. If there are no jails, no
way of disposing of prisoners of war, and a gentle servitude is the substitute, God is a great slave-driver. If men's

lusts are so greedy that even the best of them want more
wives than one, the patience of God with the slow growth
of moral ideas is translated as the establishment of polygamy. If a people are so vile and filthy that the beasts are
clean and modest in comparison, and God sends an army
to wipe them out of being, we are pointed to the white
faces of women and children lifted on the crests of the
divine wrath!

Common Sense View of the Subject—How it Eliminates Poly-
gamy, Slavery, etc.

Common sense, in asking whether the Bible is worthy of
confidence would ask whether, as matter of fact, the moral
instruction of any period of Bible record was not fully up
to the capacity of that period to receive it? It would ask
another question—namely, whether a divine tuition is different from any other, except that it is more skillful?—
whether, in fact, the critics who compare an old order of
things with the highest state of moral development are not
demanding that the people under God's training shall be a
miraculous people, throwing off prejudices as they do a
Winter garment, bearing fruit without any intermediate
period of growth and blossom, and, in general terms, upset-
ting the every-day laws of progress. It is this idealism—
than which nothing is more irrational—which creates a
large share of the moral difficulties of the Old Testament. It is the insane or reckless, the idiotic or perverse
tenacity with which men demand that the divine teaching
must not suit itself to the time in which it was given, but
must always be up to the ripest periods of progress, that
gives any opportunity for the objugations of men who
" can write a better Bible " themselves than ours.

The two great charges brought against the Bible are
polygamy and slavery. Now, admit that in all stages,

from the chimpanzee up to Darwin, they are wrong (which is by no means clear), are these charges true? The fact that polygamy and slavery existed among the people who were under drill does not prove it. The fact that there were laws regulating either of these practices does not prove it. A law regulating the social evil does not prove that the sovereign people who make the laws approve the social evil, but only that, if men and women will go wrong, society must put up some defenses against corruption. Common sense inquires whether statutory allowance is an indorsement. And if that Remarkable Man, commenting on the divorce laws of Moses, said that Moses gave those laws because the people could not bear any better laws, common sense inquires if the same may not be true of other recognized usages which are below the ideal of an advanced age.

And when one rails at the Bible for its ill-treatment of women, the railing is simply gratuitous. I have read the Old Testament more or less carefully for many years, but I do not, at this writing, remember a single word that dishonors woman as woman. I have read only a little of Brahminical writings, but I remember a sentence or two about women. "A woman is never fit for independence;" "Women have no business with the text of the Veda. * * * Sinful women must be as foul as falsehood itself. This is fixed law." Whether in the last quotation it is meant that there is no purification for a bad woman, or what else, I do not know; but I do not recall anything like it in the Old Testament. Educated common sense knows that women among the Hebrews occupied a vastly higher level than the women of all other nations. It is simply notorious, that with all the lapses from virtue, the Hebrew women were as white as snow compared with the women of the Gentile world, and honor goes always hand in hand with virtue.

More Common Sense — The Great Ingersoll Orb Approaching the Nihilistic Belt — Nebulæ.

Common sense demands that in judgment of the moral worth of the Bible, it be taken as a whole. The theory of all who receive the Old and New Testaments is that they belong together, are so to be interpreted; that one is the beginning, and the other the conclusion, of the one Bible. The one begins in the " Laurentian period," so to speak, and follows man up from a wild nomad to wealth and empire, and the decay of empire; the moral and the civil law blending and running along together for hundreds of years, then separating by the simple explosion of the civil powers. The other takes him after the wounds caused by the explosion have partly healed, and puts forth moral ideas unencumbered by any considerations of the state. The former gave moral laws to the Jew; the latter moral laws to the man; everything from first to last going on as naturally as the building of a city, or the growth of a tree. And common sense should inquire how it happens, that, while the great army of scholars who have studied these systems, believers and skeptics alike, have been filled with admiration, a man rises up now and then to vituperate the logic of events and malign the great God because He has not chosen to plant a tree with the branches in the ground and the roots in the air.

Common sense naturally asks what the meaning of this bitter outbreak may be. We have no right to men's motives. But this is a phenomenon, the cause of which we have a right to ask, as we would ask the cause of a falling meteor. The Bible is a law and order book. It teaches that one must look out how he pulls up even the tares. Are we in our historic orbit passing a belt of nihilism, a time when assassination is reform, and a bad shot at a poor czar, inheriting semi-barbarism and striving with all his might to get rid of the inheritance, is to be lamented?

You may be told that it is the horrid theology of the Bible which provokes assault. Common sense remarks that, horrid as its theology may be, its sterner features are just like the theology of nature, namely, a demand for obedience to law and "the survival of the fittest." It is nature put into language, the operation of moral causes foretold—that is all. If you want a government more just than one which judges a man according to his deeds, good or bad, and takes into account his knowledge and opportunities, why, the thing to do is to rail at nature, at cause and effect, at seed-time and harvest. For while on the better side the Bible theology is more beneficent than nature, on the hard side it is simply unmitigated natural law. Do the theologians preach that good men will be damned? Then rail at the theologians, and not at the Bible.

In closing this short article, as an addendum, let me ask a question or two for the benefit of all who have a bad opinion of the Bible, as a woman's book or a slave's book.

1. Forget the harem of Solomon, and say why Judaism was a house of refuge for thousands of Roman and Greek women, many of them of noble birth, for a century preceding the Christian era?

2. In the same line, squarely, has, or has not, the modern estate of woman been the fruit of Christian (including Judaic) teaching?

3. Did not the Bible first mitigate and finally destroy slavery in the Roman empire?

4. Did not the Bible destroy slavery in England and America? Charge all the slave-driving you will to Christian men, and give any unbeliever all he claims, and then go down to a last analysis.

5. Are not republican institutions, including (as the old republics did not) democratic ideas, directly and palpably the fruit of the teachings of that remarkable Man (whom the French infidels called the Great Democrat); whose Bible was the Old Testament, and who told His followers how to amend and finish it by a book called the New Testament ?

In whatever way these questions may be answered, the man who essays to answer them will find that it is not so easy to eliminate the genius of Moses and Jesus from the genius of the world's movement toward virtue, equality and liberty.

TELL the Prince that this (a costly copy of the Bible) is the secret of England's greatness.—*Queen Victoria.*

I HAVE always said and always will say, that the studious perusal of the Sacred Volume will make better citizens, better fathers and better husbands.—*Thomas Jefferson.*

THE Bible is equally adapted to the wants and infirmities of every human being. No other book ever addressed itself so authoritatively and so pathetically to the judgment and moral sense of mankind.—*Chancellor James Kent.*

CHRIST proved that He was the Son of the Eternal by His disregard of time. All His doctrines signify only, and the same thing, eternity.—*Napoleon Bonaparte.*

I HAVE read the Bible morning, noon and night, and have ever since been the happier and better man for such reading.—*Edward Burke.*

I DO not believe human society, including not merely a few persons in any state, but whole masses of men, ever has attained, or ever can attain, a high state of intelligence, virtue, security, liberty, or happiness without the Holy Scriptures.— *William H. Seward.*

[Photographed by Melander.]

DR. COLLYER'S REPLY.

Dr. Collyer Relates a Little Story—A Book that cost Mr. Ingersoll the Governorship of Illinois—The Volume Philosophically Considered—Heavy Blows.

I HAVE been told a gentleman went to see Mr. Ingersoll once, when he lived in Peoria, and finding a fine copy of Voltaire in his library, said, " Pray, Sir, what did this cost you?" " I believe it cost me the governorship of the State of Illinois," was the swift and pregnant answer. I can not but recall the incident as he stands in the light of his lecture. He seems to be saying, " It is my turn now, and I will do what I can to square the account. I will dethrone your God to-day amid peals of laughter; blow His being down the wind on the wings of my epigrams. I have those about me who will send my words flying all over the state. I will start a crusade which will shut up your churches some day, silence your immemorial prayers, slay all the hopes that would strive after something more than this momentary gleam between the eternities, make of no account the grand deep truth that ' life struck sharp on death makes awful lightning,' and so dwarf our human kind that when we get man where we want him he shall never again be able to look over the low billows of his green graves, and end the fight by making my own creed good once, for all that

> Man, God's last work, who seemed so fair,
> Such splendid purpose in his eyes,
> Who rolled the psalms in wintry skies,
> Who built him fanes for fruitless prayer,

> Who trusted God was love indeed,
> And love, creation's final law;
> Though nature red, in tooth and claw,
> With raven, shrieked against his creed;
> Who loved, who suffered countless ills,
> Who battled for the true and just,
> *Is* blown about the desert dust,
> And sealed within the iron hills."

Now, since we first knew Mr. Ingersoll by report, there has been a time when those who can only believe in God as a rather helpless little brother, by no means able to take care of Himself, and in themselves as big brothers, who are bound to stand up for Him, might have felt there was grave danger in such a sight as we have witnessed—of a vast array of men and women, some of them it is fair to believe of a thoughtful turn, assembled to hear the last and best word which can be said why God should be dethroned, and His presence and providence numbered among the things that seemed true enough once, but pass away inevitably in the process through which we arise from "our dead selves to higher things."

Sparks Flying in all Directions—Singular Mental Phenomenon Occasioned by $25.000 a Year.

He was clothed once in a fine austerity; went on his lonely way quite content, to give grave and serious reasons for rejecting what so many of us hold dearer than our life, and was faithful to his instinct and insight, though such ovations as were ever given him—as Dr. Dyer used to say of the old abolitionists—might take the form mainly of rotten eggs. I know of more than one man, who, in those days, nourished a deep and most tender regard for him, and found something noble in the stand he made for the best a man can do and be, who has to abide so utterly alone. But Mr. Ingersoll, roystering around as the popular advocate of atheism, at $25,000 a year, as the common report goes, is quite another sort of a man. No doubt the laborer is worthy of his hire. Those who run the thing may be trusted to see to that, and a good many of us who stand on the other side may not be much better, according to the old proverb that it is "money makes the mare go." Still, as this always turns the fine edge of *our* endeavor, and makes us weak for good when we make it at all a matter of barter and sale, so it must be with Mr. Ingersoll, making him weak for what I can not but believe to be evil. He is no more in such a case than the second batch of reformers in the old times, who argued lustily for a reformation, while still they grew rich on the Church lands. No more than your Archbishop, in the Church of England, arguing on the godliness of tythes and priestly authority. So Mr. Ingersoll, in motley, trying to laugh the deepest and most sacred convictions of men down the wind under the guise of girding at the Pentateuch (for we must thank him, I say again, for the frankness with which he tells us this is his ultimate aim), is a very different man to the quiet, manful fellow we used to hear of in Peoria long ago, who won such regard from those who could at all understand him. The man in the ring, whose sole business it is to make you laugh, makes no converts even to rough riding. And so there is ground for neither hope nor fear, as we stand on that side or this, about the advance of atheism, so long as this remains as the best method of its choicest champions. It may make headway with such men as Voltaire had to handle, and in such times; but this serious and deep-hearted race of ours never did take to this kind of thing, and never will. It is only as the crackling of the thorns under a pot.

Nor can this bitter and relentless spirit toward those who differ help the advocates of atheism any more than it does the advocates of the faith.   Robert Southey says, in a letter to Sharon Turner, touching the contentions of his time between the sects, " When I hear the dissenters talk about Churchmen, I feel like a very high Churchman myself; but when I hear Churchmen talk about dissenters, I feel that I am a dissenter, too."   It was but the bias of a nature, in which the balances were still true, in favor of the side which was dealt with most unfairly.   The plea in the mind of one who could look on both sides with a calm concern, that the result of fighting over the lamp should not be to put out the light, or of contending over the nature and properties of the spring to soil the water so that no one could drink at it, be he ever so athirst.   Lord Bacon says, " there is a superstition in avoiding superstition, when those think they do best who go farthest; but care should be taken that the good should not be purged away with the bad, which commonly happens when this is the method."   So I think it must be with such violent and utter denunciation as this, which lies within the spirit of Mr. Ingersoll's address.   It has pleased a very bright and able man in our ranks to fall into accord with him in many things he has to say, and to show how we also hold this ground.   I may be old-fashioned, and unfit for a fair judgment, but I am very much of Southey's mind, and when I hear orthodoxy denounced in such a spirit, I say I agree with Mr. Ingersoll nowhere.   Here is bigotry of a new shape, denouncing bigots; and I sway to the other side for very charity, and the desire that the most good possible should be found in any evil, and especially that one should think as well as possible of those who can not see as we do, but are still of as fine and clear a grain, and show as noble a soul of self-sacrifice—that uttermost and innermost proof a man can give that he believes he is right.

**The Clear Ring of Truth vs. the Dull Thud of the Baser Metal
—Potency of Simple Statement—The Doctor's Objections
to Ingersoll's Talk.**

Now, a man who seeks and loves the truth, must be
esteemed in every human society; but so far as my own
observation goes, the most of our fights and contentions
carried on in such a spirit as this I am trying to touch,
end in vast clouds of dust and smoke, in which the clear,
shining sun of the truth turns blood-red to our human
vision. And those who, even with the best intentions, are
forever going about, as we say, with a chip on their shoulder, are likely in the end to be voted a common nuisance.
The truth must be told, no matter who gets hurt; the
truth, or even semblance of the truth, which smites the
man who tells it, and moves his heart so that he has to cry
"Woe is me if I preach not this Gospel!" But the truth
still comes to us through clear and simple statements which
tell their own story, rather than through denial, denunciation, satire, slang, and appeals to the top-gallery. So
Channing thought, and the result is, that his best sermons
are simply statements of the truth as it had come home to
his own heart and mind. So Parker thought, and reading
his life, again, just now, I find there is nothing the man
longed for so much as that he might be quiet, and just let
the truth come itself in his great fine heart and brain, while
he regrets bitterly the evil times that compelled him to
take to other methods; and the best work he ever did for
the deep, still truth, are statements. So John Wesley
thought, when once he struck his shining path from earth
to heaven, and his sermons from 1740 to 1780, are simply
statements of the ever-growing and ever-brightening truth
God is revealing to man. And so even Calvin thought,
and his earliest and best utterances are still statements,
grim, hard, iron-clinched, but all the same the stern and

inexorable affirmation, made good for all time, that neither priest nor Pope can play fast and loose with the Most High God. Always you find the greatest and best men when they themselves are at their best making statements, exactly as Jesus does in the sermon on the mount. Saying what is in them simply and sincerely, feeling sure, as Coleridge says, that " no authority can ever prevail in opposition to the truth." So Columbus holds himself before the Council of Salamanca, when a new world is in debate. So Stephenson holds himself before the House of Lords, when he has to answer for his locomotive. So Newton affirms his discovery of the law of gravitation ; and Harvey, that of the circulation of the blood. That is the law of all truth-telling in its noblest and best shape, and then the contention, if there is one, is simply the hiss, as Stebbins, of California, said once, when he was speaking in defence of the Chinese, " is simply the hiss the white-hot truth makes when it strikes the black waters of hell."

Here, then, is my radical objection to Mr. Ingersoll's talk, apart from his final aim. It is conceived and done in a narrow and most bigoted spirit, by one who claims, above all things in the world, to be free from bigotry. The men of whom he speaks so unworthily are, take them by and large, worthy men. The things in the five books of Moses, so called, on which the fathers based their creeds, are rapidly passing into worthier meanings; and the day is not far distant when the old belief will have rotted down, and be as when an old tree rots, to become the nursing mother of a bed of violets. No man believes in such things any more, who has read and thought to any purpose; and the man who has not done this, had far better believe in the six days' work and one day's rest, rib, serpent, fall, flood, ark, manna, and all the rest of those wonders, than in Mr. Ingersoll's enormous and most fatal negation of God.

Putting the Fine Edge on Orthodoxy—Taking a Weld with Prof. Swing and Dr. Thomas—Borax and Bigotry.

Nor is that bad and bitter spirit in orthodoxy now which once found utterance in fire and the axe, as it did in far more ruthless ways in atheism when the goddess of Reason was the divinity of France. Orthodoxy, in a free-spoken land like ours, is very civil, indeed, and timid, as I think, almost to a fault, showing just the spirit which is not sure the ground may not slip from under it any moment; and so far as its finest leaders go edging away from the rocking base, as fast and as far the people for whom those men have to care will follow. Nothing could be more gentle than the way orthodoxy used Brother Swing. He was no more orthodox than you are. He might not think so, but that's the truth, patent to the whole world. Yet the church to which he was preaching, and the old standbys, as we call them, said, "This is what we are here for, and have laid out our money and time for, and, if you go back far enough, it is what our fathers shed their blood for. Dr. Swing must be true to his ancient vows, or leave." If Mr. Ingersoll should ever lay out his money, and those of his mind put theirs to it, to build a great hall in Washington or Chicago for the propagation of atheism, and employ a man to preach to them, and then if this man should depart as far backward from their way of thinking as Brother Swing departed forward from that of the Presbyterians, they will be much more catholic and inclusive than I think they are if they use that man as gently.

I do not mention this for proof of my word that orthodoxy is getting to be very civil—indeed, gentle, timid, and even wanting in a proper courage to take care of its own household, if we are to judge from the half-and-half measures they are taking with Mr. Talmadge, in Brooklyn, and the way in which they let him smite them on the mouth.

Orthodoxy has exchanged the old fetters of iron for silken bands with an elastic base. Brother Thomas, my dear and good friend, has no right to preach in a Methodist pulpit, and in the days I remember, would not have preached in one to this time. There must be a certain concert of opinion, capable of being brought within fair lines, or nobody would organize or hold anything. This is the secret of our most happy relation through all these years in this church. We hold together through a large, free, common opinion about certain grand verities. I should injure my own nature if I went over those lines. Yet men are continually going over them in the orthodox churches. But they bear and forbear, scold a little, fret a good deal, and trust the brother may see things different presently or depart in peace, and then, when there is no help for it, they lift him very gently out of the fold.

Nor is the scorn Mr. Ingersoll pours out on these ancient books befitting any man who could feel his way to their heart, apart from any theory of inspiration or the use made of them to hinder human progress. It is the spirit of the Caliph he shows, who, when the question came up what should be done with a superb library, said, "Burn it: whatever is against the Koran ought to be burnt, and whatever agrees with the Koran is not needed." With some such narrow vision he would judge these venerable monuments of the most ancient time; make an end of them to human credence; get them branded for worthless in the interests of human reason; and order himself toward them as if an iconoclast, looking over the treasures of the Louvre, should note only what is grotesque or painful, while he missed what is most beautiful and entrancing, tumble the whole into a heap, and burn it into ashes and lime. Men have misused these books, there can be no doubt of that, and turned some parts of them into bane, which, well used, might bring blessing. So they tell me, there is no place that can match Peoria in its power to turn good grain into whisky: therefore, shovel Peoria into the river, and leave the smiling prairies where the grain grows, a waste.

Nothing in the world shows a man s limitations so fatally as the play of this power which can not or will not distinguish between the use and the abuse of things, or will overlook the abiding good because of the transient evil. We tolerate it easily in the child who turns in wrath on the chair against which he has bruised himself; we look twice at the man who does this, and then draw our own conclusion. I have been told, on good authority, that Mr. Ingersoll, in his childhood and his early youth, did get badly bruised against these books. Well, the books have to take it now; but is this the sign of a large and a gracious mind? One would think he might have gotten over it before this, and come to understand them better than mere instruments of hurt. I can agree in nothing touching the Bible and the soul's life with the man who tells me his aim is to damage or destroy the faith of man in God, to the best of his ability; but if this was out of the way, one might not object to his antagonism to the misuse of Moses by those who think they do God service. Still, in any case, I find too much beauty in the books to allow me to touch them with irreverent hands. They are simply above all standards of value, with which I measure other books outside the Scriptures, in the revelation they make to me of the way men felt their way toward a sure faith in God in those old times, and so grew, in many instances, to be very noble and good at last, and, as I have said, of the way in which they tried to account for this wonderful and mysterious universe in which they found themselves when they had "learned the use of I and me, and said 'I am not what I see, and other than the things I touch.'" Nor would I lose one of

the wonders. They all tell us something we want to know
about the working of the human mind.

That is a very poor and rude matter I treasure in my
study; a broken vase of gray clay, with a few fishbone
marks on it; but if there was not another of them in the
world I would not exchange it for the Portland vase, for
this reason: That on a day, so remote I can not strike it,
some poor savage made that vase in my little town, to hold
the dust of some one dear to him, put those marks on it for
a token of what was in his mind, and then made a little
vault and hid it away until the sun of this century should
shine on it, and when I hold that vase, I find a trace of the
man who had else been lost. There is the faint beat of a
human heart lingering in the clay, and a dim remembrance
of tears, and the marks, and as if they should open my grave
two thousand years from now, and find the white cross still
fresh on my coffin, and say, "Tender, loving hands laid
that there, let us deal with it tenderly." These rude and
half-shapen things in the old books are the clue to the man
who made them, and how he felt, and what he thought.
I would not spare the least letter out of them, but would
scan them in all reverence, let who will scorn them. They
all belong to our human history, and it is only their mis-
fortune they have ever been misused. They are included
in the saying of the great and wise German, that the Bible
begins nobly with Paradise, the symbol of Faith, and con-
cludes with the eternal kingdom; and with the grand, sweet
word of Thomas Carlyle: "In the poorest cottage there is
one book wherein, for thousands of years, the spirit of man
has found light and nourishment, and an interpreting
response to whatever is deepest in him. The Book
wherein to this day the eye that will look well, the mystery
of existence reflects itself, and if not to the satisfying of
the outward sense, yet to the opening of the inward sense,
which is the far grander result."

A Touching Illustration—Eloquence and Truth—Havelock's Saints.

Of the doctrine advanced by Mr. Ingersoll, and his purpose to have done with the God Jesus believed in, and
show reason why we should have done with Him, there is
nothing to say if I have not said it steadily these many
years. A remark of Charles Hare strikes me forcibly as I
read the few words that are said on this matter, in the
address, "There is no being eloquent for atheism. In that
exhausted receiver the mind can not use its wings—the
clearest proof that it is out of its element." For when I
consider how eloquent Mr. Ingersoll has been at times, and
the moving cause of it, I can see that he also must answer
to this law. He never said grander words than those about
our boys, their mighty heart, and utter self-sacrifice, for the
noblest ends. But there never was anything done since
the world stood, in which the presence of God could be
traced, and his power felt more clearly, nor did ever men
make such sacrifice with a devouter sense that God was
within it all, than those most worthy his grand and touching eulogium. "Call out Havelock's saints," Sir Archi-
bald Campbell shouted, when hope was almost dead in the
great Sepoy rebellion in India. Something must be done,
and done on the swift instant, or there would be more woful
work among the women and children. Call out Havelock's
saints, *they* are sure to be ready, and they are never drunk.
They were of the sort that carry a Bible in their knapsack,
and turn to chapter and verse, and sing psalms from old
Rouse's version to Dundee and Elgin, and the Martyrs,
and nourish their hearts on stories of the way stout battles
were fought and grand martyrdoms endured for God among
the moors. Call out Havelock's saints, they are always
ready, and never get drunk, and they do fight like the very
angels. They were but the brothers of the great, simple

souls who fought at Ball's Bluff, and in scores of battles beside, while mothers and sisters did the praying for the moment, for they had no time except just to look up and hear that voice in the heart say, " Steady, my boy, steady, you are of a grand stock, you must tell a grand story. And they told it, and at the heart of it all was God, and a new life for the nation, and in time a new civilization that shall shed its blessing on the whole waiting world.

Atheism—Not an Institution but a "Destitution!"—The True Life.

I have no stones to throw at atheism any more than I have stones to throw at blindness. It can never be more than a very sore and sad limitation, not an institution, but a destitution. This Anglo-Saxon nature is not good soil for it; no arguments can make it take hold and grow in us any more than arguments can make roses take hold and grow on Aberdeen granite. Nor have I any exhortation save this: That as we stand as pioneers of the noblest and fairest faith we can reach, a faith which throws no strands to stay itself on the fall, or the flood, or the manna, or the sun, standing still, or any of these, old wonders, but just fronts the light and drinks it in, we shall grow ever more worthy to prove God's presence in the world, by revealing it in our life, and in the work he has given us to do. There is no argument like that which lies within a sweet and true life which looks to God forever for its inspiration and its joy. Let us be right worthy of our faith.

> Then shall this Western Goth,
> So fiercely practical, so keen of eye,
> Find out some day that nothing pays but God.
> Served whether in the smoke of battle field,
> In work obscure done honestly—or vote
> For truth unpopular—or faith maintained,
> To ruinous convictions—or good deeds,
> Wrought for good's sake, heedless of heaven or hell.

FRED. PERRY POWERS' REPLY.

— —

The Sinaitic Code — Solvent Powers of the Historic Method — Graphic Illustration of the Two Schools.

CHRISTIANITY, like a fortress on an open plain, is liable to attack from opposite directions. But it is well for the attacking parties to remember that columns of argument do not, like columns of soldiers, co-operate when moving in opposite directions. Christianity is not to be disposed of by proving that at the same time it is and is not a certain thing.

The "historic method," like every new journal, seems "to meet a long-felt want." It has been clutched greedily and employed in every conceivable shape. It proves not only that whatever is is right, but that whatever was was right, and whatever will be will be right. It has been carried to a point where it undermines personal responsibility, and with it Mr. Herbert Spencer, in the conclusion of his Sociology, enjoins the reformer and the philanthropist from activity. It eliminates ethical considerations from the mind of the historian. It closes the eyes of society to the vices of its members, and it lays its hand upon the mouth of the judge before whom stands a man who, as the result of antecedents, and in the natural effort to harmonize himself with his environment, has committed murder.

Now, it is a little singular that this invaluable historic method should be a legitimate weapon against the church, but an illegitimate weapon for the church. If the church is to be allowed to use this weapon freely it will have no difficulty in making a perfect defense for itself, its predecessor and all of its members, no matter how wild or wicked. The historic method is a solvent in which the inquisition disappears, and which at once removes those spots on the robe of religious history, the wars and massacres of the Israelites. I have no disposition to make any such extensive use of the historic method as this. But all matters of history are to be studied as historical, not as contemporaneous. And it is in the last degree uncandid for the opponents of Christianity to make the extremest use of the historic method when it suits their purpose, and then, in dealing with religious history, eliminate ordinary historic perspective. In this latter particular the enemies of the church are not alone. The Reformation brought in a revival of Judaism, and a large section of Protestant Christianity resolutely closes its eyes to the fact that the Mosaic dispensation was given several thousand years ago, and to a race wholly different in its position from any now existing.

The Mosaic dispensation is not the only thing treated in this way. The directions given by St. Paul to a particular church at a particular date are constantly appealed to in the churches as universal law, applicable to all churches and throughout all ages. If a picture with a man in the foreground and an elephant in the background were shown to two savages, one of whom knew something about elephants, and the other of whom did not, the former would insist upon it that the artist was a ignoramus for painting an elephant smaller than a man, and the other would conclude that man was a larger animal than an elephant, because he appeared so in the picture. The former represents a school of atheists who attack the ethics of the Sinaitic code, and the latter represents a school of devout believers who, receiving the Sinaitic code as a matter of revelation, feel compelled to defend it as the truth and nothing but the truth, and the truth for all times and all places. It is worth while to remember at the very outset what both parties to the war waged over the ethics of the Pentateuch seem disposed to ignore, that what are now denounced as the errors of the Sinaitic code were pointed out more than eighteen hundred years ago by the highest authority recognized by the Christian world.

In the Sermon on the Mount Jesus Christ used the following language:

Ye have heard that it hath been said, an eye for an eye, and a tooth for a tooth. But I say unto you, That ye resist not evil; but whosoever shall smite thee on thy right cheek, turn to him the other, also.—Matt. v., 38, 39.

The *lex talionis*, here repudiated, was not a rabbinical interpolation; it was an integral maxim of the Sinaitic code, as the following words, coming shortly after the Decalogue, show:

And if any mischief follows, then thou shalt give life for life, eye for eye, tooth for tooth, hand for hand, foot for foot, burning for burning, wound for wound, stripe for stripe.—Exodus xxi., 23-25.

Free divorce was another Sinaitic error, so called, and in pointing it out Christ gave us the key to the whole Mosaic dispensation, as the following passage shows:

The Pharisees also came unto Him, tempting Him, and saying unto Him, Is it lawful for a man to put away his wife for every cause? And He answered and said unto them, Have ye not read that He which made them at the beginning made them male and female, and said, for this cause shall a man leave father and mother and shall cleave to his wife, and they twain shall be one flesh? Wherefore they are no more twain, but one flesh. What, therefore, God hath joined together, let no man put asunder. They say unto Him, Why did Moses then command to give a writing of divorcement, and to put her away? He saith unto them, Moses, because of the hardness of your hearts, suffered you to put away your wives; but from the beginning it was not so. And I say unto you, Whosoever shall put away his wife, except it be for fornication, and shall marry another, committeth adultery; and whoso marrieth her which he put away doth commit adultery.—Matt. xix., 3-9.

Divine Adjustment of the Moral Law — Progressive Elimination of Polygamy, Slavery, Etc.— Mount Sinai and Mount Calvary.

The "hardness of heart" referred to is evidently the dullness of the intellectual and moral sense that characterized the almost savage slaves of the Egyptians when they came up out of Egypt. Instead of imposing on them an ethical system perfectly complete and perfectly unintelligible to them in their degraded condition, Moses, under direction of divine wisdom, gave them a moral law which they could understand, and which would develop in them a capacity for something purer and higher.

Polygamy was tolerated, not because it was the ideal system; not because the deity of the Hebrews could devise no other, but because polygamy is the natural intermediate station between promiscuity and monogamy. God chose to make a civilized people out of the Jews, not by His creative fiat, but by operating through natural laws of sociology. In due time, when men were prepared for it, the law of permanent and monogamous marriage was promulgated, but it was in advance of public sentiment, as is shown by the fact that when Christ, in the passage above quoted, forbade free divorce, and proclaimed the sanctity of the marital relation, the disciples suggested that if that was the law it was better not to marry.

So slavery was tolerated under the Mosaic law. But servitude for a short term of years was substituted for permanent and hereditary servitude, and the law threw some protection about the person of the slave. The Mosaic dispensation is not responsible for a defense of slavery. It tolerated an intermediate state between barbarism and civilization.

A fact of vast importance to notice is that this Mosaic system contained within itself the seeds which, when humanity had outgrown the old dispensation, would mature into a new dispensation so far in advance of human attainments, that after nearly nineteen centuries the human race has not begun to catch upon it. Christ expounded the Old Testament references to Himself, beginning with Moses. When Sinai had reduced society to order, and stamped out paganism, then Calvary came and appealed to all that was highest and purest in man. Even at this late day there are not many souls that really comprehend the full meaning of Calvary and whose lives give evidence of that fact. When any considerable portion of the human race has received all that Calvary can confer, a new dispensation may be expected.

In this sense the Mosaic dispensation was perfect and complete. As promulgated on Mount Sinai, it was adapted only to a certain low condition of mankind. But it contained a vital principle, which enabled it to expand as fast as civilization advanced. Starting with the Decalogue, it developed the penitential psalms and the noble exhortations of the prophets, and finally the Beatitudes. Beginning with a catalogue of penalties, it in course of time developed sorrow for sin, and at last that love to God which withholds from sin. This system of religion has developed faster than civilization has advanced. The Israelites at the foot of Mount Sinai probably knew something of the wrongfulness of murder, theft and adultery. But, to-day, in spite of great moral advances—to-day, nineteen centuries after Christ—how much does the human race really know about " hungering and thirsting after righteousness? " Let the foolish declaration that we have outgrown Christianity come from those who have been filled, and who still want something more.

The Decalogue is by no means the complete moral code that it is often represented to be, and it would be singularly

out of place in a Christian church were it not that, even
to-day, and in the United States, there are many persons
incapable of comprehending the Beatitudes which comprehend all there is in the Decalogue, and vastly more. The
seventh commandment does not apply to crimes, both
participants in which are unmarried, and the Mosaic law
treated the seduction of an unbetrothed bondmaid as a
trivial offense, sufficiently atoned for by the sacrifice of a
ram. The seduction of a free maid, if she was not be-
trothed, was atoned for by marriage. It was on account
of the "hardness of their hearts," their infancy in ethics,
that this easy-going statute regarding the sexes was enacted.
But Christ said :

Ye have heard that it was said of them of old time, "Thou shalt not
commit adultery;" but I say unto you, That whosoever looketh on a
woman to lust after her hath committed adultery with her already in
his heart.—Matt. v., 27, 28.

The Decalogue said, "Thou shalt not kill," but Jesus
Christ added to this as follows :

Whosoever is angry with his brother without a cause shall be in dan
ger of the judgment.—Matt. v., 22.

The Decalogue forbade the bearing of false witness; it
was silent as to ordinary mendacity. In the New Testament this law is extended to cover all untruthfulness.

Purpose and Potency of the Mosaic Law.

The purpose of the Mosaic law was to start the Israelites
on the path of spiritual enlightenment. It was a provi-
sional system, superseded at the right time by Christianity.
The sacrifices were fines imposed on the guilty. They were
also daily reminded of the existence of God, and the blood
pouring from the altar taught the serious nature and fatal
consequences of sin as nothing else would. Of course, to
a set of modern sophists, who deny the existence of sin,

the sacrifices are simply meaningless, revolving spectacles; but the man who hasn't studied the subject enough to understand the meaning of the Hebrew sacrifices is estopped from discussing them in public.

The barbarities of the Mosaic system form a pet subject of denunciation by gentlemen who have a repugnance to study, coupled with a mania for delivering lectures, when the latter can be done at a pecuniary profit. If a man thinks it just as well to worship the sun or a bull as to worship Jehovah, of course he will regard the penalties denounced against idolatry as tyrannical and barbarous. But no man, unless he has a purpose to accomplish thereby, can shut his eyes to the barrier that idolatry places in the way of mental or moral progress, or both. The interests of the human race demanded that paganism should be roofed out somewhere, if not everywhere. The promise to Abraham, that in his seed should all the nations of the earth be blessed, has been fulfilled, but that has been accomplished only by the most rigorous hostility to paganism among the Jews. In spite of all the stern laws of Moses, Israel again and again relapsed into paganism; yet it was an absolute necessity that if what we now know as civilization was ever to come, paganism must in some corner of the world be stamped out, and the way prepared for Christianity. To teach the Israelites what a moral contagion was idolatry, they had to be taught that it was a physical contagion, contaminating everything connected with the idolator. Had not this been done, the Israelites would have remained, like all the rest of the world, immersed in the unspeakably unclean worship of Baal and Astarte and Moloch. Cost what it might, the ravages of the pestilence had to be checked somewhere.

6

**Excessive Wickedness and Proportionate Punishment—The Court
of Heaven vs. the Court of Earth.**

Of course, the wars of the Israelites and the annihilation
of certain tribes are held to be horrible cruelties by the
sophists of the present day. But we are distinctly told
that it was for their extraordinary wickedness that these
tribes were exterminated. We are again and again told
that it was for the wickedness of the Amalekites that their
destruction was commanded. We get some glimpses of
the unmentionable vileness of some of these Canaanitish
tribes. The fact was that they were ulcers on the body of
the human race which had to be cut out. Possibly the
innocent suffered with the guilty, and possibly there were
no innocent except the infants, whom it would have
been no mercy to save after their unclean parents were
destroyed. It is probable that the moral taint had so rooted
itself in the physical system that, had the children been
spared, they would have inevitably developed into adults as
unclean as their parents. The passages sometimes quoted
to show that Jehovah was vindicative, are passages aimed
at sin. The most ample amnesty to the repentant is promised from one end of Genesis to the other end of Revelation.
The people who denounce the divine government, as manifest in the Old Testament, either deny that there is any
such thing as sin, or, which is often the case, they have
admirable reasons for being angry because sin is punished.
The gentlemen who denounce the destruction of Sodom are
necessarily apologists for the Sodomists.

When malignancy is charged against Jehovah it is important to remember that the presence of five righteous
persons would have saved Sodom. There was only one
righteous person, and not only was he enabled to escape
but he secured immunity for his family. Nineveh was

spared because the people repented. The Israelites were delivered from their enemies when they forsook their sins. On the other hand Nathan's rebuke to David is a matter of record, and Solomon's licentiousness was punished by the revolt of Jeroboam and the ten tribes. The statement that Jehovah disregarded distinctions of right and wrong, or treated the innocent and guilty alike, or took pleasure in the death even of the wicked is false, and known to be so by the persons who make it. The very sentiment of humanity which prompts certain persons to denounce the divine government of the Jews is found only where Christianity, the legitimate successor of Judaism, prevails.

What are denounced as massacres committed by the Israelites were judicial executions performed under the orders of the only court in the universe which has perfect information of the cases tried before it, and which is perfectly free from weaknesses. To object to the judgment one must either show that the condemned were innocent, which at this late day can not be shown, or one must show that the crimes were less heinous than the court held them to be, which is to become an apologist for crimes of every character, some of which are not even to be named. It is also to be remembered that the divine government is the creator of society, instead of the creature of society, as is human government. The former is, therefore, not to be judged precisely as the latter is, even though abstract justice is the same in Heaven that it is on earth. The charge of vindictiveness is absolutely without foundation; and, by the way, of all the nations known to the Jews the one we might suppose them most hostile to is the Egyptian, for it was in Egypt that the Israelites were enslaved and maltreated. Yet the divine command, coming from Moses, was that the Israelites should in no case oppress the Egyptians, and the reason was that they were once sojourners in the land of Egypt, the very reason we might suppose why they should be especially bitter toward the Egyptians.

Able Bodied Mendacity and Civilization—Love and Obedience.

There is a good deal of dense ignorance or able-bodied mendacity in circulation regarding the ethics of the New Testament. Jesus Christ and His apostles upheld neither political nor domestic despotism. But it is a fact which lecturers should understand that civil order is the first step toward civilization. Despotism is more conducive to civilization than anarchy is. Furthermore, when Paul wrote his epistles the Roman officials suspected all Christians of being hostile to the government, and it was especially necessary that the Roman power should understand by the loyalty of the Christians that He whom they called their king was a spiritual sovereign, and not a rival of the emperor.

What Paul at a particular time wrote to a particular church is by no means necessarily a universal law. What is particularly to be noted is that the exhortations to obedience on the part of the citizen, the wife, the child and the servant are coupled with and conditioned on exhortations to the ruler, the husband, the parent and the master, which certain uncandid and irrational persons, some of whom are inside the church and some of whom are outside of it, are careful to ignore. In Ephesians v. 22, Paul commands wives to submit themselves to their husbands, but in the twenty-fifth verse husbands are commanded to love their wives as Christ loves His church. Now, if the husband fulfills his part of the mutual obligation, the wife's submission will not be of a very mental character. In Ephesians vi. 1, children are commanded to obey their parents, but in the fourth verse fathers are commanded not to provoke their children to wrath, but to bring them up in the nurture and admonition of the Lord. In the next verse servants are commanded to obey their masters, but in the ninth verse we read, "And, ye masters, do the same things unto them, forbearing threatening, knowing that your Master also is in Heaven; neither is there respect of person with Him." In Hebrews xiii. 17, we read, "Obey them that have the rule over you, and submit yourselves; for they watch for your souls as they that must give account." The command to obey rules is conditioned on the discharge of their duties by the rulers.

Now, in omitting one half of each **double command**, and on the strength of the other half arraigning Christianity as the ally of domestic and political tyranny, modern "free thought" is accomplishing a great work, is it not? The distinguishing characteristic of "free thought" seems to be that it is thought freed from all subservience to facts.

Mr. Powers' Pungent Peroration.

Theology has made many shipwrecks by an excess of *a priori* reasoning, and by reasoning deductively when the means of reasoning inductively exist. But what is termed materialism is habitually doing the same thing, if it can make a point against Christianity by so doing. The enemies of Calvinism have denounced it because it promoted immorality. Yet a severer code of morals would be difficult to find than that maintained by the English Puritans, the Scotch Covenanters, and the French Huguenots, all Calvinists. Would it not be just as rational to judge Calvinism by its fruits as to judge its fruits by Calvinism?

When man has argued from the New Testament that Christianity must be the ally of despotism, and then looks about him and sees that civil liberty is not known outside of Christian lands, and has its fullest development in England and America, where Christianity in its simplest forms prevail, and where there are the fewest barriers between the human soul and the New Testament itself: when he has argued from the New Testament to show that Christianity is inimical to the best interests of womanhood, and then looks around and sees womanhood honored only in Christian countries, constantly employed by and honored in the church, must it not occur to him with painful force that he is a good deal off the track?

It would not be necessary to remind philosophers of the fact, but it is necessary to remind sophists that the Jews did a good many things that the Mosaic dispensation is not responsible for, and that it is mere idiocy to hold Christianity responsible for everything done by individuals or associations in its name. The man who can not discriminate between the legitimate results of a system, and the abuses grafted on to it by its professed adherents, is plainly unfit to debate philosophical questions.

If people made half the effort to understand the Bible that they make to discard it, they wouldn't be so funny as they are now, but they would know more.

THERE are over two hundred passages in the Old Testament which prophesied about Christ, and every one of them has come true.—*D. L. Moody.*

IN regard to the Great Book, I have only to say it is the best gift which God has given to man. All the good from the Saviour of the World is communicated through this Book. But for this Book we could not know right from wrong. All those things desirable to man are contained in it. I return you my sincere thanks for this very elegant copy of the Great Book of God which you present.—*Abraham Lincoln, on receiving a present of a Bible.*

I DEFY you all, as many as are here, to prepare a tale so simple and so touching, as the tale of the passion and death of Jesus Christ, whose influence will be the same after so many centuries.—*Denis Diderot.*

THE Bible is the best book in the world. It contains more of my little philosophy than all the libraries I have seen.—*John Adams. (Second President of United States.)*

AND, finally, I may state, as the conclusion of the whole matter, that the Bible contains within itself all that, under God, is required to account for and dispose of all forms of infidelity, and to turn to the best and highest uses all that man can learn of nature.—*Chancellor Dawson.*

THE Bible is the only cement of nations, and the only cement that can bind religious hearts together.—*Chevalier Bunsen.*

THE Bible is the Word of God—with all the peculiarities of man, and all the authority of God.—*Prof. Murphy.*

FROM the time that, at my mother's feet, or on my father's knee, I first learned to lisp verses from the sacred writings, they have been my daily study and vigilant contemplation. If there be anything in my style or thoughts to be commended, the credit is due to my kind parents in instilling into my mind an early love of the Scriptures.—*Daniel Webster.*

THE same divine hand which lifted up before the eyes of Daniel and of Isaiah the veil which covered the tableau of the time to come, unveiled before the eyes of the author of Genesis the earliest ages of the creation. And Moses was the prophet of the past, as Daniel and Isaiah and many others were the prophets of the future.—*Prof. Guyot.*

WE are persuaded that there is no book by the perusal of which the mind is so much strengthened and so much enlarged as it is by the perusal of the Bible.—*Dr. Melville.*

Chas. Edwd. Chaney

BISHOP CHENEY'S REPLY.

How the Question of Forgery Applies to the Five Books of Moses.

In looking at almost any object in the world of nature round about, it becomes remarkable only from certain points of view. The cathedral rocks that form one of the glories of the Yosemite Valley differ not much from any other great pile of jagged cliffs, except in a certain position, where the great mass of Gothic spires and arches appear clothed with evergreen ivy. Only as you reach a certain point where Profile Notch penetrates the White Mountains, do you see far up, up on the topmost cliff, the formation of a face cut in the solid granite by nature's own chisel. But the case of alleged forgery before us is extraordinary from every point of view, for forgery is generally something which concerns some brief document, something that requires only a signature in order to secure its currency. The longer and more elaborate the document which forgery produces, the more danger there must inevitably be of its final and ultimate detection. But here are five long historic books. They are full of details. They cover vast periods of time. They enter into a variety of topics. Incidentally they discuss not only questions of religion, but of law, of politics, of commerce, even of hygiene—medical laws of health. Was ever forgery committed before or since on such a gigantic scale as this? Moreover, there is no crime that is liable to be so speedily detected as forgery. The man who signs some document with another's name rarely goes down to the grave without meeting his punishment here on earth. Why, only a few weeks ago, the doors of our penitentiary, in the State of

Illinois, closed upon a prisoner who had affixed the name of another, whose name was better than his own, to a check upon which he had received the money; but only one month intervened as a gap between that crime and the punishment it merited and received.

It was a hundred years ago, that Thomas Chatterton, one of the most wonderful men, or boys, I might rather say, that England has ever produced, forged a huge mass of papers, professedly historical, that were dated away back in the thirteenth and fourteenth centuries. The style was that of the monks and chroniclers, which he had imitated with the greatest possible perfection. The references to the customs of that ancient period were such as to avoid detection, and Chatterton, in the precocity of his intellect, and in the versatility of his talent, was without a peer in English literary history. The English literary world received it as a revelation out of lost centuries. The great scholars of England were deceived. But it only took three years to expose to every eye the fraud that had been committed, and Chatterton, whom Wordsworth called the "marvelous boy," ended his career in a suicide's grave. O, brethren! who can count the years, who can enumerate the centuries which have rolled over this world of ours since the alleged forgery of this man Moses! And yet to-day, after the lapse of centuries, there are more people who believe in that forgery as the genuine work of the man whom God appointed the great law-giver and leader of Israel, there are more people who hang their hopes for time and eternity on this alleged fraud, and that which has grown out of this alleged fraud—the Gospel of our Lord Jesus Christ—than ever before in two thousand years. Am I not then justified in saying that if this be a forgery, which is contained in the five books of Moses, it is the most extraordinary forgery that has ever been committed in the world since words

expressed human thought, or human beings learned to wield
a pen?

The "Common Ground" of the Contending Parties—Logical Position of Ezra.

Now, in the first place, I desire to call your attention to
certain facts concerning the Mosaic record. In all contro-
versies in every department of human thought there are
certain points which are regarded as neutral ground. When
our great civil war shook this land from centre to circum-
ference and two mighty armies were face to face in the
Valley of the Tennessee, the stars and stripes floated in the
same breeze that wafted the stars and the bars ; the strains
of "Dixie" and "My Maryland" commingled with
"Hail Columbia" and the "Star-Spangled Banner';" the
soldiers of the different armies exchanged such commodi-
ties as they possessed, as if they had been neighbors in
peace at home. No wonder that finally it came to pass
that between these armies there was what is known as
neutral ground, on which it was agreed that the soldiers of
one side should not fire on those of the other. Now, is
there any such ground as that between those who defend
what are known as the five books of Moses, and those who
declare they were never written by Moses at all ? Is there
any point, I say, in this controversy where the skeptic and
the believer can come to stand upon one common ground ?
If we can find such a neutral ground as that, it will save
us a long, tiresome, profitless debate.

Now, such a ground I think we have in the life and history of Ezra, the writer of the book of the Old Testament,
which bears his name. It is conceded on all hands that
this man was a scribe of the Jewish law after the close of
the Babylonian captivity. After the people had returned
from the land of their exile into the land of their fathers,

he gathered into one great collection all these sacred writings that were held by the Jews to be the inspired word of God. No infidel that I am aware of has ever questioned the fact that in this collection of Ezra was contained the five books of Moses. It has been claimed by some of the least scholarly of infidels that Ezra wrote those five books. But that idea was found visionary and was long ago given up by those who opposed the truth of Christianity. But the fact remains that no one, Christian or unbeliever, to-day questions the historic fact that the five books of Moses, as we now accept them, were received as the writings of the lawgiver of the Jewish people when Ezra was at the acme of his influence after the Baylonian captivity. But they state that it was universally conceded that it was four hundred and fifty years before the birth of Christ. In other words, it was admitted that every Jew who returned out of the Babylonian captivity, held these five books to be the works of Moses, the man of God, twenty-three hundred years ago.

The Bishop Planting Signals on the Mountain Tops of History— Survey of the New Moses Air Line.

We stand, then, without dispute, without any controversy, at this point of time—four hundred and fifty years before the birth of our Lord and Saviour Jesus Christ. Now, fix that point in your memory while I attempt, like a civil engineer penetrating some wilderness, to plant the signal on some more remote mountain top of history. Now, all the ancient writings, whether Egyptian or Chaldean, corroborate the testimony of the Bible that these Hebrews were slaves in the land of Egypt. They also agree that they migrated into Southern Syria, under the leadership of a man who was called Moses—a word which meant "one drawn out of the water." It is also universally allowed that they settled in this new land, which had long before

been promised to their fathers, about the year 1450 before
Christ. We have established then our second date—a date
which no skeptic has ever called in question. When our
great tunnel that brings the pure water of Lake Michigan
into every home and household in this city was in process
of construction, the workmen began at either end. There
was a shaft out in yonder crib, and there was another on
the shore, and underneath the waves the two parties of
toilers worked toward each other. And so it is with us.
We tunnel between our two shafts. The date 450 B. C. and
the date 1450 B. C.—only one thousand years are to be accounted for. Does that seem a long period of time to you?
I admit that it does, but not in the history of nations. It
is only a trifle more than the time in which you and I are
living is removed from the time of William of Normandy,
who conquered Harold and the English barons.

Now we will cross the sea to the old tower that still
recalls the memory of William the Conqueror. We will
enter the office of public records, and in that fire-proof vault,
guarded as they guard the specie that is gathered into the
treasury of the nation, is a book in two huge volumes of
vellum. It is known as the " Doomsday Book." In the
year 1086, eight hundred years ago, remember, William the
Conqueror caused that record to be prepared. It is nearly
as old as the five books of Moses, the Pentateuch, was in
the days of Ezra the scribe. But not a page of the
" Doomsday Book " has been lost; not a line has been
altered; not a letter erased. Its pages read to-day as they
did in this old time when the Norman heel was on the
Saxon neck—eight centuries ago. The ink is as fresh
on the parchment as though that parchment were unstained
by age. Do you ask how it is that the record has remained
uncorrupted? Do you ask how it is that after all the revo-
lutions that have swept over England, after all the changes

of royal houses, and the dissolutions of powerful parties, that that has remained perfectly unaltered? The answer is a perfectly easy one to give. It is because "Doomsday Book" contains the name of every man, who, in the days of William the Conqueror, owned one rood of English soil. It contains a description of the lands throughout the realm. It gives the boundaries of every great estate, and every old English family must, therefore, find the roots of its genealogy in that old book of the early times of the Norman conquest. It gives the title to every acre of land in England. Thus, two of the strongest motives that can influence the human mind and the human will, have conspired to guard this "Doomsday Book" with a jealous and tireless care.

The possession of a great name, and the possession of landed property are wrapped up in England in the safety of that one book. Now, exactly the same motives conspired for the preservation, from all corruption, of the five books of Moses. They contain the list of those who came out of Egypt with Moses and entered into Palestine; they gave a description of the land that was apportioned to each and every name. To lose these books, which the Jews ever regarded as a precious treasure, the genealogy of their household—to suffer them to be tampered with, was to unsettle the title to every man's field from Dan to Beersheba.

If the "Doomsday Book" has survived, uncorrupted, what reason on earth is there to doubt that the Pentateuch was preserved intact during the thousand years that intervened between the time of Moses and the time of Ezra? But I need not stop here. Ezra, as I have said, was one of the captives who returned out of exile. But Daniel, long before the time of Ezra, speaks of this law of Moses. He bases his own conduct and his own private character upon it. Daniel brings us a hundred years nearer to the days when Moses gave that law to the world. When King Josiah mounted the throne of Judah he found that throne polluted by the wickedness that characterized the reign of his father, King Manasseh, and then there came an overwhelming and powerful revival of religion throughout the kingdom. Monarch and subject united in humiliation before God. Numbers of people bowed down before the Jehovah whom they had offended. But we all distinctly know that the root and the seed out of which this revival sprung was the finding of the copy of the five books of Moses, and learning there what Moses had commanded against the sin of idolatry. I have reached a point nearer yet to the time of Moses himself. I will hasten on.

Termination of the Great Air Line.

One thousand and four years before Christ, Solomon regulated the temple service and worship, but he regulated it, we are distinctly told, according to the law that was contained in the Pentateuch. And we are within four hundred and fifty years of the death of Moses. But David refers constantly to the five books of Moses in the psalms. The law of Moses was the foundation on which all the religious character of the psalms of David rest. Before David was Samuel. His entire career pre-supposes the existence of the Mosaic books. But only three hundred and fifty years intervened between Samuel and Moses. Joshua succeeded Moses as the leader of the chosen people. Again and again in his addresses to the people, did he reprove, exhort and encourage Israel, but everywhere on the basis of the books of the law of Moses. Thus, we have link by link carried back this chain of testimony to the very days in which Moses lived. Now we want no better proof than that in the secular history. Suppose the farewell address of George Washington had been made the object of skeptical criticism; suppose that it had been denied that it had been written by Washington, and if I find it alluded to in Mr. Lincoln's address at the monument-raising in Gettysburg; if I find in one of his speeches that President Polk also spoke of it; if this is true of Mr. Van Buren, and Mr. Madison before him, and if even John Adams, the successor of George Washington in the presidential chair, refers to that address—why then, every sensible man will say that it is the nearest equivalent of mathematical demonstration that can possibly be given of the genuineness of the document to which I have referred.

Genealogical Reflections.

Now, I want you to notice again that if these writings were forged, they were forged by men, who even in so doing, blackened the character of their own lineage and ancestry.   It has been well said that a man whose chief glory is in his ancestors, is very like a potato—the best part of him is under ground.   But after all there is no good man who does not rejoice—and thank God for the fact—when he is able to trace back a long line of God-fearing, pure-living, honest men and women as the seed from whence he sprang.   If I go to work and forge a genealogy for myself, I certainly will not manufacture one that describes my forefathers as the blackest set of criminals that ever escaped from a penitentiary.   No one pretends for a moment that any one but the Jews were those who could have been responsible for the Testament records ; but if they forged it they must have had some motive.   Forgers always have a motive.   There is something before their minds that is to be gained.   But what did these forgers do ?   Why they compiled a record of their own family tree, that overwhelmed their fathers with everlasting shame and contempt.   They described the ancient Hebrews as besotted idolaters in the land of Egypt. When God promised them a land, all their own, flowing with milk and honey—when all that was set before them—they were willing to give up all hope of prosperity, all hope of deliverance from slavery, if they might only have that which they sighed for—the fish and the leeks and garlic of Egypt. They are represented as bowing down to the worship of a calf, which their own hands had made out of their golden ear-rings, and doing that in the very presence of God, displayed upon Mount Sinai, and are described when they reached the borders of the promised land, when all its glory was before them, and its liberty was almost theirs, as being too cowardly to fight the battles that were necessary to gain the possession of their inheritance, till at last God refused to let one of the miserable, cowardly generation enter the land He had promised to their fathers. Yet all this is forgery, not of the Assyrians, not of the Egyptians, who were their hereditary enemies ; not of the Philistines, but themselves—the forgery of the Jews themselves. As though in the dead of night a man should steal out under cover of the darkness to the tombstone of his dead father, and with chisel and mallet in hand try to erase the honorable record of his life, and forge a lying epitaph that made him the vilest scoundrel that ever polluted the earth. Nay, if I commit a forgery on my family record, if ever I try to impose a fabulous family tree on those who know me, I don't think I shall ever trace my line to Cæsar Borgia.

Cutting the Gordian Knot.

Now again I would like to notice very briefly some of the objections to the credibility of the Mosaic writers. Now, there is nothing easier than to start difficulties on any subject which the human mind can give attention to. Let a child in its tiny fingers grasp a pin and

7

get at the silvered side of a mirror, and in five minutes it will do more damage than the most skillful laborer can remedy with the work of many hours.

Is it wonderful that the Bible has been made the subject of repeated attacks ? I no more hope to answer all the objections that can be put against a book such as the book in question, or even the books of Moses—I say I can no more hope to answer all these attacks than in this spring-time I can hope to pick off every green leaf that starts out upon every spreading tree. It were an easier and more effective way to girdle the tree itself. God girdles the tree of infidelity by revival.

If the record of experience tells any fact in the world, it is this, that a thousand objections which the head can see, vanish into thin air when the spirit of God gets hold of a man's heart. Why, there are men here to-night who remember the hour when they found difficulties upon every page of the word of God, when they objected to every principle it propounded, and now look back to the difficulties they used to find there, and wonder how it was possible that they could ever have been troubled by difficulties so palpably absurd. They did not study out one by one the replies that might have been made to these objections. When, in June, huge swarms of flies make our city like the land of Egypt in the days of old, we never undertake to kill them one by one : half a million of people would not be sufficient for that. But God's west wind blows, and they are scattered. So it is that the winds of God's spirit sweep away the swarms of difficulties that men find in the Bible. And yet I am prepared to-night to take up two or three of the objections which have been urged against the credibility of the Pentateuch. These objections resolve themselves into two different parts—the one to the facts of the history of Moses, the other to the morality of

the acts that are there recorded, or the precepts that are
there laid down. I won't have time to go over both
branches of the subject. The limits of such a sermon as
this absolutely forbid it. I speak now of the facts. At
some future time I hope to take up the moral portion of it.

Now, every time you visit the South Park, you find a
place of rest under the grateful shade of an ancient willow.
The vast expanse of its gigantic branches, the immense
girth of its trunk are the witnesses of its venerable age.
If I should take up to-morrow the report of the park com-
missioners and find there the statement that they, at vast
expense, had transplanted that willow tree from the native
soil in which it grew to adorn Chicago's pleasure-ground,
I should know beforehand that it was false; the very appearance of the tree gives the lie to the statement, and if there
were any way in which I could examine the rings that
made up the trunk, I need only count them to have a positive proof of the fact that the statement contained in the
report was false.

Now, precisely akin to that is the accusation that is often
brought against the Book of Genesis. It is said that Moses
declares that six thousand years ago God created this world
in which we are living now. But we only need to count
the geologic strata—we only need to number the rings of
the huge trunk of this earth in order to disprove the
statement.

The Bishop's Challenge—Moses and Ingersoll as Chronologists.

Now, in reply to this difficulty, which is so often urged
against the Book of Genesis, I want to say one word, and
that is, I challenge any man in this congregation—I challenge any man in the wide world that has ever read the
Bible, to find in any book of the Bible, much less in the
Book of Genesis, the statement that the creation of this

earth took place six thousand years ago. This Moses, whom Col. Ingersoll thinks was such a blunderer; whose mistakes have been the subject of his jeers and blasphemous ridicule, was a more careful man than our Peoria skeptic thinks. He certainly was careful not to fix the time at which God created this earth. Whether that creation took place six thousand or six million years ago, he does not state. He does say that "In the beginning God created the heavens and the earth." But that is all. All that he asserts is, that matter—the substance out of which the earth was made—is not eternal; it had a beginning; He did create it.

Well, then, again, the creation of man, equally with that of the world, is made the object of attack. We are told that the Bible claims that between five and six thousand years ago God placed the first pair of the human family in Eden. But when geologists have dug down into the formations that make up this globe—formations which upon mathematical calculation have taken ages and ages to produce — they find there the remains of ancient tools, weapons, ornaments and utensils that prove that man must have lived in a time far ante-distant to that of Adam.

For example, the skeleton of an Indian was exhumed some years ago, while digging for the foundation of the gas-works in the City of New Orleans, and it was alleged by one geologist of that day that it could not have been less than fifty thousand years ago that that man lived. It has been flaunted in our faces that science and religion are opposed to each other; that the Bible is against progress, and that we all must concede that the Pentateuch is but a tissue of falsehood.

Now the first answer I have to give is, that there is not one syllable in the Bible that fixes the length of time or man's existence upon this earth. Not one syllable. Moses does not tell us anything about the date that God created Adam and put him in the garden of Eden. True, we have in the New Testament, in the genealogy of Christ, a statement of the number of generations from Abraham down to the Saviour; but who knows precisely what is the meaning of the term "generations?" The word is used in a variety of senses in the Bible, and it baffles all calculation to determine how many ages intervened between Adam and Abraham. The wisest scholars have been perplexed to fix the number of centuries that rolled over the world in that period of time. To say that God placed man upon this earth six thousand years ago, is not quoting the Bible. I want you to remember that. I want you to tell it to the skeptic that picks out genealogical difficulties in the Scripture. It is only repeating the result of calculations in chronology of certain fallible men who, as fallible, were liable to be mistaken. All infidels do it in trying to fasten upon the Scripture the blunders of mistaken men. But, as is well known, the tendency of the best geologists in our day is rapidly going away from the old ideas of the vast periods of time in the construction of this earth.

Mud Calendars vs. Facts—Some Sad and Sorrowful Scientific Figuring in the Sand.

It was not very long ago that Sir Charles Lyell, the distinguished English geologist, calculated from his own standpoint the rate at which the mud is deposited in the great delta of the Mississippi. By actual figures he reached the astounding calculation that the formation of the delta of the Mississippi must have occupied not less than one hundred thousand years. And, when down underneath that deposit a skeleton was exhumed, it proved beyond all question that not less than fifty thousand years ago human feet had trod the soft soil of the delta of the Mississippi.

But unfortunately for Sir Charles Lyell, American geologists were on his track, and the United States coast survey followed in the pathway where he had been investigating. Gen. Humphrey, of the American army, measured accurately the amount of the deposit. He reviewed the figures of the English geologist, and he showed unanswerably that the whole delta of the Mississippi could not have been in process of formation longer than four thousand four hundred years. For many years geologists held that a quantity of pottery that was found some sixty feet below the surface of the soil, in the delta of the Nile, was at least twelve thousand years old. But later investigations deeper down in the same soil came upon some more patterns, which were undoubtedly of Roman origin, and under these, a brick that bore ineffaceably the stamp of Mehemet Ali, a modern pasha.

If you have visited Minneapolis, you certainly must have been struck by the formation of the banks where the Mississippi has cut its way through the rocks. Above there is layer upon layer, stratum upon stratum of limestone, and beneath them the saccharoid sandstone, white as the sugar from which it derives its name, and soft enough to be cut with a knife, lies in huge masses. On the bluff overlooking the river, there lives, in an immense house, which many years ago was a popular hotel of the ancient city of St. Anthony's Falls, a friend of mine. One day there came to him startling news. Just outside of his premises, in excavating for the foundation of a new building, the workmen had struck upon a wooden coffin, and in it they found what was recognized to be, beyond all doubt, human bones. A local geologist, a physician of the state, with some skeptical tendencies, seized upon this new foundation of the antiquity of man, and the next day the columns of an evening paper of St. Paul contained an article from this gentleman's pen about what countless ages must have elapsed to perfect that saccharoid sandstone over the coffin, and over that to have put these layers upon layers of rock.

The conclusion was, that the chronology of the Bible was utterly a mistake, and that we had, before the days of Mr. Ingersoll, one of the mistakes of Moses. On reading the article my friend felt at once it was his duty to investigate the event. He found the coffin still unremoved, for it was solidly wedged into the saccharoid sandstone, and small pieces of the bones were scattered carelessly about. My friend, whose Christian feeling is only equaled by his profound ability and scholarship, began carefully to examine these relics of pre-Adamite man. Imagine his surprise to find that the coffin which had been made so many ages before Adam was placed upon this earth, was the plank sewer of the old hotel in which he lived, and the bones were those of some innocent lamb, that a careless cook had some time ago flung into that receptacle. I honor geology, but I claim it is yet a very imperfect science, and even with all its imperfections I have yet to find a solitary principle or fact that geology has laid down that contradicts one word of the five books of Moses.

A Mistake of Ingersoll, Tom Paine & Co. Corrected—Conclusion.

I allude to one more of the Mosaic facts that is assailed by the opponents of the Gospel. It is a difficulty which Mr. Ingersoll recently brought forward in that remarkable production of his, as something which he had discovered; but Bishop Colenso, whom the Church of England some thirty years ago sent out among the Zulus, dwelt upon it long ago, and even before his time, Tom Paine had made it his weapon against the truthfulness of the Pentateuch. It is simply this: We are told that the children of Israel, according to the Bible, were in the land of Egypt, in captivity, two hundred and fifteen years. There went down

with Jacob and his sons, their wives and children, seventy
souls in all. But the Exodus finds in the army of Israel
six hundred thousand fighting men, involving a total of
men, women and children which could not have been less
than two or three millions, and it is declared that such an
increase is utterly unparalleled in the annals of history.
Our mathematicians have figured it all out to their satisfaction. Now, I want you to observe what a tissue of
blunders make up this opposition to this Great Book. First
of all turn back to the life of Abraham, the ancestor of
Jacob, and you there discover that a Hebrew family did
not consist merely of the parents and children. The servants were a part of the Hebrew household, and God distinctly made His commands imperative and unavoidable
upon Abraham, that every male youth born in his house
should receive the seal of circumcision. He therefore
became a participator in the Abrahamic covenant. Nay,
more, if he bought a servant he had to be brought into the
covenant of circumcision. God insists upon this, and thus
every servant of every Hebrew household became a Hebrew, and was reckoned in the family into which he was
adopted. Away back in the time of Abraham, if you take
up the Book of Genesis you will find he had so many of
these servants born in his own household, that three hundred
and eighteen of them, able-bodied men, soldiers, followed
him to battle, and when Jacob, in the one hundred and
thirtieth year of his age, went down into the land of Egypt
the three hundred and eighteen of Abraham's day surely
must have multiplied into thousands.

The Pentateuch, it is true, gives only the formal list of
Jacob's sons, their wives and their children. There is no
formal mention of this vast crowd of attendants, who, notwithstanding as part of the family, must have entered into
the land of Egypt with them. Thus, at the very rate of

increase that the tables of the census of the United States to-day display, these thousands might have easily amounted to three millions in two hundred and fifteen years.

I am not through with this stronghold of the enemies of the Pentateuch. As I study it seems to me that I never knew a ghost to vanish into thinner air. I would like to know where or how the critics learned that Israel was in bondage in the land of Egypt two hundred and fifteen years. Why, they learned in precisely the way that they learned that Moses said this earth was made just six thousand years ago. They have taken up certain genealogies and speculations of commentators. They have taken up the calculations of Hales and others, and they have regarded them as infallible. They have never turned to the twelfth chapter of Exodus, and I find there the statement given with precision that admits of no question that the sojourn of the children of Israel in Egypt was four hundred and thirty years: "And it came to pass, at the end of four hundred and thirty years, within the self-same day it came to pass that all the hosts of the Lord came out of the land of Egypt." Long before that, God had told Abraham that his seed should be strangers in a land that was not theirs, and that they should afflict them four hundred years. And the Jews so understood it, as shown by the fact that in the New Testament Stephen declares that God told the father of the faithful that his seed should sojourn in a strange land, and they should bring them into bondage and evil entreat them four hundred years. Now, if but seventy had gone down with Jacob into Egypt, an increase to two or three or even four millions in four and a half centuries would have been no more than what is paralleled by the history of every race on the surface of the globe.

In Italy, three hundred years ago, when men were wild over the discovery of Galileo's telescope, there was one philosopher who refused to look through the tube that pierced the vail of the starry worlds, and when he was asked the reason, "I am afraid," he said, "that I should believe Galileo's theory of the planetary motion." My brethren, look into the telescope of revelation. To know it, to study it, is to find the very truth of God.

Ingersoll's Lecture

SKULLS,

AND HIS

REPLIES TO PROF. SWING, DR. RYDER, DR. HERFORD, DR. COLLYER, AND OTHER CRITICS.

REPRINTED FROM "THE CHICAGO TIMES."

LADIES AND GENTLEMEN: Man advances just in the proportion that he mingles his thoughts with his labor — just in the proportion that he takes advantage of the forces of nature; just in proportion as he loses superstition and gains confidence in himself. Man advances as he ceases to fear the gods and learns to love his fellow-men. It is all, in my judgment, a question of intellectual development. Tell me the religion of any man and I will tell you the degree he marks on the intellectual thermometer of the world. It is a simple question of brain. Those among us who are the nearest barbarism have a barbarian religion. Those who are nearest civilization have the least superstition. It is, I say, a simple question of brain, and I want, in the first place, to lay the foundation to prove that assertion.

A little while ago I saw models of nearly everything that man has made. I saw models of all the water craft, from the rude dug-out in which floated a naked savage — one of our ancestors — a naked savage, with teeth twice as long as his forehead was high, with a spoonful of brains in the back of his orthodox head — I saw models of all the water craft of the world, from that dug-out up to a man-of-war that carries a hundred guns and miles of canvas; from that dug-out to the steamship that turns its brave prow from the port of New York, with a compass like a conscience, crossing three thousand miles of billows without missing a throb or beat of its mighty iron heart from shore to shore. And I saw at the same time the paintings of the world, from the rude daub of yellow mud to the landscapes that enrich palaces and adorn houses of what were once called the common people. I saw also their sculpture, from the rude god with four legs, a half dozen arms, several noses, and two or three rows of ears, and one little, contemptible, brainless head, up to the figures of to-day,—to the marbles that genius has clad in such a personality that it seems almost impudent to touch them without an introduction. I saw their books—books written upon the skins of wild beasts—upon shoulder-blades of sheep—books written upon leaves, upon bark, up to the splendid volumes that enrich the libraries of our day. When I speak of libraries I think of the remark of Plato: "A house that has a library in it has a soul."

I saw at the same time the offensive weapons that man has made, from a club, such as was grasped by that same savage when he crawled from his den in the ground and hunted a snake for his dinner: from that club to the boomerang, to the sword, to the cross-bow, to the blunderbuss, to the flint-lock, to the cap-lock, to the needle-gun, up to a cannon cast by Krupp, capable of hurling a ball weighing two thousand pounds through eighteen inches of solid steel. I saw, too, the armor from the shell of a turtle that one of our brave ancestors lashed upon his breast when he went to fight for his country; the skin of a porcupine, dried with the quills on, which this same savage pulled over his orthodox head, up to the shirts of mail that were worn in the middle ages, that laughed at the edge of the sword and defied the point of the spear; up to a monitor clad in complete steel. And I say orthodox not only in the matter of religion, but in everything. Whoever has quit growing he is orthodox, whether in art, politics, religion, philosophy—no matter what. Whoever thinks he has found it all out he is orthodox. Orthodoxy is that which rots, and heresy is that which grows forever. Orthodoxy is the night of the past, full of the darkness of superstition, and heresy is the eternal coming day, the light of which strikes the grand foreheads of the intellectual pioneers of the world. I saw their implements of agriculture, from the plow made of a crooked stick, atttached to the horn of an ox by some twisted straw, with which our ancestors scraped the earth, and from that to the agricultural implements of this generation, that make it possible for a man to cultivate the soil without being an ignoramus.

In the old time there was but one crop; and when the rain did not come in answer to the prayer of hypocrites a famine came and people fell upon their knees. At that time they were full of superstition. They were frightened all the time for fear that some god would be enraged at his poor, hapless, feeble and starving children. But now, instead of depending upon one crop they have several, and if there is not rain enough for one there may be enough for another. And if the frosts kill all, we have railroads and steamships enough to bring what we need from some other part of the world. Since man has found out something about agriculture, the gods have retired from the business of producing famines.

I saw at the same time their musical instruments, from the tom-tom —that is, a hoop with a couple of strings of raw-hide drawn across it— from that tom-tom, up to the instruments we have to-day, that make the common air blossom with melody, and I said to myself there is a regular advancement. I saw at the same time a row of human skulls, from the lowest skull that has been found, the Neanderthal skull— skulls from Central Africa, skulls from the bushmen of Australia— skulls from the farthest isles of the Pacific Sea—up to the best skulls of the last generation—and I noticed that there was the same difference between those skulls that there was between the *products* of those skulls, and I said to my elf: "After all, it is a simple question of intellectual development." There was the same difference between those skulls, the lowest and highest skulls, that there was between the dug-out and the man-of-war and the steamship, between the club and the Krupp gun, between the yellow daub and the landscape, between the tom-tom and an opera by Verdi. The first and lowest skull in this row was the den in which crawled the base and meaner instincts of mankind, and the last was a temple in which dwelt joy, liberty and love. And I said to myself, it is all a question of intellectual development.

Man has advanced just as he has mingled his thought with his labor. As he has grown he has taken advantage of the forces of nature; first of the moving wind, then of falling water, and finally of steam. From one step to another he has obtained better houses, better clothes, and better books, and he has done it by holding out every incentive to the ingenious to produce them. The world has said, give us better clubs and guns and cannons with which to kill our fellow Christians. And whoever will give us better weapons and better music, and better houses to live in, we will robe him in wealth, crown him in honor, and render his name deathless. Every incentive was held out to every human being to improve these things, and that is the reason we have advanced in all mechanical arts. But that gentleman in the dug-out not only had his ideas about politics, mechanics, and agriculture; he had his ideas also about religion. His idea about politics was "right makes might." It will be thousands of years, may be, before mankind will believe in the saying that "right makes might." He had his religion. That low skull was a devil factory. He believed in Hell, and the belief was a consolation to him. He could see the waves of God's wrath dashing against the rocks of dark damnation. He could see tossing in the white-caps the faces of women, and stretching above the crests the dimpled hands of children; and he regarded these things as the justice and mercy of God. And all to-day who believe in this eternal punishment are the barbarians of the nineteenth century. That man believed in a devil, too, that had a long tail terminating with a fiery dart; that had wings like a bat—a devil that had a cheerful habit of breathing brimstone, that had a cloven foot, such as some orthodox clergymen seem to think I have. And there has not been a patentable improvement made upon that devil in all the years since. The moment you drive the devil out of theology, there is nothing left worth speaking of. The moment they drop the devil, away goes atonement. The moment they kill the devil, their whole scheme of salvation has lost all of its interest for mankind. You must keep the devil and you must keep Hell. You must keep the devil, because with no devil no priest is necessary. Now, all I ask is this—the same privilege to improve upon his religion as upon his dug-out, and that is what I am going to do, the best I can. No matter what church you belong to, or what church belongs to us. Let us be honor bright and fair.

I want to ask you: Suppose the king, if there was one, and the priest if there was one at that time, had told these gentlemen in the dug-out: "That dug-out is the best boat that can ever be built by man; the pattern of that came from on high, from the great God of storm and flood, and any man who says he can improve it by putting a stick in the middle of it and a rag on the stick, is an infidel, and shall be burned at the stake;" what, in your judgment—honor bright—would have been the effect upon the circumnavigation of the globe? Suppose the king, if there was one, and the priest, if there was one—and I presume there was a priest, because it was a very ignorant age—suppose this king and priest had said: "The tom-tom is the most beautiful instrument of music of which any man can conceive; that is the kind of music they have in Heaven; an angel sitting upon the edge of a glorified cloud, golden in the setting sun, playing upon that tom-tom, became so enraptured so entranced with her own music, that in a kind of ecstasy she dropped it—that is how we obtained it; and any man who says it can be improved by putting a back and front to it, and four strings, and a bridge, and getting a bow of hair with rosin, is a blaspheming wretch, and shall die the death,"—I ask you, what effect would that have had upon music? If that course had been pursued, would the human ears, in your judgment, ever have been enriched with the divine symphonies of Beethoven? Suppose the king, if there was one, and the priest, had said: "That crooked sticks is the best plow that can be invented; the pattern of that plow was given to a pious farmer in an exceedingly holy dream, and that twisted straw is the *ne plus ultra* of all twisted things, and any man who says he can make an improvement upon that plow, is an atheist;" what, in your judgment, would have been the effect upon the science of agriculture?

Now, all I ask is the same privilege to improve upon his religion as upon his mechanical arts. Why don't we go back to that period to get the telegraph? Because they were barbarians. And shall we go to barbarians to get our religion? What is religion? Religion simply embraces the duty of man to man. Religion is simply the science of human duty and the duty of man to man—that is what it is. It is the highest science of all. And all other sciences are as nothing, except as they contribute to the happiness of man. The science of religion is the highest of all, embracing all others. And shall we go to the barbarians to learn the science of sciences? The nineteenth century knows more about religion than all the centuries dead. There is more real charity in the world to-day than ever before. There is more thought to-day than ever before. Woman is glorified to-day as she never was before in the history of the world. There are more happy families now than ever before—more children treated as though they were tender blossoms than as though they were brutes than in any other time or nation. Religion is simply the duty a man owes to man; and when you fall upon your knees and pray for something you know not of, you neither benefit the one you pray for nor yourself. One ounce of restitution is worth a million of repentances anywhere, and a man will get along faster by helping himself a minute than by praying ten years for somebody to help him. Suppose you were coming along the street, and found a party of men and women on their knees praying to a bank, and you asked them, "Have any of you borrowed any money of this bank?" "No, but our fathers, they, too, prayed to this bank." "Did they ever get any?" "No, not that we ever heard of." I would tell them to get up. It is easier to earn it, and it is far more manly.

Our fathers in the "good old times,"—and the best that I can say of the "good old times" is that they are gone, and the best I can say of the good old people that lived in them is that they are gone, too—believed that you made a man think your way by force. Well, you can't do it. There is a splendid something in man that says: "I won't; I won't be driven." But our fathers thought men could be driven. They tried it in the "good old times." I used to read about the manner in which the early Christians made converts—how they impressed upon the world the idea that God loved them. I have read it, but it didn't burn into my soul. I didn't think much about it—I heard so much about being fried forever in Hell that it didn't seem so bad to burn a few minutes. I love liberty and I hate all persecutions in the name of God. I never appreciated the infamies that have been committed in the name of religion until I saw the iron arguments that Christians used. I saw, for instance, the thumb-screw, two little innocent looking pieces of iron, armed with some little protuberances on the inner side to keep it from slipping down, and through each end a screw, and when some man had made some trifling remark, as, for instance, that he never believed that God made a fish swallow a man to keep him from drowning, or something like that, or, for instance, that he didn't believe in baptism. You know that is very wrong. You can see for yourselves the justice of damning a man if his parents had happened to baptize him in the wrong way— God can not afford to break a rule or two to save all the men in the world. I happened to be in the company of some Baptist ministers once—you may wonder how I happened to be in such company as that— and one of them asked me what I thought about baptism. Well, I told them I hadn't thought much about it—that I had never sat up nights on that question. I said: "Baptism—with soap—is a good institution." Now, when some man had said some trifling thing like that, they put this thumb-screw on him, and in the name of universal benevolence and for the love of God—man has never persecuted man for the love of man; man has never persecuted another for the love of charity—it is always for the love of something he calls God, and every man's idea of God is his own idea. If there is an infinite God, and there may be—I don't know—there may be a million for all I know—I hope there is more than one—one seems so lonesome. They kept turning this down, and when this was done, most men would say: " I will recant." I think I would. There is not much of the martyr about me. I would have told them: " Now you write it down, and I will sign it. You may have one God or a million, one Hell or a million. You stop that—I am tried."

Do you know, sometimes I have thought that all the hypocrites in the world are not worth one drop of honest blood. I am sorry that any good man ever died for religion. I would rather let them advance a little easier. It is too bad to see a good man sacrificed for a lot of wild beasts and cattle. But there is now and then a man who would not swerve the breadth of a hair. There was now and then a sublime heart willing to die for an intellectual conviction, and had it not been for these men we would have been wild beasts and savages to-day. There were some men who would not take it back, and had it not been for a few such brave, heroic souls in every age we would have been cannibals, with pictures of wild beasts tattooed upon our breasts, dancing around some dried-snake fetish. And so they turned it down to the last thread of agony, and threw the victim into some dungeon, where, in the throb.

bing silence and darkness, he might suffer the agonies of the fabled damned. This was done in the name of love, in the name of mercy, in the name of the compassionate Christ. And the men that did it are the men that made our Bible for us.

I saw, too, at the same time, the collar of torture. Imagine a circle of iron, and on the inside a hundred points almost as sharp as needles. This argument was fastened about the throat of the sufferer. •Then he could not walk nor sit down, nor stir without the neck being punctured by these points. In a little while the throat would begin to swell, and suffocation would end the agonies of that man. This man, it may be, had committed the crime of saying, with tears upon his cheeks, " I do not believe that God, the father of us all, will damn to eternal perdition any of the children of men." And that was done to convince the world that God so loved the world that He died for us. That was in order that people might hear the glad tidings of great joy to all people.

I saw another instrument, called the scavenger's daughter. Imagine a pair of shears with handles, not only where they now are, but at the points as well and just above the pivot that unites the blades a circle of iron. In the upper handles the hands would be placed; in the lower, the feet; and through the iron ring, at the centre, the head of the victim would be forced, and in that position the man would be thrown upon the earth, and the strain upon the muscle would produce such agony that insanity took pity. And this was done to keep people from going to Hell—to convince that man that he had made a mistake in his logic—and it was done, too, by Protestants—Protestants that persecuted to the extent of their power, and that is as much as Catholicism ever did. They would persecute now if they had the power. There is not a man in this vast audience who will say that the church should have temporal power. There is not one of you but what believes in the eternal divorce of church and state. Is it possible that the only people who are fit to go to heaven are the only people not fit to rule mankind?

I saw at the same time the rack. This was a box like the bed of a wagon, with a windlass at each end, and ratchets to prevent slipping. Over each windlass went chains, and when some man had, for instance, denied the doctrine of the trinity, a doctrine it is necessary to believe in order to get to Heaven — but, thank the Lord, you don't have to understand it. This man merely denied that three times one was one, or maybe he denied that there was ever any Son in the world exactly as old as his father, or that there ever was a boy eternally older than his mother—then they put that man on the rack. Nobody had ever been persecuted for calling God bad—it has always been for calling him good. When I stand here to say that, if there is a Hell, God is a fiend; they say that is very bad. They say I am trying to tear down the institu-

tions of public virtue. But let me tell you one thing; there is no reformation in fear — you can scare a man so that he won't do it sometimes,
but I will swear you can't scare him so bad that he won't want to do it.
Then they put this man on the rack and priests began turning these
levers, and kept turning until the ankles, the hips, the shoulders, the
elbows, the wrists, and all the joints of the victim were dislocated, and
he was wet with agony, and standing by was a physician to feel his
pulse. What for? To save his life? Yes. In mercy? No. But in
order that they might have the pleasure of racking him once more.
And this was the Christian spirit. This was done in the name of civilization, in the name of religion, and all these wretches who did it died in
peace. There is not an orthodox preacher in the city that has not a
respect for every one of them. As, for instance, for John Calvin, who
was a murderer and nothing but a murderer, who would have disgraced
an ordinary gallows by being hanged upon it. These men when they
came to die were not frightened. God did not send any devils into
their death-rooms to make mouths at them. He reserved them for
Voltaire, who brought religious liberty to France. He reserved them
for Thomas Paine, who did more for liberty than all the churches. But
all the inquisitors died with the white hands of peace folded over the
breast of piety. And when they died, the room was filled with the rustle
of the wings of angels, waiting to bear the wretches to Heaven.

When I read these frightful books it seems to me sometimes as though
I had suffered all these things myself. It seems sometimes as though I
had stood upon the shore of exile, and gazed with tearful eyes toward
home and native land; it seems to me as though I had been staked out
upon the sands of the sea, and drowned by the inexorable, advancing
tide; as though my nails had been torn from my hands, and into the
bleeding quick needles had been thrust; as though my feet had been
crushed in iron boots; as though I had been chained in the cell of the
Inquisition, and listened with dying ears for the coming footsteps of
release; as though I had stood upon the scaffold and saw the glittering
axe fall upon me; as though I had been upon the rack and had seen,
bending above me, the white faces of hypocrite priests; as though I
had been taken from my fireside, from my wife and children, taken to
the public square, chained; as though fagots had been piled about me;
as though the flames had climbed around my limbs and scorched my
eyes to blindness, and as though my ashes had been scattered to the four
winds by all the countless hands of hate. And, while I so feel, I swear
that while I live I will do what little I can to augment the liberties of
man, woman and child. I denounce slavery and superstition everywhere. I believe in liberty, and happiness, and love, and joy in this
world. I am amazed that any man ever had the impudence to try and

do another man's thinking. I have just as good a right to talk about theology as a minister. If they all agreed I might admit it was a science, but as they all disagree, and the more they study the wider they get apart, I may be permitted to suggest it is not a science. When no two will tell you the road to Heaven—that is, giving you the same route —and if you would inquire of them all, you would just give up trying to go there, and say: " I may as well stay where I am, and let the Lord come to me."

Do you know that this world has not been fit for a lady and gentleman to live in for twenty-five years, just on account of slavery. It was not until the year 1808 that Great Britain abolished the slave trade, and up to that time her judges, her priests occupying her pulpits, the members of the royal family, owned stock in the slave ships, and luxuriated upon the profits of piracy and murder. It was not until the same year that the United States of America abolished the slave trade between this and other countries, but carefully preserved it as between the states. It was not until the 28th day of August, 1833, that Great Britain abolished human slavery in her colonies; and it was not until the 1st day of January, 1863, that Abraham Lincoln, sustained by the sublime and heroic North, rendered our flag pure as the sky in which it floats. Abraham Lincoln was, in my judgment, in many respects, the grandest man ever president of the United States. Upon his monument these words should be written: " Here sleeps the only man in the history of the world, who, having been clothed with almost absolute power, never abused it, except upon the side of mercy."

For two hundred years the Christians of the United States deliberately turned the cross of Christ into a whipping-post. Christians bred hounds to catch other Christians. Let me show you what the Bible has done for mankind: " Servants, be obedient to your masters." The only word coming from that sweet Heaven was, " Servants, obey your masters." Frederick Douglas told me that he had lectured upon the subject of freedom twenty years before he was permitted to set his foot in a church. I tell you the world has not been fit to live in for twenty-five years. Then all the people used to cringe and crawl to preachers. Mr. Buckle, in his history of civilization, shows that men were even struck dead for speaking impolitely to a priest. God would not stand it. See how they used to crawl before cardinals, bishops and popes. It is not so now. Before wealth they bowed to the very earth, and in the presence of titles they became abject. All this is slowly, but surely changing. We no longer bow to men simply because they are rich. Our fathers worshipped the golden calf. The worst you can say of an American now is, he worships the gold of the calf. Even the calf is beginning to see this distinction.

The time will come when no matter how much money a man has, he will not be respected unless he is using it for the benefit of his fellow-men. It will soon be here. It no longer satisfies the ambition of a great man to be king or emperor. The last Napoleon was not satisfied with being the emperor of the French. He was not satisfied with having a circlet of gold about his head. He wanted some evidence that he had something of value within his head. So he wrote the life of Julius Cæsar, that he might become a member of the French academy. The emperors, the kings, the popes, no longer tower above their fellows. Compare, for instance, King William and Helmholtz. The king is one of the anointed by the Most High, as they claim—one upon whose head has been poured the divine petroleum of authority. Compare this king with Helmholtz, who towers an intellectual Colossus above the crowned mediocrity. Compare George Eliot with Queen Victoria. The queen is clothed in garments given her by blind fortune and unreasoning chance, while George Eliot wears robes of glory woven in the loom of her own genius. And so it is the world over. The time is coming when a man will be rated at his real worth, and that by his brain and heart. We care nothing now about an officer unless he fills his place. No matter if he is president, if he rattles in the place nobody cares anything about him. I might give you an instance in point, but I won't. The world is getting better and grander and nobler every day.

Now, if men have been slaves, if they have crawled in the dust before one another, what shall I say of women? They have been the slaves of men. It took thousands of ages to bring women from abject slavery up to the divine height of marriage. I believe in marriage. If there is any Heaven upon earth it is in the family by the fireside, and the family is a unit of government. Without the family relation is tender, pure and true, civilization is impossible. Ladies, the ornaments you wear upon your persons to-night are but the souvenirs of your mother's bondage. The chains around your necks, and the bracelets clasped upon your white arms by the thrilled hand of love, have been changed by the wand of civilization from iron to shining, glittering gold. Nearly every civilization in this world accounts for the devilment in it by the crimes of woman. They say woman brought all the trouble into the world. I don't care if she did. I would rather live in a world full of trouble with the women I love, than to live in Heaven with nobody but men. I read in a book an account of the creation of the world. The book I have taken pains to say was not written by any God. And why do I say so? Because I can write a far better book myself. Because it is full of barbarisms. Several ministers in this city have undertaken to answer me —notably those who don't believe the Bible themselves. I want to ask these men if ...

Every minister in the City of Chicago that answers me, and those who have answered me had better answer me again — I want them to say, and without any sort of evasion — without resorting to any pious tricks — I want them to say whether they believe that the Eternal God of this universe ever upheld the crime of polygamy. Say it square and fair. Don't begin to talk about that being a peculiar time, and that God was easy on the prejudices of those old fellows. I want them to answer that question and to answer it squarely, which they haven't done. Did this God, which you pretend to worship, ever sanction the institution of human slavery? Now, answer fair? Don't slide around it. Don't begin and answer what a bad man I am, nor what a good man Moses was. Stick to the text. Do you believe in a God that allowed a man to be sold from his children? Do you worship such an infinite monster? And if you do, tell your congregation whether you are not ashamed to admit it. Let every minister who answers me again tell whether he believes God commanded his general to kill the little dimpled babe in the cradle. Let him answer it. Don't say that those were very bad times. Tell whether He did it or not, and then your people will know whether to hate that God or not. Be honest. Tell them whether that God in war captured young maidens and turned them over to the soldiers; and then ask the wives and sweet girls of your congregation to get down on their knees and worship the infinite fiend that did that thing. Answer! It is your God I am talking about, and if that is what God did, please tell your congregation what, under the same circumstances, the devil would have done. Don't tell your people that is a poem. Don't tell your people that is pictorial. That won't do. Tell your people whether it is true or false. That is what I want you to do.

In this book I have read about God's making the world and one man. That is all he intended to make. The making of woman was a second thought, though I am willing to admit that as a rule second thoughts are best. This God made a man and put him in a public park. In a little while He noticed that the man got lonesome; then He found He had made a mistake, and that He would have to make somebody to keep him company. But having used up all the nothing He originally used in making the world and one man, He had to take a part of a man to start a woman with. So He causes sleep to fall on this man—now understand me, I do not say this story is true. After the sleep had fallen on this man the Supreme Being took a rib, or, as the French would call it, a cutlett, out of him, and from that He made a woman; and I am willing to swear, taking into account the amount and quality of the raw material used, this was the most magnificent job ever accomplished in this world. Well, after He got the woman done she was brought to the man, not to see how she liked him, but to see how he liked her. He liked her and they started housekeeping, and they were told of certain things they might do and of one thing they could not do—and of course they did it. I would have done it in fifteen minutes, I know it. There wouldn't have been an apple on that tree half an hour from date, and the limbs would have been full of clubs. And then they were turned out of the park and extra policemen were put on to keep them from getting back. And then trouble commenced and we have been at it ever since. Nearly all of the religions of this world account for the existence of evil by such a story as that.

Well, I read in another book what appeared to be an account of the same transaction. It was written about four thousand years before the other. All commentators agree that the one that was written last was the original, and the one that was written first was copied from the one that was written last. But I would advise you all not to allow your creed to be disturbed by a little matter of four or five thousand years. It is a great deal better to be mistaken in dates than to go to the devil. In this other account the Supreme Brahma made up his mind to make the world and a man and woman. He made the world, and he made the man and then the woman, and put them on the Island of Ceylon. According to the account it was the most beautiful island of which man can conceive. Such birds, such songs, such flowers, and such verdure! And the branches of the trees were so arranged that when the wind swept through them every tree was a thousand Æolian harps. Brahma, when he put them there, said: "Let them have a period of courtship, for it is my desire and will that true love should forever precede marriage." When I read that, it was so much more beautiful and lofty than the other, that I said to myself: "If either one of these stories ever turns out to be true, I hope it will be this one."

Then they had their courtship, with the nightingale singing and the stars shining and the flowers blooming, and they fell in love. Imagine that courtship! No prospective fathers or mothers-in-law; no prying and gossiping neighbors; nobody to say, "Young man, how do you expect to support her?" Nothing of that kind—nothing but the nightingale singing its song of joy and pain, as though the thorn already touched its heart. They were married by the Supreme Brahma, and he said to them, "Remain here; you must never leave this island." Well, after a little while the man—and his name was Adami, and the woman's name was Heva—said to Heva: "I believe I'll look about a little." He wanted to go West. He went to the western extremity of the island where there was a little narrow neck of land connecting it with the mainland, and the Devil, who is always playing pranks with us, produced a mirage, and when he looked over to the mainland, such hills and vales, such dells and dales, such mountains crowned with snow, such cataracts clad in bows of glory did he see there, that he went back and told Heva: " The country over there is a thousand times better than this; let us migrate." She, like every other woman that ever lived, said : " Let well enough alone; we have all we want; let us stay here." But he said: " No, let us go;" so she followed him, and when they came to this narrow neck of land, he took her on his back like a gentleman, and carried her over. But the moment they got over they heard a crash, and, looking back, discovered that this narrow neck of land had fallen into the sea. The mirage had disappeared, and there was naught but rocks and sand, and then the Supreme Brahma cursed them both to the lowest Hell.

Then it was that the man spoke—and I have liked him ever since for it—" Curse me, but curse not her; it was not her fault, it was mine." That's the kind of a man to start a world with. The Supreme Brahma said : " I will save her but not thee." And then spoke out of her full-ness of love, out of a heart in which there was love enough to make all her daughters rich in holy affection, and said : " If thou wilt not spare him, spare neither me; I do not wish to live without him, I love him." Then the Supreme Brahma said—and I have liked him ever since I read it—" I will spare you both, and watch over you and your children forever." Honor bright, is that not the better and grander story ?

And in that same book I find this: " Man is strength, woman is beauty; man is courage, woman is love. When the one man loves the one woman, and the one woman loves the one man, the very angels leave Heaven, and come and sit in that house, and sing for joy." In the same book this : " Blessed is that man, and beloved of all the gods, who is afraid of no man, and of whom no man is afraid." Magnificent char-acter! A missionary certainly ought to talk to that man. And I find this: " Never will I accept private, individual salvation, but rather will I stay and work, strive and suffer, until every soul from every star has been brought home to God." Compare that with the Christian that expects to go to Heaven while the world is rolling over Niagara to an eternal and unending Hell. So I say that religion lays all the crime and troubles of this world at the beautiful feet of woman. And then the church has the impudence to say that it has exalted women. I believe that marriage is a perfect partnership; that woman has every right that man has—and one more—the right to be protected. Above all men in the world I hate a stingy man—a man that will make his wife beg for money. " What did you do with the dollar I gave you last week ? " " And what are you going to do with this ? " It is vile. No gentleman will ever be satisfied with the love of a beggar and a slave—no gentle-man will ever be satisfied except with the love of an equal. What kind of children does a man expect to have with a beggar for their mother? A man can not be so poor but that he can be generous, and if you only have one dollar in the world and you have got to spend it, spend it like a lord—spend it as though it were a dry leaf, and you the owner of unbounded forests—spend it as though you had a wilderness of your own. That's the way to spend it.

I had rather be a beggar and spend my last dollar like a king, than be a king and spend my money like a beggar. If it has got to go let it go. And this is my advice to the poor. For you can never be so poor that whatever you do you can't do in a grand and manly way. I hate a cross man. What right has a man to assassinate the joy of life? When you go home you ought to go like a ray of light—so that it will, even in the night, burst out of the doors and windows and illuminate the darkness. Some men think their mighty brains have been in a turmoil; they have been thinking about who will be Alderman from the Fifth Ward; they have been thinking about politics, great and mighty questions have been engaging their minds, they have bought calico at five cents or six, and want to sell it for seven. Think of the intellectual strain that must have been upon that man, and when he gets home everybody else in the house must look out for his comfort. A woman who has only taken care of five or six children, and one or two of them sick, has been nursing them and singing to them, and trying to make one yard of cloth do the work of two, she, of course, is fresh and fine and ready to wait upon this gentleman—the head of the family—the boss!

I was reading the other day of an apparatus invented for the ejectment of gentlemen who subsist upon free lunches. It is so arranged that when the fellow gets both hands into the victuals, a large hand descends upon him, jams his hat over his eyes—he is seized, turned toward the door, and just in the nick of time an immense boot comes from the other side, kicks him in italics, sends him out over the sidewalk and lands him rolling in the gutter. I never hear of such a man—a boss—that I don't feel as though that machine ought to be brought into requisition for his benefit.

Love is the only thing that will pay ten per cent of interest on the outlay. Love is the only thing in which the height of extravagance is the last degree of economy. It is the only thing, I tell you. Joy is wealth. Love is the legal tender of the soul —and you need not be rich to be happy. We have all been raised on success in this country. Always been talked with about being successful, and have never thought ourselves very rich unless we were the possessors of some magnificent mansion, and unless our names have been between the putrid lips of rumor we could not be happy. Every little boy is striving to be this and be that. I tell you the happy man is the successful man. The man that has won the love of one good woman is a successful man. The man that has been the emperor of one good heart, and that heart embraced all his, has been a success. If another has been the emperor of the round world and has never loved and been loved, his life is a failure. It won't do. Let us teach our children the other way, that the happy man is the successful man, and he who is a happy man is the one who always tries to make some one else happy.

The man who marries a woman to make her happy; that marries her as much for her own sake as for his own; not the man that thinks his wife is his property, who thinks that the title to her belongs to him — that the woman is the property of the man; wretches who get mad at their wives and then shoot them down in the street because they think the woman is their property. I tell you it is not necessary to be rich and great and powerful to be happy.

A little while ago I stood by the grave of the old Napoleon—a magnificent tomb of gilt and gold, fit almost for a dead deity—and gazed upon the sarcophagus of black Egyptian marble, where rest at last the ashes of the restless man. I leaned over the balustrade and thought about the career of the greatest soldier of the modern world. I saw him walking upon the banks of the Seine, contemplating suicide—I saw him at Toulon—I saw him putting down the mob in the streets of Paris —I saw him at the head of the army of Italy—I saw him crossing the bridge of Lodi with the tri-color in his hand—I saw him in Egypt in the shadows of the pyramids—I saw him conquer the Alps and mingle the eagles of France with the eagles of the crags. I saw him at Marengo —at Ulm and Asterlitz. I saw him in Russia, where the infantry of the snow and the cavalry of the wild blast scattered his legions like Winter's withered leaves. I saw him at Leipsic in defeat and disaster—driven by a million bayonets back upon Paris—clutched like a wild beast—banished to Elba. I saw him escape and retake an empire by the force of his genius. I saw him upon the frightful field of Waterloo, where chance and fate combined to wreck the fortunes of their former king. And I saw him at St. Helena, with his hands crossed behind him, gazing out upon the sad and solemn sea. I thought of the orphans and widows he had made—of the tears that had been shed for his glory, and of the only woman who ever loved him, pushed from his heart by the cold hand of ambition. And I said I would rather have been a French peasant and worn wooden shoes. I would rather have lived in a hut with a vine growing over the door, and the grapes growing purple in the kisses of the Autumn sun. I would rather have been that poor peasant with my loving wife by my side, knitting as the day died out of the sky— with my children upon my knees and their arms about me. I would rather have been that man and gone down to the tongueless silence of the dreamless dust, than to have been that imperial impersonation of force and murder known as Napoleon the Great. It is not necessary to be rich in order to be happy. It is only necessary to be in love. Thousands of men go to college and get a certificate that they have an education, and that certificate is in Latin and they stop studying, and in two years to save their life they couldn't read the certificate they got.

It is mostly so in marrying. They stop courting when they get married. They think, we have won her and that is enough. Ah! the difference before and after! How well they look! How bright their eyes! How light their steps, and how full they were of generosity and laughter! I tell you a man should consider himself in good luck if a woman loves him when he is doing his level best! Good luck! Good luck! And another thing that is the cause of much trouble is that people don't count fairly. They do what they call putting their best foot forward. That means lying a little. I say put your worst foot forward. If you have got any faults admit them. If you drink, say so and quit it. If you chew and smoke and swear, say so. If some of your kindred are not very good people, say so. If you have had two or three that died on the gallows, or that ought to have died there, say so. Tell all your faults, and if after she knows your faults she says she will have you, you have got the dead wood on that woman forever. I claim that there should be perfect equality in the home, and I can not think of anything nearer Heaven than a home where there is true republicanism and true democracy at the fireside. All are equal.

And then, do you know, I like to think that love is eternal; that if you really love the woman, for her sake, you will love her no matter what she may do; that if she really loves you, for your sake, the same; that love does not look at alterations, through the wrinkles of time, through the mask of years—if you really love her you will always see the face you loved and won. And I like to think of it. If a man loves a woman she does not ever grow old to him, and the woman who really loves a man does not see that he grows old. He is not decrepit to her. He is not tremulous. He is not old. He is not bowed. She always sees the same gallant fellow that won her hand and heart. I like to think of it in that way, and as Shakspeare says: "Let Time reach with his sickle as far as ever he can; although he can reach ruddy cheeks and ripe lips, and flashing eyes, he can not quite reach love." I like to think of it. We will go down the hill of life together, and enter the shadow one with the other, and as we go down we may hear the ripple of the laughter of our grandchildren, and the birds, and spring, and youth, and love will sing once more upon the leafless branches of the tree of age.

I love to think of it in that way—absolute equals, happy, happy, and free, all our own.

But some people say: "Would you allow a woman to vote?" Yes, if she wants to; that is her business, not mine. If a woman wants to vote, I am too much of a gentleman to say she shall not. But they say woman has not sense enough to vote. It don't take much. But it seems to me there are some questions,.as for instance, the question of peace and war, that a woman should be allowed to vote upon. A woman that has sons to be offered on the altar of that Moloch, it seems to me that such a grand woman should have as much right to vote upon the question of peace and war as some thrice-besotted sot that reels to the ballot box and deposits his vote for war. But if women have been slaves, what shall we say of the little children born in the sub-cellars; children of poverty, children of crime, children of wealth, children that are afraid when they hear their names pronounced by the lips of the mother, children that cower in fear when they hear the footsteps of their brutal father, the flotsam and jetsam upon the rude sea of life, my heart goes out to them one and all.

Children have all the rights that we have and one more, and that is to be protected. Treat your children in that way. Suppose your child tells a lie. Don't pretend that the whole world is going into bankruptcy. Don't pretend that that is the first lie ever told. Tell them, like an honest man, that you have told hundreds of lies yourself, and tell the dear little darling that it is not the best way; that it soils the soul. Think of the man that deals in stocks whipping his children for putting false rumors afloat! Think of an orthodox minister whipping his own flesh and blood, for not telling all it thinks! Think of that! Think of a lawyer beating his child for avoiding the truth! when the old man makes about half his living that way. · A lie is born of weakness on one side and tyranny on the other. That is what it is. Think of a great big man coming at a little bit of a child with a club in his hand! What is the little darling to do? Lie, of course. I think that mother Nature put that ingenuity into the mind of the child, when attacked by a parent, to throw up a little breastwork in the shape of a lie to defend itself. When a great general wins a battle by what they call strategy, we build monuments to him. What is strategy? Lies. Suppose a man as much larger than we are as we are larger than a child five years of age, should come at us with a liberty pole in his hand, and in tones of thunder want to know "who broke that plate," there isn't one of us, not excepting myself, that wouldn't swear that we never had seen that plate in our lives, or that it was cracked when we got it.

Another good way to make children tell the truth is to tell it yourself. Keep your word with your child the same as you would with your banker. If you tell a child you will do anything, either do it or give the child the reason why. Truth is born of confidence. It comes from the lips of love and liberty. I was over in Michigan the other day. There was a boy over there at Grand Rapids about five or six years old, a nice, smart boy, as you will see from the remark he made—what you might call a nineteenth century boy. His father and mother had promised to take him out riding. They had promised to take him out riding for about three weeks, and they would slip off and go without him. Well, after a while, that got kind of played out with the little boy, and the day before I was there they played the trick on him again. They went out and got the carriage, and went away, and as they rode away from the front of the house, he happened to be standing there with his nurse, and he saw them. The whole thing flashed on him in a moment. He took in the situation, and turned to his nurse and said, pointing to his father and mother: "There goes the two d——t liars in the State of Michigan!" When you go home fill the house with joy, so that the light of it will stream out the windows and doors, and illuminate even the darkness. It is just as easy that way as any in the world.

I want to tell you to-night that you can not get the robe of hypocrisy on you so thick that the sharp eye of childhood will not see through every veil, and if you pretend to your children that you are the best man that ever lived—the bravest man that ever lived—they will find you out every time. They will not have the same opinion of father when they grow up that they used to have. They will have to be in mighty bad luck if they ever do meaner things than you have done. When your child confesses to you that it has committed a fault, take that child in your arms, and let it feel your heart beat against its heart, and raise your children in the sunlight of love, and they will be sunbeams to you along the pathway of life. Abolish the club and the whip from the house, because, if the civilized use a whip, the ignorant and the brutal will use a club, and they will use it because you use the whip.

Every little while some door is thrown open in some orphan asylum, and there we see the bleeding back of a child whipped beneath the roof that was raised by love. It is infamous, and the man that can't raise a child without the whip ought not to have a child. If there is one of you here that ever expect to whip your child again, let me ask you something. Have your photograph taken at the time and let it show your face red with vulgar anger, and the face of the little one with eyes swimming in tears, and the little chin dimpled with fear, looking like a piece of water struck by a sudden cold wind. If that little child should die, I can not think of a sweeter way to spend an Autumn afternoon than to take that photograph and go to the cemetery, when the maples are clad in tender gold, and when little scarlet runners are coming from the sad heart of the earth, and sit down upon that mound, and look upon that photograph, and think of the flesh, now dust, that you beat. Just think of it. I could not bear to die in the arms of a child that I had whipped. I could not bear to feel upon my lips, when they were withered beneath the touch of death, the kiss of one that I had struck. Some Christians act as though they really thought that when Christ said, "Suffer little children to come unto me," He had a rawhide under His coat. They act as though they really thought that He made that remark simply to get the children within striking distance.

I have known Christians to turn their children from their doors, especially a daughter, and then get down on their knees and pray to God to watch over them and help them. I will never ask God to help my children unless I am doing my level best in that same wretched line. I will tell you what I say to my girls: "Go where you will; do what crime you may; fall to what depth of degradation you may; in all the storms and winds and earthquakes of life, no matter what you do, you never can commit any crime that will shut my door, my arms or my heart to you. As long as I live you shall have one sincere friend." Call me an antheist; call me an infidel because I hate the God of the Jew—which I do. I intend so to live that when I die my children can come to my grave and truthfully say: " He who sleeps here never gave us one moment of pain."

When I was a boy there was one day in each week too good for a child to be happy in. In these good old times Sunday commenced when the sun went down on Saturday night, and closed when the sun went down on Sunday night. We commenced Saturday to get a good ready. And when the sun went down Saturday night there was a gloom deeper than midnight that fell upon the house. You could not crack hickory nuts then. And if you were caught chewing gum, it was only another evidence of the total depravity of the human heart. Well, after a while we got to bed sadly and sorrowfully after having heard Heaven thanked that we were not all in Hell. And I sometimes used to wonder how the mercy of God lasted as long as it did, because I recollected that on several occasions I had not been at school, when I was supposed to be there. Why I was not burned to a crisp was a mystery to me. The next morning we got up and we got ready for church—all solemn, and when we got there the minister was up in the pulpit, about twenty feet high, and he commenced at Genesis about " The fall of man," and he went on to about twenty thirdly; then he struck the second application, and when he struck the application I knew he was about half way through. And then he went on to show the scheme how the Lord was satisfied by punishing the wrong man. Nobody but a God would have thought of that ingenious way. Well, when he got through that, then came the catechism

—the chief end of man. Then my turn came, and we sat along on a little bench where our feet came within about fifteen inches of the floor, and the dear old minister used to ask us:

"Boys, do you know that you ought to be in Hell?"

And we answered up as cheerfully as could be expected under the circumstances:

"Yes, sir."

"Well, boys, do you know that you would go to Hell if you died in your sins?"

And we said: "Yes, sir."

And then came the great test:

"Boys"—I can't get the tone, you know. And do you know that is how the preachers get the bronchitis. You never heard of an auctioneer getting the bronchitis, nor the second mate on a steamboat—never. What gives it to the minister is talking solemnly when they don't feel that way, and it has the same influence upon the organs of speech that it would have upon the cords of the calves of your legs to walk on your tip-toes, and so I call bronchitis "parsonitis." And if the ministers would all tell exactly what they think they would all get well, but keeping back a part of the truth is what gives them bronchitis.

Well the old man—the dear old minister—used to try and show us how long we would be in Hell if we would only locate there. But to finish the other. The grand test question was:

"Boys, if it was God's will that you should go to Hell, would you be willing to go?"

And every little liar said:

"Yes, sir."

Then, in order to tell how long we would stay there, he used to say:

"Suppose once in a billion ages a bird should come from a far distant clime and carry off in its bill one little grain of sand, the time would finally come when the last grain of sand would be carried away. Do you understand?

"Yes, sir."

"Boys, by that time it would not be sun-up in Hell."

Where did that doctrine of Hell come from? I will tell you; from that fellow in the dug-out. Where did he get it? It was a souvenir from the wild beasts. Yes, I tell you he got it from the wild beasts, from the glittering eye of the serpent, from the coiling, twisting snakes with their fangs mouths; and it came from the bark, growl and howl of wild beasts; it was born of a laugh of the hyena and got it from the depraved chatter of malicious apes. And I despise it with every drop of my blood and defy it. If there is any God in this universe who will damn his children for an expression of an honest thought I wish to go to Hell. I would rather go there than go to Heaven and keep the company of a God that would thus damn his children. Oh! it is an infamous doctrine to teach that to little children, to put a shadow in the heart of a child to fill the insane asylums with that miserable, infamous lie. I see now and then a little girl—a dear little darling, with a face like the light, and eyes of joy, a human blossom, and I think, " is it possible that little girl will ever grow up to be a Presbyterian?" Is it possible, my goodness, that that flower will finally believe in the five points of Calvinism or in the eternal damnation of man?" Is it possible that that little fairy will finally believe that she could be happy in Heaven with her baby in Hell? Think of it! Think of it! And that is the Christian religion!

We cry out against the Indian mother that throws her child into the Ganges to be devoured by the alligator or crocodile, but that is joy in comparison with the Christian mother's hope, that she may be in salvation while her brave boy is in Hell.

I tell you I want to kick the doctrine about Hell—I want to kick it out every time I go by it. I want to get Americans in this country placed so they will be ashamed to preach it. I want to get the congregations so that they won't listen to it. We can not divide the world off into saints and sinners in that way. There is a little girl, fair as a flower, and she grows up until she is twelve, thirteen, or fourteen years old. Are you going to damn her in the fifteenth, sixteenth or seventeenth year, when the arrow from Cupid's bow touches her heart and she is glorified —are you going to damn her now? She marries and loves, and holds in her arms a beautiful child. Are you going to damn her now? When are you going to damn her? Because she has listened to some Methodist minister and after all that flood of light failed to believe? Are you going to damn her then? I tell you God can not afford to damn such a woman.

. A woman in the State of Indiana forty or fifty years ago who carded the wool and made rolls and spun them, and made the cloth and cut out the clothes for the children, and nursed them, and sat up with them nights and gave them medicine, and held them in her arms and wept over them—cried for joy and wept for fear, and finally raised ten or eleven good men and women with the ruddy glow of health upon their cheeks, and she would have died for any one of them any moment of her life, and finally she, bowed with age and bent with care and labor, dies, and at the moment the magical touch of death is upon her face, she looks as though she never had had a care, and her children burying her cover her face with tears. Do you tell me God can afford to damn that kind of a woman? One such act of injustice would turn Heaven itself into Hell. If there is any God, sitting above him in infinite serenity we have the figure of justice. Even a God must do justice; even a God must worship justice; and any form of superstition that destroys justice is infamous! Just think of teaching that doctrine to little children! A little child would go out into the garden, and there would be a little tree laden with blossoms, and the little fellow would lean against it, and there would be a bird on one of the bows, singing and swinging, and thinking about four little speckled eyes warmed by the breast of its mate,—singing and swinging, and the music in happy waves rippling out of the tiny throat, and the flowers blossoming, the air filled with perfume, and the great white clouds floating in the sky, and the little boy would lean up against the tree and think about Hell and the worm that never dies. Oh! the idea there can be any day too good for a child to be happy in!

Well, after we got over the catechism, then came the sermon in the afternoon, and it was exactly like the one in the fore-noon, except the other end to. Then we started for home—a solemn march—"not a soldier discharged his farewell shot"—and when we got home if we had been real good boys we used to be taken up to the cemetery to cheer us up, and it always did cheer me, those sunken graves, those leaning stones, those gloomy epitaphs covered with the moss of years always cheered me. When I looked at them I said: "Well, this kind of thing can't last always." Then we came back home, and we had books to read which were very eloquent and amusing. We had Josephus, and the "History of the Waldenses," and "Fox's Book of Martyrs," Baxter's "Saint's Rest," and "Jenkyn on the Atonement." I used to read Jenkyn with a good deal of pleasure, and I often thought that the atone-ment would have to be very broad in its provisions to cover the case of a man that would write such a book for the boys. Then I would look to see how the sun was getting on, and sometimes I thougt it had stuck from pure cussedness. Then I would go back and try Jenkyn's again. Well, but it had to go down, and when the last rim of light sank below the horizon, off would go our hats and we would give three cheers for liberty once again.

I tell you, don't make slaves of your children on Sunday.

The idea that there is any God that hates to hear a child laugh! Let your children play games on Sunday. Here is a poor man that hasn't money enough to go to a big church and he has too much independence to go to a little church that the big church built for charity. He don't want to slide into Heaven that way. I tell you don't come to church, but go to the woods and take your family and a lunch with you, and sit down upon the old log and let the children gather flowers and hear the leaves whispering poems like memories of long ago, and when the sun is about going down, kissing the summits of far hills, go home with your hearts filled with throbs of joy. There is more recreation and joy in that than going to a dry goods box with a steeple on top of it and hearing a man tell you that your chances are about ninety-nine to one for being eternally damned. Let us make this Sunday a day of splendid pleasure, not to excess, but to everything that makes man purer and grander and nobler. I would like to see now something like this: Instead of so many churches, a vast cathedral that would hold twenty or thirty thousand of people, and I would like to see an opera produced in it that would make the souls of men have higher and grander and nobler aims. I would like to see the walls covered with pictures and the niches rich with statuary; I would like to see something put there that you could use in this world now, and I do not believe in sacrificing the present to the future; I do not believe in drinking skimmed milk here with the promise of butter beyond the clouds. Space or time can not be holy any more than a vacuum can be pious. Not a bit, not a bit; and no day can be so holy but what the laugh of a child will make it holier still.

Strike with hand of fire, on, weird musician, thy harp, strung with Apollo's golden hair! Fill the vast cathedral aisles with symphonies sweet and dim, deft toucher of the organ's keys; blow, bugler, blow until thy silver notes do touch and kiss the moonlit waves, and charm the lovers wandering 'mid the vine-clad hills. But know your sweetest strains are discords all compared with childhood's happy laugh—the laugh that fills the eyes with light and every heart with joy! O, rippling river of laughter, thou art the blessed boundary line between the beasts and men, and every wayward wave of thine doth drown some fretful fiend of care. O Laughter, rose lipped daughter of Joy, there are dimples enough in thy cheeks to catch and hold and glorify all the tears of grief.

Don't plant your children in long, straight rows, like posts. Let them have light and air and let them grow beautiful as palms. When I was a little boy children went to bed when they were not sleepy, and always got up when they were. I would like to see that changed, but they say we are too poor, some of us, to do it. Well, all right. It is as easy to wake a child with a kiss as with a blow; with kindness as with a curse, And, another thing; let the children eat what they want to. Let them commence at whichever end of the dinner they desire. That is my doctrine. They know what they want much better than you do. Nature is a great deal smarter than you ever were.

All the advance that has been made in the science of medicine, has been made by the recklessness of patients. I can recollect when they wouldn't give a man water in a fever—not a drop. Now and then some fellow would get so thirsty he would say: " Well, I'll die any way, so I'll drink it," and thereupon he would drink a gallon of water, and thereupon he would burst into a generous perspiration, and get well—

and the next morning when the doctor would come to see him they would tell him about the man drinking the water, and he would say:
" How much ?"

" Well, he swallowed two pitchers full."

" Is he alive ?"

" Yes."

So they would go into the room and the doctor would feel his pulse and ask him :

" Did you drink two pitchers of water?"

" Yes."

" My God! what a constitution you have got."

I tell you there is something splendid in man that will not always mind. Why, if we had done as the kings told us five hundred years ago, we would all have been slaves. If we had done as the priests told us we would all have been idiots. If we had done as the doctors told us we would all have been dead. We have been saved by disobedience. We have been saved by that splendid thing called independence, and I want to see more of it, day after day, and I want to see children raised so they will have it. That is my doctrine. Give the children a chance. Be perfectly honor bright with them, and they will be your friends when you are old. Don't try to teach them something they can never learn. Don't insist upon their pursuing some calling they have no sort of faculty for. Don't make that poor girl play ten years on a piano when she has no ear for music, and when she has practiced until she can play " Bonaparte crossing the Alps," and you can't tell after she has played it whether Bonaparte ever got across or not. Men are oaks, women are vines, children are flowers, and if there is any Heaven in this world, it is in the family. It is where the wife loves the husband, and the husband loves the wife, and where the dimpled arms of children are about the necks of both. That is Heaven, if there is any—and I do not want any better Heaven in another world than that, and if in another world I can not live with the ones I loved here, then I would rather not be there. I would rather resign.

Well, my friends, I have some excuses to make for the race to which I belong. In the first place, this world is not very well adapted to raising good men and good women. It is three times better adapted to the cultivation of fish than of people. There is one little narrow belt running zigzag around the world, in which men and women of genius can be raised, and that is all. It is with man as it is with vegetation. In the valley you find the oak and elm tossing their branches defiantly to the storm, and as you advance up the mountain side the hemlock, the pine, the birch, the spruce, the fir, and finally you come to little dwarfed trees, that look like other trees seen through a telescope reversed—every limb·

twisted as through pain—getting a scanty substance from the miserly crevices of the rocks. You go on and on, until at last the highest crag is freckled with a kind of moss, and vegetation ends. You might as well try to raise oaks and elms where the mosses grow, as to raise great men and great women where their surroundings are unfavorable. You must have the proper climate and soil.

There never has been a man or woman of genius from the southern hemisphere, because the Lord didn't allow the right climate to fall upon the land. It falls upon the water. There never was much civilization except where there has been snow, and ordinarily decent Winter. You can't have civilization without it. Where man needs no bedclothes but clouds, revolution is the normal condition of such a people. It is the Winter that gives us the home; it is the Winter that gives us the fireside and the family relation and all the beautiful flowers of love that adorn that relation. Civilization, liberty, justice, charity and intellectual advancement are all flowers that bloom in the drifted snow. You can't have them anywhere else, and that is the reason we of the north are civilized, and that is the reason that civilization has always been with Winter. That is the reason that philosophy has been here, and, in spite of all our superstitions, we have advanced beyond some of the other races, because we have had this assistance of nature, that drove us into the family relation, that made us prudent; that made us lay up at one time for another season of the year. So there is one excuse I have for my race.

I have got another. I think we came from the lower animals. I am not dead sure of it, but think so. When I first read about it I didn't like it. My heart was filled with sympathy for those people leave nothing to be proud of except ancestors. I thought how terrible this will be upon the nobility of the old world. Think of their being forced to trace their ancestry back to the Duke Orang-Outang or to the Princess Chimpanzee. After thinking it all over I came to the conclusion that I liked that doctrine. I became convinced in spite of myself. I read about rudimentary bones and muscles. I was told that everybody had rudimentary muscles extending from the ear into the check. I asked: "What are they?" I was told: "They are the remains of muscles; that they became rudimentary from the lack of use." They went into bankruptcy. They are the muscles with which your ancestors used to flap their ears. Well, at first, I was greatly astonished, and afterward I was more astonished to find they had become rudimentary. How can you account for John Calvin unless we came up from the lower animals? How could you account for a man that would use the extremes of torture unless you admit that there is in man the elements of a snake, of a vulture, a hyena, and a jackal? How can you account for the religious creeds of to-day? How can you account for that infamous doctrine of Hell, except with an animal origin? How can you account for your conception of a God that would sell women and babes into slavery?

Well, I thought that thing over and I began to like it after a while, and I said: "It is not so much difference who my father was as who his son is." And I finally said I would rather belong to a race that commenced with the skulless vertebrates in the dim Laurentian seas, that wriggled without knowing why they wriggled, swimming without knowing where they were going, that come along up by degrees through millions of ages, through all that crawls, and swims, and floats, and runs, and growls, and barks, and howls, until it struck this fellow in the dug-out. And then that fellow in the dug-out getting a little grander, and each one below calling every one above him a heretic, calling every one who had made a little advance an infidel or an atheist, and finally the heads getting a little higher and donning up a little grander and more splendidly, and finally produced Shakspeare, who harvested all the field of dramatic thought and from whose day until now there have been none but gleaners of chaff and straw. Shakspeare was an intellectual ocean whose waves touched all the shores of human thought, within which were all the tides and currents and pulses upon which lay all the lights and shadows, and over which brooded all the calms, and swept all the storms and tempests of which the soul is capable. I would rather belong to that race that commenced with that skulless vertebrate; that produced Shakspeare, a race that has before it an infinite future, with the angel of progress leaning from the far horizon, beckoning men forward and upward forever. I would rather belong to that race than to have descended from a perfect pair upon which the Lord has lost money every moment from that day to this.

Now, my crime has been this: I have insisted that the Bible is not the word of God. I have insisted that we should not whip our children. I have insisted that we should treat our wives as loving equals. I have denied that God—if there is any God—ever upheld polygamy and slavery. I have denied that that God ever told his generals to kill innocent babes and tear and rip open women with the sword of war. I have denied that, and for that I have been assailed by the clergy of the United States. They tell me I have misquoted; and I owe it to you, and maybe I owe it to myself, to read one or two words to you upon this subject. In order to do that I shall have to put on my glasses; and that brings me back to where I started—that man has advanced just in proportion as his thought has mingled with his labor. If man's eyes hadn't failed he would never have made any spectacles, he would never have had the telescope, and he never would have been able to read the leaves of Heaven.

Mr. Ingersoll's Reply to Dr. Collyer.

Now, they tell me—and there are several gentlemen who have spoken on this subject—the Rev. Mr. Collyer, a gentleman standing as high as anybody, and I have nothing to say against him, because I denounce a God who upheld murder, and slavery and polygamy, he says that what I said was slang. I would like to have it compared with any sermon that ever issued from the lips of that gentleman. And before he gets through he admits that the Old Testament is a rotten tree that will soon fall into the earth and act as a fertilizer for his doctrine.

Is it honest in that man to assail my motive? Let him answer my argument! Is it honest and fair in him to say I am doing a certain thing because it is popular? Has it got to this, that, in this Christian country, where they have preached every day hundreds and thousands of sermons—has it got to this that infidelity is so popular in the United States?

If it has, I take courage. And I not only see the dawn of a brighter day, but the day is here. Think of it! A minister tells me in this year of grace, 1879, that a man is an infidel simply that he may be popular. I am glad of it. Simply that he may make money. Is it possible that we can make more money tearing up churches than in building them up? Is it possible that we can make more money denouncing the God of slavery than we can praising the God that took liberty from man? If so, I am glad.

I call publicly upon Robert Collyer—a man for whom I have great respect—I call publicly upon Robert Collyer to state to the people of this city whether he believes the Old Testament was inspired. I call upon him to state whether he believes that God ever upheld these institutions; whether he believes that God was a polygamist; whether he believes that God commanded Moses or Joshua or any one else to slay little children in the cradle. Do you believe that Robert Collyer would obey such an order? Do you believe that he would rush to the cradle and drive the knife of theological hatred to the tender heart of a dimpled child? And yet when I denounce a God that will give such a hellish order, he says it is slang.

I want him to answer; and when he answers he will say he does not believe the Bible is inspired. That is what he will say, and he holds these old worthies in the same contempt that I do. Suppose he should act like Abraham. Suppose he should send some woman out into the wilderness with his child in her arms to starve, would he think that mankind ought to hold his name up forever, for reverence?

Robert Collyer says that we should read and scan every word of the Old Testament with reverence; that we should take this book up with

reverential hands. I deny it. We should read it as we do every other
book, and everything good in it, keep it; and everything that shocks
the brain and shocks the heart, throw it away. Let us be honest.

Mr. Ingersoll's Reply to Prof. Swing.

Prof. Swing has made a few remarks on this subject, and I say the
spirit he has exhibited has been as gentle and as sweet as the perfume of a
flower. He was too good a man to stay in the Presbyterian church.
He was a rose among thistles. He was a dove among vultures—and they
hunted him out, and I am glad he came out. I tell all the churches to
drive all such men out, and when he comes I want him to state just
what he thinks. I want him to tell the people of Chicago whether he
believes the Bible is inspired in any sense except that in which Shakspeare was inspired. Honor bright I tell you that all the sweet and
beautiful things in the Bible would not make one play of Shakspeare, all
the philosophy in the world would not make one scene in Hamlet, all
the beauties of the Bible would not make one scene in the Midsummer
Night's Dream; all the beautiful things about woman in the Bible
would not begin to create such a character as Perdita or Imogene or
Miranda. Not one.

I want him to tell whether he believes the Bible was inspired in any
other way than Shakspeare was inspired. I want him to pick out
something as beautiful and tender as Burns' poem to Mary in Heaven.
I want him to tell whether he believes the story about the bears eating
up children; whether that is inspired. I want him to tell whether he
considers that a poem or not. I want to know if the same God made
those bears that devoured the children because they laughed at an old
man out of hair. I want to know if the same God that did that is the
same God who said, " Suffer little children to come unto me, for such is
the kingdom of Heaven." I want him to answer it, and answer it
fairly. That is all I ask. I want just the fair thing.

Now, sometimes Mr. Swing talks as though he believed the Bible,
and then he talks to me as though he didn't believe the Bible. The day
he made this sermon I think he did, just a little, believe it. He is like
the man that passed a ten dollar counterfeit bill. He was arrested, and
his father went to see him and said, " John, how could you commit such
a crime? How could you bring my gray hairs in sorrow to the grave?"
" Well," he says, " father, I'll tell you. I got this bill and some days I
thought it was bad and some days I thought it was good, and one day
when I thought it was good I passed it."

I want it distinctly understood that I have the greatest respect for
Prof. Swing, but I want him to tell whether the 109th psalm is inspired.

I want him to tell whether the passages I shall afterward read in this book are inspired. That is what I want.

Ingersoll's Reply to Brooke Herford, D.D.

Then there is another gentleman here. His name is Herford. He says it is not fair to apply the test of truth to the Bible—I don't think it is myself. He says although Moses upheld slavery, that he improved it. They were not quite as bad as they were before, and Heaven justified slavery at that time. Do you believe that God ever turned the arms of children into chains of slavery? Do you believe that God ever said to a man: "You can't have your wife unless you will be a slave! You can not have your children unless you will lose your liberty; and unless you are willing to throw them from your heart forever, you can not be free?" I want Mr. Herford to state whether he loves such a God. Be honor bright about it. Don't begin to talk about civilization, or what the church has done or will do. Just walk right up to the rack and say whether you love and worship a God that established slavery. Honest! And love and worship a God that would allow a little babe to be torn from the breast of its mother and sold into slavery. Now tell it fair, Mr. Herford, I want you to tell the ladies in your congregation that you believe in a God that allowed women to be given to the soldiers. Tell them that, and then if you say it was not the God of Moses, then don't praise Moses any more. Don't do it. Answer these questions.

The Ingersoll Gattling Gun Turned on Dr. Ryder.

Then here is another gentleman, Mr. Ryder, the Rev. Mr. Ryder, and he says that Calvinism is rejected by a majority of Christendom. He is mistaken. There is what they call the Evangelical Alliance. They met in this country in 1875 or 1876, and there were present representatives of all the evangelical churches in the world, and they adopted a creed, and that creed is that man is totally depraved. That creed is that there is an eternal, universal Hell, and that every man that does not believe in a certain way is bound to be damned forever, and that there is only one way to be saved, and that is by faith, and by faith alone; and they would not allow anybody to be represented there that did not believe that, and they would not allow a Unitarian there, and would not have allowed Dr. Ryder there, because he takes away from the Christian world the consolation naturally arising from the belief in Hell.

Dr. Ryder is mistaken. All the orthodox religion of the day is Calvinism. It believes in the fall of man. It believes in the atonement. It believes in the eternity of Hell, and it believes in salvation by faith; that is to say, by credulity.

That is what they believe, and he is mistaken; and I want to tell Dr. Ryder to-day, if there is a God, and He wrote the Old Testament, there is a Hell. The God that wrote the Old Testament will have a Hell. And I want to tell Dr. Ryder another thing, that the Bible teaches an eternity of punishment. want to tell him that the Bible upholds the doctrine of Hell. I want to tell him that if there is no Hell, somebody ought to have said so, and Jesus Christ himself should not have said: "I will at the last day say: 'Depart from me, ye cursed, into everlasting fire prepared for the devil and his angels.'" If there was not such a place, Christ would not have said: "Depart from me, ye cursed, and these shall go hence into everlasting fire." And if you, Dr. Ryder, are depending for salvation on the God that wrote the Old Testament, you will inevitably be eternally damned.

There is no hope for you. It is just as bad to deny Hell as it is to deny Heaven. It is just as much blasphemy to deny the devil as to deny God, according to the orthodox creed. He admits that the Jews were polygamists, but, he says, how was it they finally quit it? I can tell you—the soil was so poor they couldn't afford it. Prof. Swing says the Bible is a poem. Dr. Ryder says it is a picture. The Garden of Eden is pictorial; a pictorial snake and a pictorial woman, I suppose, and a pictorial man, and maybe it was a pictorial sin. And only a pictorial atonement.

Ingersoll's Reply to Rabbi Bien.

Then there is another gentleman, and he a rabbi, a Rabbi Bien, or Bean, or whatever his name is, and he comes to the defense of the Great Law-giver. There was another rabbi who attacked me in Cincinnati, and I couldn't help but think of the old saying, that a man got off when he said the tallest man he ever knew, his name was Short. And the fattest man he ever saw, his name was Lean. And it is only necessary for me to add that this rabbi in Cincinnati was Wise.

The rabbi here, I will not answer him, and I will tell you why. Because he has taken himself outside of all the limits of a gentleman; because he has taken it upon himself to traduce American women in language the beastliest I ever read; and any man who says that the American women are not just as good women as any God can make, and pick his mud to-day, is an unappreciative barbarian.

I will let him alone because he denounced all the men in this country, all the members of Congress, all the members of the Senate, and all the judges upon the Bench; in his lecture he denounced them as thieves and robbers. That won't do. I want to remind him that in this country the Jews were first admitted to the privileges of citizens; that in this country they were first given all their rights, and I am as much in favor of their having their rights as I am in favor of having my own. But when a rabbi so far forgets himself as to traduce the women and men of this country, I pronounce him a vulgar falsifier, and let him alone.

Strange, that nearly every man that has answered me, has answered me mostly on the same side. Strange, that nearly every man that thought himself called upon to defend the Bible was one who did not believe in it himself. Isn't it strange? They are like some suspected people, always anxious to show their marriage certificate. They want at least to convince the world that they are not as bad as I am.

Now, I want to read you just one or two things, and then I am going to let you go. I want to see if I have said such awful things, and whether I have got any scripture to stand by me. I will only read two or three verses. Does the Bible teach man to enslave his brother? If it does, it is not the word of God, unless God is a slaveholder.

Moreover, all the children of the strangers that do sojourn among you, of them shall ye buy of their families which are with you, which they beget in your land, and they shall be your possession. Ye shall take them as an inheritance for your children after you to inherit them. They shall be your bondmen forever. (Old Testament.)

Upon the limbs of unborn babes this fiendish God put the chains of slavery. I hate him.

Both thy bondmen and bondwomen shall be of the heathen round about thee, and them shall ye buy, bondmen and bondwomen.

Now let us read what the New Testament has. I could read a great deal more, but that is enough.

Servants, be obedient to them that are your masters, according to the flesh in fear and trembling, in singleness of your heart, as unto Christ.

This is putting the dirty thief that steals your labor on an equality with God.

Servants, be subject to your masters with all fear; not only to the good and gentle but also to the froward.

For this is thankworthy, if a man for conscience toward God endure grief, suffering wrongfully.

The idea of a man on account of conscience toward God stealing another man, or allowing him nothing but lashes on his back as legal-tender for labor performed.

Let as many servants as are under the yoke count their own masters worthy of all honor, that the name of God and His doctrine be not blasphemed.

How can you blaspheme the name of God by asserting your independence? How can you blaspheme the name of a God by striking fetters from the limbs of men? I wish some of your answers would tell you that. "And they that have believing masters let them not despise them." That is to say, a good Christian could own another believer in Jesus Christ; could own a woman and her children, and could sell the child away from its mother. That is a sweet belief. O, hypocrisy!

Let them not despise them because they are brethren, but rather do them service because they are faithful and beloved, partakers of the benefit.

Oh, what slush! Here is what they tell the poor slave, so that he will serve the man that stole his wife and children from him:

For we brought nothing into this world, and it is certain we can carry nothing out. Having food and raiment let us be therewith content.

Don't you think that it would do just as well to preach that to the thieving man as to the suffering slave? I think so. Then this same Bible teaches witchcraft, that spirits go into the bodies of the man, and pigs; and that God himself made a trade with the devil, and the devil traded him off—a man for a certain number of swine, and the devil lost money because the hogs ran right down into the sea. He got a corner on that deal.

Now let us see how they believed in the rights of children:

If a man have a stubborn and a rebellious son which will not obey the voice of his father, or the voice of his mother, and that, when they have chastened him, will not harken unto them, then shall his father and his mother lay hold on him, and bring him out unto the elders of his city, and unto the gate of his place. And they shall say unto the elders of his city, This, our son, is stubborn and rebellious, he will not obey our voice, he is a glutton and a drunkard. And all the men of his city shall stone him with stones, that he die, so shalt thou put evil away.

That is a very good way to raise children. Here is the story of Jephthah. He went off and he asked the Lord to let him whip some people, and he told the Lord if He would let him whip them, he would sacrifice to the Lord the first thing that met him on his return; and the first thing that met him was his own beautiful daughter, and he sacrificed her. Is there a sadder story in all the history of the world than that? What do you think of a man that would sacrifice his own daughter? What do you think of a God that would receive that sacrifice? Now, then, they come to women in this blessed gospel, and let us see what the gospel says about women. Then you ought all to go to church, girls, next Sunday and hear it. "Let the woman learn in silence with all subjection; suffer not woman to think nor usurp authority over man, for Adam was formed first, not Eve."

Don't you see?

"Adam was not deceived, but the woman being deceived was in the transgession. Notwithstanding all this she shall be saved in child-bearing if she continues in faith and charity and holiness with sobriety." (That is Mr. Timothy.) "But I would have you know that the head of every man is Christ, and the head of the woman is the man, and the head of Christ is God."

I suppose that every old maid is acephalous.

"For a man indeed ought not to cover head, forasmuch as he is the image and glory of God; but the woman is the glory of man. For the man is not of the woman, but woman of the man. Neither was the man created for the woman, but the woman for the man. Wives, submit yourselves unto your own husband as unto the Lord, for the husband is the head of the wife even as Christ is the head of the Church."

Do you hear that! You didn't know how much we were above you. When you go back to the Old Testament, to the great law-giver, you find that the woman has to ask forgiveness for having borne a child. If it was a boy, thirty-three days she was unclean; if it was a girl sixty-six. Nice laws! Good laws! If there is a pure thing in this world, if there is a picture of perfect purity, it is a mother with her child in her arms. Yes, I think more of a good woman and a child than I do of all the gods I have ever heard these people tell about. Just think of this:

When thou goest forth to war against thine enemies, and the Lord thy God hath delivered them into thine hands, and thou hast taken them captive, and seest among the captive a beautiful woman and hast a desire unto her that thou wouldst have her to thy wife, then thou shalt bring her home to thine house, and she shall shave her head, and pare her nails.

Wherefore, ye must needs be subject not only for love, but for conscience sake, and for this cause pay ye tribute, for they are God's ministers.

I despise this wretched doctrine. Wherever the sword of rebellion is drawn in favor of the right, I am a rebel. I suppose Alexander, czar of Russia, was put there by the order of God, was he? I am sorry he was not removed by the nihilist that shot at him the other day.

I tell you in a country like that, where there are hundreds of girls not 16 years of age prisoners in Siberia, simply for giving their ideas about liberty, and we telegraphed to that country congratulating that wretch that he was not killed, my heart goes into the prison, my heart goes with the poor girl working as a miner in the mines, crawling on her hands and knees getting the precious ore out of the mines, and my sympathies go with her, and my symphathies cluster around the point of the dagger.

Does the Bible describe a God of mercy? Let me read you a verse or two.

I will make my arrows drunk with blood, and my sword shall devour flesh. Thy foot may be dipped in the blood of thine enemies.

And the tongue of thy dogs in the same.

And the Lord thy God will put out those nations before thee by little and little; thou mayest not consume them at once, lest the beasts of the field increase upon thee.

But the Lord thy God shall deliver them unto thee, and shall destroy them with a mighty destruction, until they be destroyed.

And He shall deliver their kings unto thine hand, and thou shalt destroy their name from under Heaven; then shall no man be able to stand before thee, until thou have destroyed them.

I can see what he had her nails pared for. Does the Bible teach polygamy?

The Rev. Dr. Newman, consul general to all the world—had a discussion with Elder Heber or Kimball, or some such wretch in Utah—

whether the Bible sustains polygamy, and the Mormons have printed that discussion as a campaign document. Read the order of Moses in the 31st chapter of Numbers. A great many chapters I dare not read to you. They are too filthy. I leave all that to the clergy. Read the 31st chapter of Exodus, the 31st chapter of Deuteronomy, the life of Abraham, and the life of David, and the life of Solomon, and then tell me that the Bible does not uphold polygamy and concubinage!

Let them answer. Then I said that the Bible upheld tyranny. Let me read you a little: "Let every soul be subject to the higher powers—the powers that be are ordained of God."

George III. was king by the grace of God, and when our fathers rose in rebellion, according to this doctrine, they rose against the power of God; and if they did they were successful.

And so it goes on telling of all the cities that were destroyed, and of the great-hearted men, that they dashed their brains out, and all the little babes, and all the sweet women that they killed and plundered—all in the name of a most merciful God. Well, think of it! The Old Testament is filled with anathemas, and with curses, and with words of revenge, and jealousy, and hatred, and meanness, and brutality.

Have I read enough to show that what I said is so? I think I have. I wish I had time to read to you further of what the dear old fathers of the church said about woman—wait a minute, and I will read you a little. We have got them running.

St. Augustine in his 22d book says: "A woman ought to serve her husband as unto God, affirming that woman ought to be braced and bridled betimes, if she aspire to any dominion, alleging that dangerous and perilous it is to suffer her to precede, although it be in temporal and corporeal things. How can woman be in the image of God, seeing she is subject to man, and hath no authority to teach, neither to be a witness, neither to judge, much less to rule or bear the rod of empire."

Oh, he is a good one. These are the very words of Augustine. Let me read some more. "Woman shall be subject unto man as unto Christ." That is St. Augustine, and this sentence of Augustine ought to be noted of all women, for in it he plainly affirms that women are all the more subject to man. And now, St. Ambrose, he is a good boy. "Adam was deceived by Eve—called Heva—and not Heva by Adam, and therefore just it is that woman receive and acknowledge him for governor whom she called sin, lest that again she slip and fall with womanly facility." Don't you see that woman has sinned once, and man never? If you give woman an opportunity, she will sin again, whereas if you give it to man, who never, never, never betrayed his trust in the world, nothing bad can happen. "Let women be subject to their own husbands as unto the Lord, for man is the head of woman, and Christ is the head of the

·congregation." They are all real good men, all of them. " It is not permitted to woman to speak; let her be in silence; as the law said: unto thy husband shalt thou ever be, and he shall bear dominion over thee."

So St. Chrysostom. He is another good man. " Woman," he says, " was put under the power of man, and man was pronounced lord over her; that she should obey man, that the head should not follow the feet. False priests do commonly deceive women, because they are easily persuaded to any opinion, especially if it be again given, and because they lack prudence and right reason to judge the things that be spoken; which should not be the nature of those that are appointed to govern others. For they should be constant, stable, prudent, and doing everything with discretion and reason: which virtues woman can not have in equality with man."

I tell you women are more prudent than men. I tell you, as a rule, women are more truthful then men. I tell you that women are more faithful than men—ten times as faithful as man. I never saw a man pursue his wife into the very ditch and dust of degradation and take her in his arms. I never saw a man stand at the shore where she had been morally wrecked, waiting for the waves to bring back even her corpse to his arms; but I have seen woman do it. I have seen woman with her white arms lift man from the mire of degradation, and hold him to her bosom as though he were an angel.

And these men thought woman not fit to be held as pure in the sight of God as man. I never saw a man that pretended that he didn't love a woman; that pretended that he loved God better than he did a woman, that he didn't look hateful to me, hateful and unclean. I could read you twenty others, but I haven't time to do it. They are all to the same effect exactly. They hate woman, and say man is as much above her as God is above man. I am a believer in absolute equality. I am a believer in absolute liberty between man and wife. I believe in liberty, and I say, " Oh, liberty, float not forever in the far horizon—remain not forever in the dream of the enthusiast, the philanthropist and poet; but come and make thy home among the children of men."

I know not what discoveries, what inventions, what thoughts may leap from the brain of the world. I know not what garments of glory may be woven by the years to come. I can not dream of the victories to be won upon the field of thought; but I do know that, coming down the infinite sea of the future, there will never touch this " bank and shoal of time " a richer gift, a rarer blessing than liberty for man, woman and child.

I never addressed a more magnificent audience in my life, and I thank you, I thank you a thousand times over.

Ingersoll's Catechism and Bible Class.

Nothing is more gratifying than to see ideas that were received with scorn, flourishing in the sunshine of approval. Only a few weeks ago I stated that the Bible was not inspired; that Moses was mistaken, that the "flood" was a foolish myth; that the Tower of Babel existed only in credulity; that God did not create the universe from nothing, that He did not start the first woman with a rib; that He never upheld slavery; that He was not a polygamist; that He did not kill people for making hair-oil: that He did not order His Generals to kill the dimpled babes; that He did not allow the roses of love and the violets of modesty to be trodden under the brutal feet of lust; that the Hebrew language was written without vowels; that the Bible was composed of many books written by unknown men; that all translations differed from each other, and that this book had filled the world with agony and crime.

At that time I had not the remotest idea that the most learned clergymen in Chicago would substantially agree with me—in public. I have read the replies of the Rev. Robert Collyer, Dr. Thomas, Rabbi Kohler, Rev. Brooke Herford, Prof Swing, and Dr. Ryder, and will now ask them a few questions, answering them in their own words:

First, Rev. ROBERT COLLYER: Question. What is your opinion of the Bible? Answer. "It is a splendid book. It makes the noblest type of Catholics and the meanest bigots. Through this book men give their hearts for good to God, or for evil to the Devil. The best argument for the intrinsic greatness of the book is that it can touch such wide extremes, and seem to maintain us in the most unparalleled cruelty, as well as the most tender mercy; that it can inspire purity like that of the great saints and afford arguments in favor of polygamy. The Bible is the text book of ironclad Calvinism and sunny Universalism. It makes the Quaker quiet and the Millerite crazy. It inspired the Union soldier to live and grandly die for the right, and Stonewall Jackson to live nobly and die grandly for the wrong."

Q. But, Mr. Collyer, do you really think that a book with as many passages in favor of wrong as right, is inspired? A. "I look upon the Old Testament as a rotting tree. When it falls it will fertilize a bank of violets."

Q. Do you believe that God upheld slavery and polygamy? Do you believe that He ordered the killing of babes and the violation of maidens? A. "There is three-fold inspiration in the Bible, the first peerless and perfect, the Word of God to man; the second simply and purely human, and then below this again, there is an inspiration born of an evil heart, ruthless and savage there and then as anything well can be. A three-fold inspiration, of Heaven first, then of the Earth, and then of Hell, all in the same book, all sometimes in the same chapter, and then, besides, a great many things that need no inspiration."

Q. Then, after all, you do not pretend that the Scriptures are really inspired? A. "The Scriptures make no such claim for themselves as the Church makes for them. They leave me free to say this is false, or this is true. The truth even within the Bible dies and lives, makes on this side and loses on that."

Q. What do you say to the last verse in the Bible, where a curse is threatened to any man who takes from or adds to the book? A. "I have but one answer to this question, and it is: Let who will have written this, I can not for an instant believe that it was written by a divine inspiration. Such dogmas and threats as these are not of God, but of man, and not of any man of a free spirit and heart eager for the truth, but a narrow man who would cripple and confine the human soul in its quest after the whole truth of God, and back those who have done the shameful things in the name of the Most High."

Q. Do you not regard such talk as "slang?"

(Supposed) Answer. If an infidel had said that the writer of Revelations was narrow and bigoted, I might have denounced his discourse as "slang," but I think that Unitarian ministers can do so with the greatest propriety.

Q. Do you believe in the stories of the Bible, about Jael, and the sun standing still, and the walls falling at the blowing of horns? A. "They may be legends, myths, poems, or what they will, but they are not the Word of God. So I say again, it was not the God and Father of us all who inspired the woman to drive that nail crashing through the king's temple after she had given him that bowl of milk and bid him sleep in safety, but a very mean Devil of hatred and revenge that I should hardly expect to find in a squaw on the plains. It was not the ram's horns and the shouting before which the walls fell flat. If they went down at all, it was through good solid pounding. And not for an instant did the steady sun stand still or let his planet stand still while barbarian fought barbarian. He kept just the time then he keeps now. They might believe it who made the record. I do not. And since the whole Christian world might believe it, still we do not who gather in this church. A free and reasonable mind stands right in our way. Newton might believe it as a Christian and disbelieve it as a philosopher. We stand then with the philosopher against the Christian, for we must believe what is true to us in the last test, and these things are not true."

SECOND, REV. DR. THOMAS. Question. What is your opinion of the Old Testament? Answer. "My opinion is that it is not one book, but many—thirty-nine books bound up in one. The date and authorship of most of these books are wholly unknown. The Hebrews wrote without vowels and without dividing the letters into syllables, words or sentences. The books were gathered up by Ezra. At that time only two of the Jewish tribes remained. All progress had ceased. In gathering up the sacred book, copyists exercised great liberty in making changes and additions."

Q. Yes, we know all that, but is the Old Testament inspired? A. " There may be the inspiration of art, of poetry, or oratory; of patriotism—and there are such inspirations. There are moments when great truths and principles come to men. They seek the man and not the man them."

Q. Yes, we all admit that, but is the Bible inspired? A. " But still I know of no way to convince any one of spirit and inspiration and God only as His reason may take hold of these things."

Q. Do you think the Old Testament true? A. " The story of Eden may be an allegory; the history of the children of Israel may have mistakes."

Q. Must inspiration claim infallibility? A. " It is a mistake to say that if you believe one part of the Bible you must believe all. Some of the thirty-nine books may be inspired, others not; or there may be degrees of inspiration."

Q. Do you believe that God commanded the soldiers to kill the children and the married women and save for themselves the maidens, as recorded in Numbers 31:2? Do you believe that God upheld slavery? Do you believe that God upheld polygamy? A. " The Bible may be wrong in some statements. God and right can not be wrong. We must not exalt the Bible above God. It may be that we have claimed too much for the Bible, and thereby given not a little occasion for such men as Mr. Ingersoll to appear at the other extreme, denying too much."

Q. What then shall be done? A. " We must take a middle ground. It is not necessary to believe that the bears devoured the forty-two children, nor that Jonah was swallowed by the whale."

THIRD, REV. DR. KOHLER. Question. What is your opinion about the Old Testament? Answer. " I will not make futile attempts of artificially interpreting the letter of the Bible so as to make it reflect the philosophical, moral and scientific views of our time. The Bible is a sacred record of humanity's childhood."

Q. Are you an orthodox Christian? A. " No. Orthodoxy, with its face turned backward to a ruined temple or a dead Messiah, is fast becoming like Lot's wife, a pillar of salt."

Q. Do you really believe the Old Testament was inspired? A. " I greatly acknowledge our indebtedness to men like Voltaire and Thomas Paine, whose bold denial and cutting wit were so instrumental in bringing about this glorious era of freedom, so congenial and blissful, par ticularly to the long-abused Jewish race."

Q. Do you believe in the inspiration of the Bible? A. "Of course there is a destructive axe needed to strike down the old building in order to make room for the grander new. The divine origin claimed by the Hebrews for their national literature was claimed by all nations for their old records and laws as preserved by the priesthood. As Moses, the Hebrew law-giver, is represented as having received the law from God on the holy mountain, so is Zoroaster, the Persian, Manu, the Hindoo, Minos, the Cretan, Lycurgus, the Spartan, and Numa, the Roman."

Q. Do you believe all the stories in the Bible? A. "All that can and must be said against them is that they have been too long retained around the arms and limbs of grown-up manhood to check the spiritual progress of religion; that by Jewish ritualism and Christian dogmatism they became fetters unto the soul, turning the light of Heaven into a misty haze to blind the eye, and even into a Hell fire of fanaticism to consume souls."

Q. Is the Bible inspired? A. "True, the Bible is not free from errors, nor is any work of man and time. It abounds in childish views and offensive matters. I trust that it will, in a time not far off, be presented for common use in families, schools, synagogues and churches, in a refined shape, cleansed from all dross and chaff, and stumbling-blocks on which the scoffer delights to dwell."

Fourth, Rev. Mr. Herford. Question. Is the Bible true? Answer. "Ingersoll is very fond of saying 'The question is not, is the Bible inspired, but is it true?' That sounds very plausible, but you know as applied to any ancient book it is simply nonsense."

Q. Do you think the stories in the Bible exaggerated? A. "I dare say the numbers are immensely exaggerated."

Q. Do you think that God upheld polygamy? A. "The truth of which simply is, that four thousand years ago polygamy existed among the Jews, as everywhere else on earth then, and even their prophets did not come to the idea of its being wrong. But what is there to be indignant about in that?"

Q. And so you really wonder why any man should be indignant at the idea that God upheld and sanctioned that beastliness called polygamy? A. "What is there to be indignant about in that?"

Fifth, Prof. Swing. Question. What is your idea of the Bible? Answer. "I think it a poem."

Sixth, Rev. Dr. Ryder. Question. And what is your idea of the sacred Scriptures? Answer. "Like other nations, the Hebrews had their patriotic, descriptive, didactic and lyrical poems in the same varieties as other nations; but with them, unlike other nations, what-

10

ever may be the form of their poetry, it always possesses the character-istic of religion."

Q. I suppose you fully appreciate the religious characteristics of the Song of Solomon? No answer.

Q. Does the Bible uphold polygamy? A. "The law of Moses did not forbid it, but contained many provisions against its worst abuses, and such as were intended to restrict it within narrow limits."

Q. So you think God corrected some of the worst abuses of polyg-amy, but preserved the institution itself?

I might question many others, but have concluded not to consider those as members of my Bible class who deal in calumnies and epithets. From the so-called " replies " of such ministers it appears that, while Christianity changes the heart, it does not improve the manners, and that one can get into Heaven in the next world without having been a gentleman in this.

It is difficult for me to express the deep and thrilling satisfaction I have experienced in reading the admissions of the clergy of Chicago. Surely the battle of intellectual liberty is almost won when ministers admit that the Bible is filled with ignorant and cruel mistakes; that each man has the right to think for himself, and that it is not necessary to believe the Scriptures in order to be saved.

From the bottom of my heart I congratulate my pupils on the advance they have made, and 'hope soon to meet them on the serene heights of perfect freedom.

INGERSOLL AT HIS BROTHER'S GRAVE

The funeral of Hon. Ebon C. Ingersoll, brother of Col. Robert G. Inger-soll, of Illinois, took place at his residence in Washington, D. C., June 2, 1879. The ceremonies were extremely simple, consisting merely of viewing the remains by relatives and friends, and a funeral oration by Col. Robert G. Ingersoll, brother of the deceased. A large number of distinguished gentlemen were present, including Secretary Sherman, Assistant Secretary Hawley, Senators Blaine, Voorhees, Paddock, Alli-son, Logan, Hon. Thomas Henderson, Gov. Pound, Hon. Wm. M. Mor-rison, Gen. Jeffreys, Gen. Williams, Col. James Fishback, and others. The pall-bearers were Senators Blaine, Voorhees, David Davis, Paddock and Allison, Col. Ward, H. Lamon, Hon. Jeremiah Wilson of Indiana, and Hon. Thomas A. Boyd of Illinois.

Soon after Mr. Ingersoll began to read his eloquent characterization of the dead, his eyes filled with tears. He tried to hide them behind his eye-glasses, but he could not do it, and finally he bowed his head upon the dead man's coffin in uncontrolable grief. It was after some delay and the greatest efforts at self-mastery, that Col. Ingersoll was able to finish reading his address, which was as follows:

Colonel Ingersoll's Funeral Oration.

My Friends: I am going to do that which the dead often promised he would do for me. The loved and loving brother, husband, father, friend, died where manhood's morning almost touches noon, and while the shadows still were falling toward the West. He had not passed on life's highway the stone that marks the highest point, but being weary for a moment he laid down by the wayside, and, using his burden for a pillow, fell into that dreamless sleep that kisses down his eyelids still. While yet in love with life and raptured with the world, he passed to silence and pathetic dust. Yet, after all, it may be best, just in the happiest, sunniest hour of all the voyage, while eager winds are kissing every sail, to dash against the unseen rock, and in an instant hear the billows roar a sunken ship. For, whether in mid-sea or among the breakers of the farther shore, a wreck must mark at last the end of each and all. And every life, no matter if its every hour is rich with love and every moment jeweled with a joy, will, at its close, become a tragedy, as sad, and deep, and dark as can be woven of the warp and woof of mystery and death. This brave and tender man in every storm of life was oak and rock, but in the sunshine he was vine and flower. He was the friend of all heroic souls. He climbed the heights and left all superstitions far below, while on his forehead fell the golden dawning of a grander day. He loved the beautiful and was with color, form and music touched to tears. He sided with the weak, and with a willing hand gave alms ; with loyal heart and with the purest hand he faithfully discharged all public trusts. He was a worshipper of liberty and a friend of the oppressed. A thousand times I have heard him quote the words : " For justice all place a temple and all season summer." He believed that happiness was the only good, reason the only torch, justice the only worshipper, humanity the only religion, and love the priest. He added to the sum of human joy, and were every one for whom he did some loving service to bring a blossom to his grave he would sleep to-night beneath a wilderness of flowers. Life is a narrow vale between the cold and barren peaks of two eternities. We strive in vain to look beyond the heights. We cry aloud, and the only answer is the echo of our wailing cry. From the voiceless lips of the unreplying dead there comes no word; but in the night of death hope sees a star and listening love can hear the rustle of a wing. He who sleeps here, when dying, mistaking the approach of death for the return of health, whispered with his latest breath, " I am better now." Let us believe, in spite of doubts and dogmas and tears and fears that these dear words are true of all the countless dead. And now, to you who have been chosen from among the many men he loved to do the last sad office for the dead, we give his sacred dust. Speech can not contain our love. There was—there is—no gentler, stronger, manlier man.

BEECHER'S COMMENTS.

Henry Ward Beecher's Comments on Mr. Ingersoll's Faith, and Funeral Discourse.

" The root element of faith is in the imagination. The tendency of our age, or in certain lines of it, is a rising tendency among the educated to give to the evidence of the physical senses not only greater weight than comes with the imagination, but to deny to the imagination all use except that of producing pleasure. To a certain extent we are indebted for this to the perversion of religious views. The ascetic school banished the imagination from religion and made it a mere minion of pleasure and turned the thoughts of men to what are called weightier things. We are told in the serious words of the ascetic teachers that life is too important to trifle away. They have stripped off the wings of the imagination to make quills to write their dull treatises withal. There is also danger from the scientific or materialistic tendencies of the age, the votaries of which hold that all things must be proven by tangible evidence—that the soul is but matter. But taking the materialistic view that the soul is but matter, it is matter so different from ordinary matter that it is to be judged by entirely different laws. But without taking that ground and adhering as I do to the ground that it is a spiritual matter, the necessity is much stronger for applying the true principle in dealing with its consideration.

" There is a growing tendency towards materialism in the German mind, and this has long been the tendency of the French mind. It has made inroads into the sturdy old English mind, and it has with ten thousand other immigrants that we could have spared come across the seas and gained a foothold here. But to apply to the imagination the same rules you apply to things that have no imagination is impolitic, unphilosophical and unwise. There are a great many men who say with Tyndall: ' If you present God as a poem I can accept it, but if you present Him as a fact I resist it; I say there is no evidence; it is not proven.' There are realities which can not be proven. No formula can demonstrate the sentiment of honor; yet honor demonstrates itself, and the intellect discerns things by the aid of the imagination that it can not discern without it. Reasonings are no more than spider-webbings.

" That which comforts must be accepted as true, although it can not be proven by any direct line of evidence. Take, for instance, the pictures of the Virgin Mary which are the objects of such veneration to devout

Roman Catholics. They are not really the Virgin Mary; they don't even look like her; but they are a representation of the tenderness of the mother towards the child, and that tenderness is a reality. I, too, hang the pictures in my parlor and in my bedroom, and I, too, am a worshipper of the Virgin. I worship the tender, loving spirit of God out of which theology has cheated us. Put that in theology and you would not want any pictorial illustration. So as to ministering angels; I never thought of an angel except with wings. I never saw an angel painted with wings that it did not look like an old hen to me. So with ministering angels. The moment you apply to them all that belongs to them that moment you destroy them.

"A French philosopher once said very truly: ' Everybody believes in God until you attempt to prove his existence.' Take the existence of the soul in heaven—that is a mere question of reason without evidence such as belongs to regulated forms of matter—and it is full of obscurities But let it hang in the realm of imagination and it is not only the product of the imagination of one man, but of all the nations through the growth of time. It is the imagination that has been reaped and threshed and winnowed and grown into the very bread of life. It is not any poem or notion; it is the work, the final work of the imagination of the human race, speaking all languages, under all governments; it is the result to which men come—that death doesn't stop human life; it goes on unending.

"Mr. Ingersoll is a man of great merit and power and he has made himself perhaps as widely known as almost any other man in this generation by his contemning of, I will not say religion, but of those views of religion handed down to us by the teachers of Christianity. He has great power of the imagination—a flaming wit—and has said a great many things, not wise, but by which wise men may profit. He has uttered a great many criticisms on the subject of Christianity which are just criticisms, yet taking his views of religion as a whole, they lack completeness; it is a special plea, a fault-finding plea, which sees only one side. Now, while I accord to him the extremest liberty of discussion and disclaim any right to interfere with this liberty, we have a right to whatever of instruction there may be, and I think he can instruct us by his latest utterance. He has lost a brother dearly beloved, a good man who lived happily with his family and was respected by the community, and at that brother's funeral, Mr. Ingersoll made one of the most exquisite, yet one of the most sad and mournful, sermons that I ever read.

"Was ever anything uttered by the lips of man more pathetic? But we have not only a hope, we have the certainty—we know that if our earthly tabernacle is lost we have a building not made with hands eternal in the heavens. To us the sweet voice comes under burdens, under sorrows, in pain, in persecution, in the prison dungeon—the voice of the spirit and the bride says come and the voice of the whole Church of God cries out to us 'it is real, it is real—come;' and when this noble brother of Mr. Ingersoll felt the touch of death, I don't doubt he felt the touch of God the second time, and saw in the eternal world things which he had counted but shadows here. Even skepticism and that which had been provocative of skepticism in others says when it comes to the death of hope : 'In spite of doubts or dogmas, let us hope that there is a better world.' "

ARNOLD'S COMMENTS.

Hon. Isaac N. Arnold's Comments on Ingersoll's Funeral Oration.

The sad, pathetic, and almost hopeless cry of Robert G. Ingersoll over the grave of his brother has been widely read. It is eloquent with feeling, and shows that his heart is tender and affectionate; and one can not but sympathize with a grief which is not soothed by any hope of a reunion hereafter. He says, speaking of death: " Whether in mid-sea or among the breakers of the farther shore, a wreck must mark at last the end of each and all; and every life . . will at its close become a tragedy as sad, and deep, and dark as can be woven of the warp and woof of mystery and death. And Life is a narrow vale between the cold and barren peaks of two eternities. We strive in vain to look beyond the hights. We cry aloud, and the only answer is the echo of our wailing cry."

This, then, is the despairing moan of one of the brightest infidels of our country—of one who is doing more to destroy faith in God and immortality than any other! How striking the contrast between such a " wreck," as Ingersoll calls it, and the joyous, hopeful death of a . Christian.

I have lately been reading an account of the last hours of Sir Walter Scott. As death approached this great and healthy-minded Scotchman, he asked Lockhart to read to him.

" What shall I read ?" said Lockhart.

" Need you ask ?" said Sir Walter. " There is but *one* Book." And the words that have comforted the dying and soothed the living for eighteen hundred years fell gratefully upon his ear:

Let not your heart be troubled. In my Father's house are many mansions. I go to prepare a place for you.

" Lockhart," were the last words of Scott, " Lockhart, I have but a moment to speak to you; my dear, be a good man; be virtuous, be religious! Nothing else will give you any comfort when you come to lie here."

Ingersoll sadly says over the remains of his beloved brother, " We cry aloud, and the only answer is the echo of our wailing cry;" and, speaking of his dead brother, he says: " He climbed the hights, and left all superstition far below."

If such are the results of " climbing the hights;" if to climb is only to look into the black gulf of despair, to hear over the grave only the " echoes of our wailing cry," who would not rather stay in the warm valley of faith and hope?

I would kindly ask Ingersoll, Are not faith and hope better than doubt and despair? And, if so, why make it your life's mission to ridicule, satirize, and destroy the faith and hope of the thousands who find in their religion the only refuge from the sufferings and sorrows of this life? Why labor to make your brother of humanity believe that he is but—

> The pilgrim of a day?
> Spouse of the worm and brother of the clay,
> Frail as the leaf in Autumn's yellow bower,
> Dust in the wind, or dew upon the flower?

*   *   *   *   *   *   *

> A child without a sire.
> Whose mortal life and transitory fire
> Light to the grave his chance-created form,
> As ocean wrecks illuminate the storm.

And then—

> To night and silence sink forevermore!

If these—

> The pompous teachings ye proclaim,
> Lights of the world and demi-gods of fame,
> The laurel wreath that murderer rears,
> Blood nursed and watered by the widow's tears,
> Seems not so foul, so tainted, and so dread,
> As the daily nightshade round the skeptic's head.

Infidelity is indeed the " deadly nightshade," deadly alike to happiness and to virtue. There are exceptions like Ingersoll, who have inherited from their Christian ancestors natures so generous that their sturdy virtues have resisted the deadly influence.

But every blow this modern apostle of infidelity strikes against Christianity is a blow in favor of vice and immorality. To the young man whose faith Ingersoll by his wit and eloquence has shaken, I would say, listen to his cry of despair over his dead brother, and compare it with the Christian's triumphant death and joyous hope, and choose the truth.